MERRY CHRISTMAS CUPID

HARTBRIDGE CHRISTMAS SERIES
BOOK 3

N.R. WALKER

COPYRIGHT

BLURB

After a year of tragedy, forty-four-year-old Gunter Zuniga is leaving heartbreak behind and moving to the peaceful and picturesque town of Hartbridge, Montana. He buys an old house in need of some work, which he naively thinks he can manage now that he's single and retired—he has nothing but time.

Clay Henderson runs the local sawmill with his dad, and it's the busiest time of year. Firewood and Christmas trees are in high demand, and a delivery of firewood to the old house on Cedar Bark Road leaves him curious about the new man in town.

Clay has never had time for romance and Gunter certainly isn't looking, but Hartbridge has a way of working its Christmas magic; the jingle of Christmas bells, snow, and love are ringing in the air. And Gunter and Clay are about to get the best Christmas gift they never asked for.

MERRY CHRISTMAS

Cupid

N.R. WALKER

CHAPTER ONE

GUNTER

I PULLED the car up beside the house, not deterred by the snow already sticking to the ground. I looked up at the front porch and grinned. The house was a folk Victorian style, with a cute awning, double-hung windows, and intricate wood-carved trims. It was gorgeous.

Well, it would be.

If it weren't in such disrepair.

Ridiculously excited, I climbed the steps, took out the keys I'd just collected from the realtor, and unlocked the front door. Letting the door swing inward, I stepped inside.

The front living room was small and cozy. The original fireplace hadn't seen a lick of warmth in years. The wooden floorboards were blanketed in dust, but sunlight cracked in through the bare windows, making dust motes spin like allergy galaxies through the empty room.

The tall ceilings made the room feel bigger but the house had a chill in its bones. Being empty and unloved for a few years would do that.

I knew exactly how it felt.

Walking through the arch to the kitchen and running

my hand across the countertop, I then had to wipe my hand on my jeans. I didn't care. In fact, it made me smile.

Maybe I hadn't stopped smiling yet.

My new house. My new life.

In Hartbridge, Montana.

The tiny, little town where Dad and I'd stopped last Christmas, the bed and breakfast having been kind enough to give us a room at the last minute.

The tiny, little town I'd come back to in June, very much alone instead of with my husband who'd decided the day after my father's funeral was the perfect time to announce he was leaving and wanted a divorce.

"Life's too short to be unhappy," he'd said.

So I'd arrived to spend the weekend in Hartbridge feeling all kinds of lost, and I left having found a new sense of purpose.

A charming town full of friendly faces, smiles, and warm hellos. The perfect place for me to start again.

I found a house—a very rundown house—on the outskirts of town. I'm sure the realtor thought I was crazy, but I wanted it. Given I was no longer employed, no longer married, I had nothing but time to fix it up.

To make it really mine.

I turned on the kitchen faucet. A pipe somewhere clunked and whined, a puff of resistance coughed into the sink, followed by a trickle of water, but after a few moments, a decent stream poured out.

I wasn't game to try the hot water faucet. I hadn't even turned on the power on yet. I wanted a plumber and electrician to look at it first. They were scheduled to come out the next day, so I wasn't in any hurry to burst a pipe or start an electrical fire.

Old houses, especially those left unlived in for a time, were known for such things.

Apparently.

Not that I had any clue.

I could barely change a light bulb.

Had I bitten off more than I could chew? Absolutely.

I was way in over my head . . . I was so out of my depth, not even the coast guard could find me.

But what I was, more than overwhelmed or scared, was determined.

I was *going* to make this place mine.

Before I'd even had another look at the bathroom, a loud rumbling noise got closer and closer, and I realized it was a truck approaching.

I guess I had new house sounds to learn now.

An old red dump truck with Henderson's Sawmill written in cracked yellow on the side panel came slowly down the drive, and I checked my watch. A little early, but I'd take that over being late.

I walked out onto the porch, and the driver's window rolled down. "Morning," I said cheerfully.

All I could see in the darkened cab of the truck was a brown beard and a wide smile. "Where would you like it?" he said over the rumble of the engine.

Looking at the load of chopped firewood in the back of the truck, which I assumed he was referring to, I pointed past my car, down the side of the house. "Uh, there's a shelter . . . thing . . ." I yelled over the sound of the truck. "I think that's for firewood?"

Well, it was now.

He gave a wave and the truck rumbled louder and chugged down the side of my house. He turned the truck away, backed it up, cut the engine, and tipped the bed up.

I stood back and watched the load of firewood tumble to the ground, and when it was done, the bed went back down, the cab door opened, and the man got out.

He was a giant.

Well, not literally.

At about six-foot-four, he was also at least three feet wide. His shoulders and arms . . . He had Popeye arms. He had short brown thick, woolly hair and a scruffy brown beard. He wore denim overalls over a red plaid shirt as if he'd stepped right out of an old *Mountain Lumberjack* magazine.

As stereotypical as it could get, but somehow . . . perfect.

His smile was wide and warm, and his greeny-blue eyes were bright and friendly. He offered me his huge hand, which I shook.

Without knowing why, I liked him immediately.

"Clayton Henderson," he said, his voice deep. "Folks around here call me Clay."

"Gunter Zuniga. Nice to meet you, Clay."

He looked back at the load of firewood. "You'll be okay to stack this? You coulda got the smaller bundles already wrapped, but you wanted a full load?"

"I did," I said. It would probably take me half a day to stack it, but it was what I was here for. It was crazy how excited I was to get this place into shape. "And it'll be fine. I'll get it done."

He looked at the side of the house and up to the roof. "Rumor has it you're the new owner," he said. Then he shrugged apologetically. "Small town. People gonna talk."

I turned to the side of the house—at the peeled paint, the falling-down fascia, the broken skirting boards—and put my hands on my hips and sighed. "Yep. Just got the keys today. I have a lot of work to do."

Clay looked at me, then at the house, then back at me. "Did you clean out the chimney flue yet? If you're gonna use that firewood—she's been sitting empty awhile now, and you gotta be careful—"

"Oh no, I'm not staying here," I said. Was he concerned for me? I wasn't used to strangers caring so much. I wasn't used to even not-strangers caring, to be honest. "Not yet, anyway. I'm staying at the bed and breakfast for a few weeks. Until I can get the place cleaned up and livable."

He seemed genuinely relieved. "Oh, okay. Did you want me to take a look at your flue for ya? Won't take a second."

Oh.

It's a small town, Gunter. Get used to friendly people doing friendly things. Don't upset the locals on day one.

"Oh. If it's no bother, that'd be great."

With a nod, he followed me to the front porch and up the steps. I was very aware of how he looked at the disrepair: at the cracked paint, the few boards in the porch that had seen better days.

"Leave your boots on," I offered. "The floor is a mess."

As soon as we were inside, I turned to see him smiling at the old beams that ran across the ceiling. "She's a classic," he said. There was no mocking, no hint of sarcasm. "Can I ask what kind of work you'll be doing?"

"Uh."

"Cosmetic or structural?"

"Oh. Cosmetic only. I bought it because it was old and full of character. I'd like to keep as much of that as I can."

He seemed to sigh with relief, happy to hear that. "I was

just going to say, if you're ripping out posts or beams, I'll come take them away for ya." Then he added, "She's old-school. Bet the frame and trusses are hand-hewn. Beautiful work."

It took me a second to remember he was from a sawmill, which explained his excitement. "I'm afraid structural changes are out of my realm of expertise. I had a building inspection before I bought it. They said it was sound, aside from a few cosmetic changes. The plumbing was updated in the seventies, I think. The electrical was rewired around the same time, so it's not as bad as it could be. I mean, it's not new by any stretch. I have a lot of work ahead of me. And I'm short on time because the bed and breakfast will be busy with Christmas and I told them I'd be out by then. Admittedly, it's not the best time of year. So I have about three to four weeks to make it livable."

I looked around the room toward the kitchen through the arch. "Well, the kitchen will need updating. And the bathroom. I have a plumber coming to look at it tomorrow, and the hot water. I mean, the tiles they chose in the seventies were a crime."

Clay smiled at me. "You said the inspector said there was no water damage, so the tiling and plumbing must be good. Just paint the tiles, change the fixtures, and you got yourself a new bathroom. Well, a usable bathroom for a coupla years, till you get settled." He shrugged again. "If you're short on time."

That was a good idea. It really would save a lot of time.

"Stop in and see Ren at the hardware store," he said with a nod. "He'll getcha everything you need."

"Oh, perfect. I actually have a list. Mostly cleaning stuff. Sandpaper. Paint. That kind of stuff. I was going there first thing tomorrow morning."

"You got yourself a big job. Not afraid of hard work then."

I grinned at him. "I'm so excited to get started. I was literally waiting outside the realtors before they opened."

"Where are you coming from? You're not a local."

"Mossley. Down the mountain."

"Ah." He nodded slowly. "Hartbridge called to you, huh?"

I was still smiling. "Something like that."

He stood there staring at me for a beat too long and then jolted away. "Right. Your fireplace . . ." He went to it and kneeled down.

"The floor's all dusty," I said apologetically.

He didn't seem to care. "Don't suppose you got a mirror and a flashlight here anywhere?"

"Uh . . . no. The only thing I have here is the load of wood you dropped off and my luggage in the car . . ." I tried to think if I had a mirror in my bags. I shook my head. "I have a flashlight on my phone, if that helps."

"Nah. Old fashioned way it is then." He ran his huge hand over the bricks in the bottom of the firebox. "Well, there's no creosote. Looks like it was cleaned pretty good. No critter poop either, which is a good sign." Then he lay down on his back, his head in the fireplace so he could look up the chimney. He really was a very big man. "The damper looks decent. Can't see any blockages, but I can't see the lining properly without any gear." Then he shuffled out, the inspection over, and got to his feet. "No birds nests, so that's good. Unless you like smoked pigeon."

I made a face. "No."

He laughed, a deep rumbly sound. "I can swing past tomorrow with some gear to have a better look. You're gonna need a grate though." He gestured to the empty fireplace. When I didn't say anything, he added, "To put the wood on in the fire."

"Oh yes, of course."

He met my gaze and held it for a long moment. "Right, then," he said, dusting his hands off and heading toward the door. "Work to do."

I followed him out. "Thank you so much."

He was down the steps and rounding the corner of the house toward his truck. "My pleasure. Tomorrow, yeah?"

He didn't wait for a reply.

A second later, the truck rumbled loudly to life, and with a wave, he drove out. I stood there smiling until the red truck had disappeared through the trees.

I think I'd just made my first friend in Hartbridge.

MANY HOURS LATER, I pulled my car up to the bed and breakfast and was met by Jayden. He was wiping his hands on his apron, smiling widely as he came down the steps to greet me.

I groaned as I got out of my car; the knot in my back was in dire need of a hot shower.

"Are you okay?" he asked, concerned.

I waved him off. "Oh yes. I spent all day moving and stacking a truckload of firewood at the house."

"Oh, you got the keys already?"

"This morning."

"You're technically a local now."

"Isn't there some twenty-year waiting period for being called a local in a small town?"

He grinned at that. "Probably. But it's real good to see

you again. I'm glad you're here. Let me help you with your bags."

Once we had my things in my room, Jayden left me to it. "Tacos for dinner. And maybe a margarita or two."

"Perfect." So, so perfect.

"And you can tell me all about your house and show me all the photos. I want to know everything."

"Sounds great."

I really liked Jayden. And Cass, his partner. Jayden had been so kind to me the first time I'd come here with my father, and then the second time when it was just me. I'd told him about the funeral, about the separation from my husband, and Jayden had taken it upon himself to be my merrymaker, always there with a wide smile, with food, and with something to make me laugh.

When I'd hinted that I could see myself moving to Hartbridge, he'd even helped me with some real estate searches and advice. He'd taken me into town, shown me around, introduced me to a few new faces. I knew he didn't do that for all their bed and breakfast clientele . . .

So maybe I had *two* friends in Hartbridge already.

It was a nice feeling.

One steaming-hot shower later and dressed in comfier clothes, I found Jayden in the kitchen. He was, true to his word, making margaritas.

"Figured you'd want an early dinner if you've been working hard all day," he said.

I showed him my hands, how red they were. Thankfully not blistered, but still sore. "Wore the wrong gloves."

"Ouch."

"I'll have to go to the hardware store in the morning."

Just then, Cass came inside from the back. Handsome

as ever, his smile wide, he shook my hand. "Glad you made it."

"He has the keys to his house already," Jayden volunteered. "And I was just about to tell him that I can help him out tomorrow. We can have breakfast here, then hit up the hardware store for whatever you need, then I can go see your new place. I'm good with cleaning and organizing."

"Oh." I was not expecting that. "You don't have to—"

Cass laughed and kissed the side of Jayden's head. "Gunter, I hope you like being organized and bossed around. He will have a list or two."

Jayden grinned at me, and it made me laugh. "The company would be great."

He handed me a margarita. "Awesome!"

I sipped the drink. It was delicious. "Oh, I met Clay Henderson today," I said. "He seems nice."

Cass nodded. "He is a nice guy."

Jayden frowned. "Do I know him?"

"Yes. Cliff's son. At the sawmill. Cliff delivered the Christmas trees, but you met Clay at the spring festival. He did the sapling giveaway."

Jayden's face lit up with recognition. "Oh yes. He was cute! In a total teddy-bear, garden-gnome kind of way."

Cass' eyes went wide in a you-can't-say-that way. "Jayden!"

But it made me laugh. "He totally does look like a teddy-bear garden gnome."

Big and cute.

I didn't say it out loud, but apparently I didn't have to.

"Oh?" Jayden quirked an eyebrow at me. "And just how *do* you find teddy-bear garden gnomes?"

I shook my head and sipped my margarita. "I'm definitely not looking. He was just kind enough to check my chimney."

Jayden snorted. "Oh really?"

I ignored the innuendo, but . . . "And he offered to come back tomorrow." I cleared my throat. "To give it a better look."

Cass pressed his lips into a line so he didn't smile too big, but Jayden's smile was so huge, not even his drink could hide it. "Sounds like you don't even have to be looking," he said, "when he's already looking at you."

"Jay," Cass murmured, a gentle warning.

"What?" he said, unbothered. He winked at me without shame. "Christmastime in Hartbridge is known for its romance magic."

CHAPTER TWO

CLAY

THERE WERE plenty of things I was: big, good at my job, and bisexual.

The thing I wasn't?

Was out.

Now, I'd known I'd liked guys the same as I liked girls since high school. I hadn't even known bisexuality was a thing until I read about David Bowie in a teen magazine.

Sure, it helped me understand what I was and that it was okay. I mean, if David Bowie was bi, it had to be okay, right?

But I never made a point of telling anyone.

I was a big goofy teenager, like a hound dog that hadn't grown into his paws yet. I played some different sports for a few years, and I liked hanging with the guys more than I did trying to impress girls. Not that it mattered. I left school as soon as I could.

Dad needed me to help at the sawmill, and I was way better with a lathe than I was with a math book. Hell, I'd been on the end of a shovel and broom since I could walk, and all of three years old, I'd go to bed with curls of wood shavings and sawdust in my hair.

Dad and I still worked together after all these years. And we worked together well. We got in, did the hard work, and we did okay. I helped him modernize a bit and helped him understand the importance of sustainability.

My dad was a good, good man. People all over town always shook his hand when they saw him, if that was a measure.

But he was a man's man. And when my mom died when I was twenty-one, it dang near broke my dad. Keeping busy got him through it, and me, of course, but he said to me that one day the mill would be all mine, and he hoped I'd have a son I could pass it down to.

Future generations of Henderson's was all he ever wanted.

And so, while the bisexual closet door was already closed, the lock slid home.

It wasn't like I was denying myself of anything. I still liked women just fine. Living life as fifty percent of the real me was enough. But it wasn't like that half of me was getting any either. My dating life in Hartbridge wasn't just bad. It was nonexistent.

It wasn't even that women didn't want a six-foot-something hairy, bearded man. It was that I worked all the time. When I wasn't working, I was fixing machinery or servicing the truck. I also lived at the sawmill. With my dad.

Not exactly prime dating material.

I hadn't really missed dating. I wasn't particularly lonely. I kept myself busy, and I had a good life.

I'd had some sexual encounters, all with women. And truth be told, I hadn't considered men in a long time. But I got a strange pang under my ribs when I saw Ren at the hardware store, kissing his husband. And I got a weird sense of longing when I saw Cass Campion holding his boyfriend's hand in the diner.

But I could let it go.

I *had* let it go. A long time ago. I'd made my peace with that.

Until I saw the new guy in town.

I had a delivery job to the old Nolan house down on Cedar Bark Road. We'd heard it'd sold to some out of towner, and I'd wondered about it. Thought for sure it woulda been some developer set on bulldozing the old house down.

But out walked a guy, maybe mid-forties, with short gray hair and round red-rimmed glasses. He wore jeans and boots and a red windbreaker and an excited smile.

He didn't look like a developer to me.

And he spoke with a gentle tone but he was clearly real smart. If anything, he was maybe a touch naïve. Like a city slicker who thought he could just fix up an old house in the middle of the mountains in his spare time.

But oh boy, was he handsome.

He had pretty blue eyes and I asked if he wanted me to check his fireplace.

I had no business going inside a customer's house. No business at all. But I was curious to see the inside, and I wasn't disappointed. The inside of the house was classic 1900s Montanan. Maybe 1910.

Then Gunter spoke about what he wanted to do to the place. To restore it. To make it his home. And that strange pang behind my ribs grew a little bit bigger.

"I have a lot of work ahead of me," he'd said. Yeah, he did. But he didn't seem too bothered about that. In fact, he seemed to like the idea.

And the weird sense of longing settled square in my chest.

So of course I didn't hightail it outta there like I should have. Nope. No siree. What did I do?

I offered to come back the next day.

Yep.

Sucker for punishment, apparently.

I shook my head as I got out of the truck and went to see if I was needed in the main shed.

Dad was on the main header. He had an order of ninety-eight foot 2X4s and twenty 2X6es to get through today. One of the big hemlock logs was already gone, a pile of neat building lumber in its place. He was busy and he had ear protection on, so I left him to it and went straight back to loading up another order of firewood.

I gave a wave to Eddie, one of the full-timers who was helping Dad, and as I got back into my truck, Rusty followed me in the front-end loader.

Rusty, also a full-time employee, had been working at the mill since he was a teenager. He had his fortieth birthday just last year, and was only five years older than me. Given we'd seen each other five days a week for twenty-something years, we'd become pretty good friends.

I never really had to ask him to do anything. He just knew what needed to be done.

I brought my truck around, Rusty loaded the back, and I took the order sheet for the delivery. I gave a wave as I headed back out, and Rusty was already driving off to his next job.

The lumberyard never stopped. Especially in winter and the holidays.

Like I had time to be making random house calls to be checking on handsome newcomers to town.

I certainly didn't have to be the one to volunteer to pick up some more chain oil from the hardware store the next morning on the off chance said handsome newcomer would be there first thing like he'd said he might.

It didn't help that I dreamed about him. About how a man might feel in my arms, how he might smell.

Taste.

I'd gone and lost my dang mind.

And yet, there I was pulling onto Main Street right at eight o'clock. I'd already done a full morning's work, so it wasn't like I was slacking. And I figured I'd make a stop at Carl's Diner and pick up some morning tea for the guys at work.

The bell above the door chimed as I walked into the hardware store. Ren poked his head out from behind an aisle. He was carrying a box with screws in it. "Morning, Clay," he said cheerfully.

"Morning," I replied. There didn't appear to be anyone else in the store yet. I wondered how long I could pretend to be busy before a certain newcomer might turn up. You know, before it got weird.

It's already weird, Clay.

"Whatcha in for this morning?" Ren asked.

"Ah, just some chain oil."

"Gotcha. Ten gallons?"

"Yeah, that'd be great. Might just browse a while," I said. *So lame.* "Got some projects in mind. Might take a look if that's all right."

"Sure thing. I'll leave the oil by the service counter. Come up when you're done."

I must have spent a good fifteen minutes looking at nothing in particular. There wasn't anything I needed. All my projects were done with offcuts, and I had all the gear I could ever need at the mill.

This was so ridiculous.

I was waiting in the store on the slim off chance someone might show up, just so I could what? See him? I'd already lined up to see him about his chimney. I didn't need to be waiting at the dang hardware store.

I was just getting to the counter when the door chimed. I turned, stupidly excited, only to see Mrs. Greenly come in. I tried to hide my disappointment as she rushed in and not some cute new guy.

"Oh, Clay, I was hoping to catch you," she said. "I was just walking past and saw your truck out front. Can you put us down for a firewood delivery? I've been meaning to call," she said, then gave Ren an apologetic wave as she backed out of the store. "Sorry, I'm already late. Will you call Richard to let us know when you can bring it? Thanks again. Say hello to your dad."

Then with a wave she was gone, the door chime ringing in the silence.

I turned to Ren. "Sorry about that."

He laughed. "Want me to write her order down for you?"

I snorted. "Nah. I got it, thanks."

"Did you find what you were looking for?"

I froze. "What?" How did he know? Was I too obvious?

Ren looked confused. "You were browsing for a project or something?"

Oh.

"Oh. Nah, I'm still undecided. Dunno what I'm doing."

Wasn't that the truth.

He rang up the chain oil and I paid. "You'll still be running a seedling program this spring?" Ren asked.

"Absolutely. I usually line it up with the conservation team in Missoula for Arbor Day. When I put my order in for reforestation."

"It's a great idea. Happy to help out again this year, if you want to put a sign-up sheet in the store."

"That'd be great, Ren. Thanks."

I wasn't gonna say anything. I'd be stupid to say something . . . but since I'd already gone and lost my mind. "Listen," I began. "Say, I know you and your hus—"

The door chiming again interrupted me. Stopped me. It was old Mr. Winslow, shuffling inside with his walking stick, and honestly, thank the heavens above because I had no idea what I was about to say.

Something absolutely horrifying.

"You okay, Clay?" Ren asked quietly. "You were about to say something."

"Oh no. It's nothing," I said, taking the oil, backing out. "Nothing important. I'll be in touch about those seedlings."

He watched me all curious-like. Probably because I was acting three-parts crazy. But soon Mr. Winslow was in his ear and I was outside in the crisp air.

Heaven help me.

Was I just about to seriously ask him how to go about asking if another guy might be . . . interested?

I think I was.

I mean, Ren was openly gay. And he was married. To a man. He would know these things.

And I was pretty sure Gunter was gay.

Not that I was being judgmental or nothing, but some part of me thought he was—but oh my god. What if Gunter wasn't even gay? Or bi? Or whatever. What if I was getting all bent outta shape for a guy who would never . . . could never . . .

I tossed the oil into the cab of my truck and shook my head the whole way across the street.

I was losing my dang mind.

I should call and tell him I couldn't see him about his chimney today. Or any day. I had his number at work, from when he'd ordered the firewood. I could call him and tell him it wasn't a good idea. I was too busy and this was all too crazy, and I'd be doing myself a favor if I got him outta my mind, sooner the better, and just go back to being boring old Clay, the straight guy. I didn't need to be outing myself for no one. No one needed to know about me being bisexual. No one at all.

Right, I told myself, I would call him and cancel and pretend nothing ever happened. That settled, I pulled open the door to Carl's Diner . . .

And walked straight into Gunter.

Literally.

"Oh!" He took a surprised step back. He was with the guy from the bed and breakfast. Cass's boyfriend. He had to step back too, but Gunter stepped into the other guy and overbalanced.

"Sorry," I said, reaching for Gunter's arm to keep him from falling. "Gunter. Are you okay? I didn't see you there."

He looked up at me and I still had my hand on his arm, and I swear, for a whole second, the world stopped turning.

"Clayton," he breathed, and I'd never been happier to be full-named. He smiled right at me. "I'm fine."

The guy he was with cleared his throat. "Jayden," he said, shuffling a box of pastries with one hand so he could offer me a handshake. "We've never met before, officially."

He had a bit of an accent.

"Clay Henderson," I said, shaking his hand. I met Gunter's eyes. "Or Clayton's fine."

Jayden smiled like he knew something I didn't. "Nice to meet you."

Gunter nudged him but spoke to me. "I was just telling Jayden how you kindly offered to look over my chimney and fireplace."

"Yeah, about that," I said. *Tell him you don't think it's a good idea. Tell him you can't. Tell him anything. Ignore the way he's looking at you. Ignore the blue of his eyes. Ignore the pink of his lips . . .*

"Is after lunch okay?"

Good job, Clayton.

"Perfect," Jayden answered. "Hamish and I are helping him this morning, cleaning up and whatever, but I have to be back by midday and Hamish has a thing on this arvo so he's driving me back into town. That'll leave plenty of time for you to . . . inspect his chimney."

Gunter nudged him a little harder this time.

"We should go," Jayden said, grinning now.

I opened the door for them and Jayden went out first.

"I'll see you this afternoon some time," Gunter said.

I nodded. "What's an arvo?" Jayden had said it.

He shrugged. "I have no idea."

"Around two o'clock okay?"

"Perfect."

Was he just standing there staring at me? Or was I just standing there staring at him?

"Close the door, you're letting in the cold," Carl called out from behind the counter.

Gunter nodded and ducked his head as he walked out, and I breathed for the first time since I walked in.

What the hell had just happened? Why was my heart thumping so hard?

"Young Mr. Henderson," Carl said. "What can I get for you today?"

I had to make myself not smile like a lunatic. "A mixed dozen of your best pastries, please."

"WHAT'S THIS FOR?" Dad asked me as I slid the box of goodies onto the breakroom table. And when I say *table*, I mean, it was the table I'd made senior year at high school as my end-of-year project. It was knotty pine, banged up, stained with coffee and working hands, but it was sturdy as hell.

And there was a fridge, a coffee machine, and a sink in the breakroom too. It wasn't anything new or trendy, but it'd done us just fine all these years.

"And what's got you smilin' like that?"

"Nothing," I said. "I was at the hardware store, looked across the street, and thought you know what? Some of Carl's pastries sound good."

He studied me, but before he could say anything else, the other guys walked in. "Tell me you got a bear claw," Rusty said.

I opened the box, and two pots of coffee later, we had a happy bunch of guys whistling while they worked.

It was a good reminder to do it more often.

I took a quick break at lunch, preferring to get stuff done, knowing I'd be slacking off for an hour or so later. I was coming back from checking the kiln when I noticed Dad watching me, shaking his head. "You keep smiling like that, people'll wonder what you're up to."

"It's nothing," I said. "Just woke up in a good mood today."

"Hm-mm." He didn't believe me for one second but at least he didn't push.

And when I was loading up my truck just after one o'clock, Rusty got out of the front loader and met me at the back of my truck. I lifted the tailgate and he slid one bolt lock into place. I did the other.

"I saw you threw in the ladder," he said, casual as ever.

"Ah, yeah, I just . . ." Shit. "Said I'd have a look at a chimney when I delivered the wood. No big deal."

He gave a nod.

"All part of the service."

He smiled at that. "I bet."

Goddammit.

"Anyone I know?" He looked out across the lumber-yard. "I mean, this is Hartbridge. It's gotta be someone I know."

"It's not like that."

"So tell us who it is. Is it Carrie-lee King?"

"Nope."

"Janet? From the—"

"No."

"Gimme something, Clay."

"I told ya, it ain't like that." I clapped his shoulder. "I'll be an hour or so."

He shot me a look. "An hour?"

"Yeah," I said, climbing into my truck. "I gotta check a chimney."

He rolled his eyes, but I shut the door and that was the end of that.

It wasn't lost on me that his immediate assumptions were women. And I guess I'd never done anything for him to assume otherwise. But it made it awkward.

Would he care if he knew I was bi?

Not sure, but I wouldn't think so. He liked Ren and Hamish from the hardware store just fine and never said a bad word about either of them. Never made jokes behind their backs, not even when it was just us. Never even raised an eyebrow when we found out Ren was dating a guy. So yeah, I think Rusty would be fine.

But would my dad?

Unsure.

My dad was a good man, and he never meant harm or ill will on anyone. He liked Ren and Hamish just fine too and was always up for a chat at the store. But he's a bit old-school and was born and bred in these mountains.

And it's different when it's your own son.

Would I even have to tell him? Probably not.

I was getting way ahead of myself. I had no idea if Gunter was even into guys or if he was single. Just because he'd reminded me that I was still attracted to men didn't mean anything.

God, I needed to stop thinking about him. That'd be a real good start . . .

I delivered the load of wood on Bridge Street and headed out to Cedar Bark Road, trying not to think about him the whole way to his house. Which of course made me think about him the whole way.

So maybe I could stop thinking about him after seeing him this one last time.

Maybe I could ask him what his story was. If he was straight, then this silly infatuation ended today.

I turned into his driveway, and as soon as I saw his car parked beside his house, my nerves ratcheted up a notch or two. And that huge load of wood I'd dropped off just yesterday was already stacked, neat and organized.

I didn't know why that made me so happy.

I cut the engine, and by the time I climbed out and shut my door, Gunter was on his front porch. "Afternoon." I nodded toward the wood pile. "Not afraid of hard work, I see."

"I did it yesterday," he said proudly. Then he winced. "And my back has been reminding me all day that I'm no longer in my twenties, and I haven't been for some time."

I chuckled as I slid the ladder out and leaned it up against the side of his house. "Sounds familiar."

"I really do appreciate you coming back out today," he said. "You certainly didn't have to."

"It's no problem at all." I grabbed my flashlight from the cab of my truck. "It won't take a few minutes. Then we'll know if it's all right to use some of that firewood."

"Oh, I have a mirror," he said. "We took it down from the bathroom wall today."

"Perfect. I'll just check your chimney first," I said. I was feeling a bit nervous and I needed a second to get myself together. Maybe being up a ladder wasn't the best place for that. Especially when he came down to hold the ladder for me.

"Let me hold you steady," he said. "I don't want you falling."

I almost laughed because, man, if only he knew.

If only he knew.

CHAPTER THREE

GUNTER

I HAD SPENT the entire day trying to convince Jayden that he was reading far more into my interactions with Clay than what was actually there.

The way he'd looked at me in the diner.

The way he'd stared.

Maybe even blushed a little. It was hard to tell with his beard and all.

His smile was just him being polite.

Nothing more.

And I wasn't looking for romance. I certainly wasn't looking for love.

"But that's just it," Jayden had replied. "You're in Hartbridge at Christmastime. I'm telling you, the Christmas bells and holiday lights they put up in this town have romantic powers."

Hamish held up his left hand with his shining new wedding ring as if it were proof. "It's true."

I'd had to make them leave before Clay arrived, otherwise it would have been terribly embarrassing. I was grateful for their help, and I honestly felt that I'd made two wonderful friends, but I wasn't having them here asking embarrassing questions or dropping horrifying hints.

I would no doubt be recounting the whole encounter to Jayden when I got back to the bed and breakfast.

And I could admit Clay was a very attractive man. In a rugged mountain-man kind of way. Certainly not the type to ever turn my head before, but he had pretty eyes that glittered when he smiled.

And a great body, from what I could see from the bottom of the ladder. The overalls weren't too flattering and the big coat he wore made him appear heavier than what he was.

But no. I wasn't looking.

"So." I cleared my throat. "What are you looking for, exactly?"

"Cracks in the mortar. These old chimney stacks are built to last forever, but it's always good to check."

He climbed down and I still held on to the ladder. He was taller than I realized, now that we were standing so close. His eyes really were a pretty greeny-blue . . .

"I, um . . ." He cleared his throat. "I need to move the ladder."

I quickly pulled my hand back. "Oh, sure."

He moved around to the far side of the chimney and made sure it was stable before he climbed up again. I held onto the ladder again, deliberately not looking at his legs as he went up.

"I can't see right up to the top," he said, stepping back down. "But what I can see all looks good."

I made sure I let go of the ladder this time. "That's great."

"I'm sure the building inspector checked it when you bought it, but you should still check it every year."

"Every year." I nodded. "Got it."

He stared at me, and I stared right back.

Clay swallowed hard. "You said you had a mirror?"

"Yes!" I turned toward the front patio. "Inside. Good idea."

Why was I stupefied around him?

Because Jayden filled your head with nonsense.

Trying to get myself together, I held the front door for him. "Don't worry about your boots. The floor will be the last thing I do."

He walked in and looked around. "You've been busy today again."

"I think I'll be busy for a long time," I said. "My to-do list is as long as my arm. But today was sanding, mostly. All the window frames and door jambs."

He nodded toward the kitchen or, more to the point, where the kitchen used to be. "And demolition, I see."

"Oh." I walked over to the old swollen and misshapen plywood cupboards now stacked in a pile on the floor. "Well, if by demolition you mean that I gave it one hard shove and it basically fell apart, then yes."

He looked at it and grimaced. "Oh."

I laughed. "Yeah. I was hoping something might be reusable, for a cupboard in the back shed even, but no. Well, maybe the old sink . . ." I pointed to the two pipes protruding from the wall under the window. "But the good news is the plumber's happy. He actually doesn't have much to fix, thankfully. Aside from the radiators and installing the new boiler. And the electrician is all good to go. New light fixtures, a ceiling fan or two. He will have to hardwire in some smoke detectors and replace the old fuse box with a new circuit breaker. The original is, well . . . original. Oh, and new wiring for the stove, of course. But I don't need to replace the transformer from the main, so that's great news. And the carpenter came and measured up for the built-ins. He's ready to start too. It's been a busy morning."

He was smiling at me.

I tried not to feel bad. "Sorry, I'm just excited. It's all coming together. I know it will slow down, especially at this time of year with Christmas coming up. And Ren at the hardware store wasn't sure what might have delayed delivery, but he was hopeful everything I wanted should be in this week. And I want to buy local if I can. If this is going to be my home, I need to support the local businesses, right? As opposed to ordering stuff online or driving back down to Mossley or even Missoula. I'd rather not."

He was still smiling. "Yeah. Local is good."

"I'm still unsure about the bathroom. I'm kinda torn. Do I just paint the tiles like you suggested? Or do I rip it all out and do a brand-new one while I'm doing everything else?" I shrugged. "If I paint over them, it puts me weeks ahead and I'll have a bathroom to use from day one, and that's a good thing, considering I don't currently have a kitchen. The plumber said the waterproofing membrane was still fine—there are no leaks. But I will probably have to look at replacing it at some point. So do I just do it now while I'm doing everything else?" I sighed. "I can't decide. To be honest, I think the plumber would rather not have to do a complete rebuild in the weeks before Christmas. I asked him if painting the tiles was a better option instead of ripping out the entire room, and he couldn't say yes fast enough," I said with a laugh. "I mean, either way, he still has a lot to do . . ."

I tried to stop talking.

"Sorry."

"Don't apologize. Passion and excitement are nothing to be sorry for."

I met his gaze. "I am excited. It's the first place I've got on my own, and I can make it as *me* as I want." I felt childish for admitting that to him.

I wasn't sure why I did.

He stared at me for a long moment and then nodded. "Then you should make it the very *you-est* you possibly can."

I grinned. Then I remembered what he was here for. "Oh, the mirror. It's in the bathroom. This way."

I went through the mudroom to the second entrance of the bathroom. "Gotta love these old designs that were built for functionality. The other door opens to the hall and bedrooms."

"Oh, wowzers."

I turned to see what'd made him stop and say that. The bathroom was just—

"That's a lot of brown."

I laughed. "And that's why I want to get rid of it. Or paint it at the very least."

"Yes, paint. Any color that hides—" He gestured to the walls, the floor, the shower. "—that."

"What? You don't like six different shades of brown in one room?" I chuckled. "The seventies were full of bold design choices. I could pair these tiles with orange blinds and yellow accents, don't you think? Maybe lime green. And a shag bath mat."

Clay smiled. "Well, you could. Then the Brady Bunch could just move right in."

"Exactly," I said with a laugh. I picked up the mirror, which was leaning against the basin. "Complete with brown plastic medicine cabinet and sliding mirror. Which I very cheerfully took off the wall today."

"Here, let me take that." He seemed to hold it with considerably less effort than me, and he looked around, taking in the details. "A quick paint job, new fixtures, fancy new basin. It'd be good as new."

"And a new toilet," I added. I pointed my chin at the atrocity and grimaced. "I mean, it flushes and all the pipes are fine, but no amount of cleaning can save that."

Clay laughed, a deep rumbling sound. "I was trying to be polite and not mention it."

Jeez. He was even more handsome when he laughed.

"Anyway," I said, trying to distract myself. I went out into the hall and headed back toward the living room, assuming he'd follow. "Enough of me babbling away about what needs to be done. I don't want to keep you any longer."

"It's no problem at all. I'm almost done for the day anyway. Had an early start." He laid the mirror down in the fireplace. "Well, I gotta get back before all the guys finish up for the day. We're kinda busy and got a lot going on this time of year. But it helps that I live there."

"You live at the sawmill?"

He nodded. "On site, yup. All my life."

"That's kind of cool."

"Well, maybe." He didn't seem too convinced. "I live there with my dad. Just him and me. We have separate houses," he added quickly. "He has the main house and I have the smaller one, but it suits me just fine."

His words hit me right in the heart. "You live with your dad?"

He gave a nod but seemed a bit embarrassed. "Yeah."

"I love that. My dad passed away earlier this year."

Clay's expression softened. "I'm sorry to hear that."

"It wasn't unexpected, but still . . . thank you."

"My grandpa passed away a few months back," he said. "My dad's dad. He was in a home. Had been for a while."

"Doesn't make it any easier," I said softly.

"Nope." He pulled on his beard. "Is that what brought you to Hartbridge?"

I nodded. "Kind of. It's a long story. But my marriage ended the day after my father's funeral, and aside from being a shock and terrible timing, it was a huge wake-up call for me."

He stared, eyes wide. "The day after your father's funeral?" He shook his head. "Well, I'll be . . . that's just awful . . . Of all the timing they coulda chose, they went with that?"

I smiled sadly. "Yeah. It was a shock. And he, uh—"

Shit.

I said he.

I just said he.

And in that very split second, in my mind, I stopped myself. I wasn't hiding anything anymore. If Clay didn't like it, then it was too bad for him.

"He?"

Were his cheeks red? It was hard to tell under the beard, but I wasn't embarrassed about being gay.

No more hiding anything.

"Yes. My ex-husband. He never did much think about other people."

Clay's eyes met mine and he held my gaze. "Well, he sounds like a fool."

Relief flooded through me. And something else. Nerves. Or excitement. Something I wasn't ready to pull apart yet. But nevertheless, I found myself smiling at him.

"He is a fool. And an ass."

He grinned. "I was trying to be polite again."

With a happy shrug, I gestured to the very empty and somewhat demolished house. "And so here I am. A new house, a new life, and I'm very excited to start. Although I'm sure if you see me in a week's time when everything's going wrong, I probably won't be so excited."

"Nah, nothing will go wrong. A few hiccups, maybe. Sounds to me like you're in store for some good in your life. Your house will be a home in no time."

I wasn't prepared for how his words and the sincerity behind them would hit me. My smile was a little teary and I squeezed his arm. "Thank you."

There was a hint of color underneath his beard; I was beginning to think it was indeed a blush. "So, tell me about your new kitchen."

I think I gasped. "Really?" I didn't wait for his answer. I was already scrolling through pictures on my phone. I held it for him to see. "I have photos of what it'll look like. Simple white cabinetry. The kitchen people are supposed to be here the week after next, before the floor goes down." I gestured to where the old kitchen had been. "Sink will be below the window, where the water pipes are, naturally. Range along this wall. Island in the middle."

"Nice."

"And I'll have my dining table here," I said, pointing to the small area to the left of the kitchen. "Cabinet over there, and I have artwork for the walls. Although the view out the back windows is pretty spectacular." I stopped to appreciate the greenery that was my backyard. "I mean, it's just trees at the moment. But it sure beats looking at a brick wall."

I sighed loudly, and when I looked at Clay, he was smiling at me.

"Your excitement's contagious," he said. "I can't wait to see what you do with the place."

That made me laugh. "You know, it's crazy, but to have people happy for me is so strange. My brother thinks I'm insane, and my ex . . . well, he'd just roll his eyes if I ever got excited about anything. And I've been here for just a few days and already you, Jayden, and Hamish are like 'oh my god, tell me all about your plans,' and I gotta say . . ." I put my hand to my heart. "It's just really lovely."

Clay was quiet for a few seconds, and it was hardly surprising, given the word-vomit I'd just unloaded on him. "Your brother thinks you're insane?"

I gave a nod. "Edward. He's in Texas. Owns a pretty big car dealership down there. When our dad passed away, Edward and I split everything, and then, of course, when Scott left me, Edward tried to convince me to move south. He can't understand why anyone would want to live where it snows."

That earned me a smile. "Well, I'm gonna assume Edward's never seen a sunrise over the mountains when they're covered in a blanket of the whitest snow you've ever seen."

My heart thumped at his words—*I can't remember when someone had said such poetic things to me*—and my voice came out as a whisper. "No, he hasn't."

"And your ex, Scott? He'd roll his eyes at you?"

I shrugged. "Sometimes, yeah."

"We've already covered the part where he's an ass, right?"

I chuckled. "We have."

"Good. Just wanted to be thorough." He smiled at me, those pretty greenish-blue eyes shining. Then he nodded out the window to the line of trees. "You said it's just trees at the moment. What did you mean?"

I walked to the window. "I love the trees. It's part of the reason I bought this place. Well, the no nosy neighbors looking over the fence was a factor too. I want to keep the trees clear of the house. You know, for a firebreak. And because of bears."

"Not a fan?"

"Oh sure. They're cute and all. I'm very happy for them to live long and fulfilling bear-lives," I said. "Just not in my backyard. Actually, somewhere else entirely would be a great start."

"Poor Yogi."

"Yogi can get his pic-a-nic basket from someone else."

Clay laughed. "I dunno if bears mind too much about the cover of trees if pic-a-nic baskets are on offer. But the firebreak around your house is a good idea. How many acres you got here?"

"Eight."

"Nice." He seemed surprised by that, and he pulled on his beard a little. "I can help ya with the clearing if you want? It won't be until after Christmas, most likely, because we're so busy. Could probably do January at the earliest. Then it'll depend on the snow and what needs to be done and where. But I can take a look for ya, if you want."

"Oh, that'd be perfect!" I replied. "I'll be busy with the interior until then anyway. Then I'll start on the exterior in the spring. And gardens. And a new driveway. And about a thousand other things I'll be doing for the next few years."

He grinned at me. "I never heard anyone be so thrilled about that much work."

I snorted and it made him laugh. *Super classy, Gunter.*

"It's crazy, huh?" I replied. "But like I said before: new life, new me."

"Nah. New life, real you."

And there he was again with those hard-hitting words. Right in the solar plexus. I had to blink back tears. "Oh my god, you just keep saying the best things. The real me. It's about time, huh?"

He stared at me for a long second and I was just about to apologize for being so emotional, but then it was Clay who looked a little glassy-eyed. "Yeah, it's about time."

I wasn't sure what to say. "Are you okay?"

He nodded quickly and faked a smile. "Yeah. About that chimney. Better take a look and get back to work."

"Oh yes, of course," I said. I'd forgotten that was why he was here. "I didn't mean to keep you."

Or dump my entire life story on you.

"It's no problem." He did the mirror and flashlight trick with the chimney, looking for blockages or creosote, the damper and the flue lining. I did more nodding and agreeing than understanding as he pointed things out, but he said it was in pretty good order.

"And I see you bought yourself a grate," he said.

"Yes, because you told me to. Ren asked me what size, and I only had your shoulders as a reference." He raised his eyebrows, so I explained, "When you were here yesterday and you laid down to look up the chimney, your shoulders barely fit."

"And what did Ren say?"

"He just laughed and he showed me what he had in stock. I took the biggest. And the heaviest. It weighs a ton."

Clay bent down, picked the grate up as if it weighed nothing, and slid it into the fireplace. "There you go. Ready for your first fire."

"Oh, thank you."

His eyes met mine for a brief second before he looked away. He chewed on his bottom lip as if he was nervous or uncomfortable or something and held onto his flashlight like it was a lifeline. He opened his mouth as if to speak but instead gave a nod and headed for the door. I followed him out to his truck, wondering what had gone so wrong.

"Thanks again," I tried. "You can send me the bill for your time. Same email as the invoice for the firewood."

He seemed shocked by this. "Oh no, it was just . . . I was just . . . being helpful. No charge."

"Clay, did I say something to upset you? Or offend you? If I did, I'm—"

"No, no." He shook his head. "Of course not. I just . . . I, uh . . ."

He opened his truck door but didn't get in. He just stood there. He ran his hand down his face, pulling on his beard, which I was starting to think he did when he was nervous.

He looked like he wanted to say something but wasn't sure how. Or if he should. He was clearly struggling.

"Okay then," I began. "If you're ever driving past, stop by. I don't have a kitchen so I can't offer you coffee, but—"

"I'm bisexual."

Oh.

He blurted it out like it was bubbling inside him, dying to get out . . . and I understood then.

Exactly what that meant.

I offered him a kind smile. "And I'm guessing you haven't told many people."

He laughed, a little maniacally. "That would be no one. You're the first. And I dunno why I'm even saying it now. It's just you said your ex was a guy, so you're gay or bi or . . .

something. And then you said you finally got to living your life and being the real you. Because it was about time."

That was when he got glassy-eyed . . . *God, Gunter. You should have seen the signs.*

I walked up to him and gave his arm a squeeze. "Thank you for telling me," I said gently. "And now—if no one else knows—you can be the real you around me. Because it's about time?"

He nodded, teary-eyed. "It is." Then he laughed at the sky, shaking off his emotions. "I dunno why now. I dunno why you. Why I had to tell you. I don't even know. I spent my whole life content to never say nothing to no one. Just gonna be me and my dad and the sawmill, and I was okay with that. Then you move here to start over and be the real you. And I dunno . . . it just hit me. I've never been the real me."

"Well, now you can be." I cursed myself for not having anything in the house to offer him. "Man, I wish I had a coffee machine, at least. We could go to the diner for coffee? If you want to chat. I don't have any chairs, though I've got some porch steps we could sit on? If you don't mind the cold."

He smiled sadly. "I do have to get back to the mill."

"Well, give me your phone." I held out my hand and he handed it over. "I'll add my number, and you can text me or call me if you ever want to talk. Okay?"

He smiled sheepishly when I gave him back his phone. "Thanks. I'm sorry for dumping this all on you. Feel kinda foolish."

"Hey, don't apologize. I dumped my entire life story on you earlier, and you did a big thing just now." I put my hand to my heart. "Clay, your secret is safe with me. And if you want to drop by anytime to talk, that's perfectly fine with me, and if anyone questions what you're doing at the new guy's house so much, you tell them you're quoting on removing trees or delivering firewood or fixing chimneys or something. I'll be happy to tell them the same." Then I shrugged. "Or I can tell them to mind their own business, we can work out our stories later."

He gave me a genuine smile. "Thank you, Gunter."

"Thank you," I replied. "For checking my chimney and for dropping by. And for getting to be the real you."

He gave me a teary nod and quickly climbed into his truck, though he was smiling again as he drove out.

I watched him go, then locked up the house and drove back to the bed and breakfast. As soon as Jayden saw me, he pounced. "Oh my god, what happened? And why are you smiling like that?"

With Clay's secret firmly locked away, I shrugged. "Nothing. It's just been a productive day." I turned my attention to the clipboards on the counter. "What have you got there?"

He studied me for a long scrutinizing moment. "Hm. Organizing menus and stock orders for Christmas." He tapped the list with his pen, a smile on his lips. "Oh, and Cass wants me to call Henderson's to order some Christmas trees. Wouldn't happen to have Clay's phone number handy, would you?"

I tried not to smile. "Maybe. For professional reasons. He's going to clear some trees for me."

He hummed and did a little wiggle-dance. "I'm telling you. Hartbridge at Christmastime. Like it or not, Cupid hides in the Christmas trees, taking potshots at people. No one's safe."

CHAPTER FOUR

CLAY

I LAY IN BED, staring at the ceiling. The ebb and flow between relief and panic kept me awake.

I hadn't intended to tell Gunter. Hell, I was just kinda hoping to find out if he was into men. His ex was a man, so that answered that. But he was so honest with me. Now that he was in Hartbridge with his new life, his new house, he was finally happy.

The real him.

It was about time.

Those words rattled around in my head, in my chest, like a freaking pinball machine.

Because I hadn't ever been the real me.

And of course, he'd taken the news well. Of course he was nice about it. As far as coming out to someone, it went well. He was supportive and even a little proud?

Anyway. It was done now.

No going back.

Would I tell other people?

Would I even have to? Would I ever be with a man?

Sure, I'd like to try that, but I didn't know if it would ever happen.

The hard truth was . . . I just didn't know.

There wasn't any point in derailing my life for no reason. The likelihood of me ever finding a man that was interested in me was pretty fucking slim. I mean, there was Gunter . . .

And the likelihood of a man like that—super smart, older, richer—there was just no way.

But if he did? Would I derail my life for a man like that? Well . . .

Yeah. Even just one night.

God, what I'd do for one night.

My thoughts went straight to sex. Imagining the touch, the stubble and hard muscles, the smell of a man, the taste . . .

I ignored the warm pool in my belly, the need in my balls.

It wasn't helping my state of mind at all.

Rubbing one out to fantasies of a man—of Gunter—would only get me in trouble.

I rolled over and grabbed my phone from my bedside table. He said I could text him . . . So I did.

Thank you for today

I hit Send before I could change my mind.

I waited for a reply but none came through. It was 10:47 p.m. after all. So I slid my phone back on the bedside table and sighed. I stared at the wall for a while, convincing myself to forget it. Just go back to the old me, the single straight guy.

The lonely guy.

The half-of-me guy.

I was almost asleep when my phone beeped with a message, the screen lighting up my room. I snatched up the phone, smiling at Gunter's name.

> You're welcome. How are you feeling about today?

Okay

I was better now that he'd replied. I wasn't so alone.

Kinda going back and forth.

He was much faster at texting than me.

> That's perfectly normal. What you told me today was a big deal. It's okay to feel a little wobbly.

I snorted at the word wobbly.

Like learning to ride a bike with training wheels?

> LOL Yes! Exactly like that. But you'll be racing soon.

I smiled at my phone. I wanted to hug it. I didn't realize just how much I needed the support.

Thanks. It means a lot.

> Anytime. And my offer for coffee still stands.

His words burned in my chest. I even felt a bit jittery, which was crazy.

I wanted to reply with an excited yes, but I wasn't sure if or when I could, so I settled for something that hopefully met in the middle.

Deal

Just hoped it was cool without sounding too eager.

No reply came through for a little bit and I wondered if he was staring at his phone like I was, not wanting to end the conversation yet not sure what to say next.

Before I could panic and say something stupid, his text bubble appeared, and those three little dots danced for the longest time. Was he writing a novel? Or was he as stuck for something to say as I was?

I'll be lighting the fire at the house tomorrow, just so you know. Testing out the chimney. I have to scrub walls and it's supposed to snow. I need the walls to dry. And I'd like to not freeze to death.

I was smiling at my phone like a fool.

Will there be a fire lighting ceremony?

Should there be?

Yes.

Olympics style. I like it!

What time do proceedings start?

LOL Probably 9am?

I'll try to swing by.

Then I'll try to have coffee.

I was still smiling. My worries from earlier seemed so far away and so stupid. I was tired now, my mind wasn't such a mess. Funny how putting down a heavy burden did that.

Goodnight Gunter

There was no way to say just how much his texts had helped me. So I just added thank you even though it was nowhere near enough, and hit Send.

And thank you.

Night, Clay.

Worrying myself sick about coming out or not could wait another day. I fell asleep smiling.

I TIMED a delivery of some beams and rough lumber out to a ranch on Old Larch Road to be done by nine. Purely coincidental that it happened that way.

Yeah, right.

Even I wasn't fooling myself. I liked Gunter. And I'd never liked a man before. Not really.

And me liking Gunter was just an infatuation. I was

sure of that. Now that the bisexual side of me was awake, of course I was gonna latch onto the first guy I noticed.

I was ignoring the fact it was probably Gunter who woke my bisexuality up. Maybe it would have come out of hibernation all by itself. There was no way to tell.

But that was all beside the point.

The real point to this whole fiasco was that me liking Gunter was purely a crush, a passing phase that would run its course and be all said and done. Then I could look back and laugh at how ridiculous I was being.

Until he walked out onto his front porch, wearing his red coat, red-rimmed glasses, and a huge smile, holding a take-out cup of coffee.

The butterflies it gave me, how happy it made me . . . yep, utterly ridiculous.

"Good morning," he said brightly. "Oh my goodness, it's cold out here. The snow is pretty, but that wind, oh my god. Come inside, quick." I was too busy noticing the man on the porch instead of the snow. It was barely an inch or two, a light dusting, really. Regardless, he ushered me in, closed the door behind me, and handed over the coffee. "I wasn't sure how you liked it, but Jayden said you preferred white with two."

I wasn't sure what he meant. "Jayden said what?"

"Your coffee. At the diner. He was working there today and he said you take your coffee white with two sugars."

"Oh."

"Is that wrong? Because I have black. We can swap if you prefer?"

I chuckled. "No, I just wasn't sure where that conversation was going. You know, the old coffee preference analogy."

Gunter laughed. "Oh, no. Bit early in the day for that."

Apparently not for my mind . . . "Ah yes, cream and two sugars." I sipped it. "It's perfect, thank you."

Smiling, he sipped his coffee, then placed it carefully on the windowsill. "I really need to bring up a table or something," he mumbled, then gestured to the fireplace. "But look. Ta-da!"

The grate was in place and there was a good stack of kindling expertly placed with some scrunched up newspapers and fire starters. There were smaller logs in a bucket beside the hearth, not a piece out of place. Everything about him was neat and orderly, and I liked that.

"I've put a decent supply of firewood in the mudroom for now. To keep it dry while I get everything else organized," he said. He pulled a utility lighter from his pocket, and with a cheeky grin, he clicked it on. "Are you ready?"

I gave a nod. "Got a fire extinguisher in the truck if you need."

He snorted. "Thanks? Fingers crossed we don't." He leaned down, the lighter just about to touch the newspaper.

"Wait," I said. He flicked the lighter off.

"What's wrong?"

"Nothing. You just need to make a speech. This is the Olympic lighting, right?"

"A speech?"

"Yep." I shrugged and strung some random words together. "Say something like 'Today I light this fire to warm this house, to make it a home. This first fire of this first year of my new life. May there be many more.'"

Gunter looked at me, swallowed hard and fanned his face, his eyes teary. "Oh my god, Clay. Don't make me cry! That was . . . that was such a sweet thing to say."

I gently patted his shoulder. "You okay?"

Please don't cry, please don't cry, please don't cry.

"Yes, of course," he said, smiling now. He let out a sigh and his eyes searched mine. "You say the best things, Clay. I don't know how you make everything sound special."

"Special?" I chuckled behind my coffee. "Well, I dunno about special . . ." I wasn't gonna admit this but being honest with him felt right. "When my mom passed away, she left a whole bunch of poetry books she'd collected over the years. When she was sick, she would read them and they gave her a real sense of joy. She found peace in 'em, so when she was sick, I'd read them to her. Then when she passed, I kept reading 'em. And she was right. Makes you see the world with kinder eyes."

He got teary again. His chin even wobbled, but he nodded quickly. "There you go again . . . with the perfect words at the perfect time."

It reminded me that he'd only lost his dad a little while back. "Sorry. I shouldn't have said—"

He put his hand on my arm, shook his head, and blinked away his tears. "No. It was perfect. I love it. So please don't apologize. If we could all see the world with kinder eyes, it'd be a better place, right?"

My heart thumped oddly against my ribs. "True."

Gunter inhaled deeply and seemed to remember the lighter in his hand. "Okay. Let's light this fire." He kneeled beside the hearth and gave me a smile. "Today I light this fire to warm this house, to make it a home. This first fire of this first year of my new life. May there be many more."

He flicked the lighter on and put the flame to the newspaper and kindling. The fire starters caught, and slowly but surely the fire began to take hold.

Gunter leaned back on his haunches and grinned up at me. "I made fire!"

It made my heart do that stupid thumping thing again.

Or maybe it was his smile. Or his eyes . . . I was half a second away from saying something completely stupid or way outta line, so I nodded to the front door. "I'll go check the chimney."

The chimney didn't need checking. Smoke wasn't billowing into the room so it had to be going up the dang chimney, but getting out of the house seemed like a good idea.

I went down the steps and walked out a few yards so I could see the roof properly and, sure enough, smoke was coming out the top of the chimney.

Gunter stood on his porch and I gave him a thumbs up. "Looks good."

He gave a little clap, then came down to join me. He stood beside me, facing the house, and he was grinning. The joy he got from the smallest things made me like him even more.

Like him?

I barely knew him.

I knew he was single and gay. I knew he'd moved here for a new start and he wasn't afraid of hard work. He hadn't mentioned a job but he obviously had money. I knew he was kind, and he seemed like a decent guy. He wanted to support local businesses. He wanted to restore the house. He wanted to keep as many trees as possible.

I knew he made me feel all warm and woozy.

He made me . . . want to be with a man. I wanted to try it. I wanted to know what it was like. I wanted to feed that half of me that I'd starved for far too long.

"You okay?" he asked.

Oh shoot. Was I staring? Did I zone out?

"Yeah, of course," I lied. "But I should get going or they'll send out a search party for me."

"Yes, of course," he replied. "I really do appreciate you being here today." A breeze picked up and he turned to face the wind. "Boy, that wind's got some bite. You better get out of the cold." Then he shot a look back to the house. "Oh, lemme just grab your coffee for you. It'll keep you warm on the drive home."

I wasn't going to say no. Not to the coffee. Not to spending an extra minute with him.

I followed him back to the porch, and in his rush, he went to take the steps two at a time, and as his foot went down, he slid. His hand went out to grab the railing, but he missed, his arm flailing in the air, and before I knew it, he was falling backward.

And right into my arms.

CHAPTER FIVE

GUNTER

"WHAT DO you mean you fell on top of him?" Jayden asked. He put a cup of coffee down in front of me, his eyes as wide as his smile. We were in his kitchen just before dinner. It had been a long and eventful day.

"I slipped on the step," I repeated. "Went to grab the railing. Missed. Somehow got kind of turned around mid-fall and landed on him."

"And you weren't hurt?"

"Nope."

"And you didn't hurt him?"

I shook my head. "He caught me and held me, our faces this close." I said with my palm an inch from my nose.

He gasped and covered his mouth with his hand. "Just like in a movie. In those amazingly cheesy romcoms that can't possibly happen in real life."

I nodded. "Exactly. And let me tell you, he's strong. And broad. And Jayden," I leaned in. "I can confirm, underneath that plaid and overalls, he is *all* man."

Cass cleared his throat behind us. I spun around almost dying of embarrassment and Jayden burst out laughing.

"Talking about anyone I know?" Cass said with a smile.

Jayden pulled him in close, still smiling. "Gunter had a very close encounter with a certain lumberjack. It involved a well-timed fall down some steps into the very strong and capable arms of Clay Henderson."

"Ooh, just like in the movies," Cass said. He swiped Jayden's coffee and took a sip. "I gotta go shower. Then I can come do dinner."

"No need. I bought what was left of yesterday's lasagna home from the diner. Carl told me to take it." He looked at me. "Is that okay?"

Was he kidding? "It sounds absolutely perfect."

Cass kissed the side of Jayden's head and it shot an ache through me. I missed that intimacy. I missed that kind of love. "I'll leave you two to talk about poor Clay Henderson."

"From what Gunter was saying, there's not much *poor* about him." Jayden gave me a cheeky nudge. "Was he big?"

"Jayden!" Cass said.

I laughed, embarrassed. "Big chest. Big arms, big hands," I said. "That's as much as I'm saying."

Truth was, that was all I remember feeling. Those huge arms wrapped around me, holding me to his chest, his face barely an inch from mine. And those damn greenish-blue eyes.

"And after he caught you, saved you heroically, like a damsel in distress—" Jayden put the back of his hand to his forehead. "—what did he do?"

Cass rolled his eyes and left us to gossip.

It was stupid. I felt foolish and childish, but this *was* the stuff from a cheesy rom-com movie. And I'd be lying if I said it didn't feel good.

I sipped my coffee and smiled at Jayden. "Well, he took me inside, out of the cold, and fussed over me. He thought I might have hurt myself, and it's a miracle that I didn't."

"If he hadn't caught you, you would have for sure."

"Without a doubt."

"So he saved your life!"

I admired Jayden's enthusiasm. "Well, he saved me from spraining something. Or breaking my wrist. Or twisting my knee. I don't even know how I fell," I admitted. "The step was slippery in the snow, and my feet just went out from under me. He definitely saved me from hurting myself."

"And he fussed all over you?"

I nodded, smiling at the memory. "He kneeled down in front of me by the fire and made sure nothing was broken, at least. Checked my ankles and knees."

"Did he check your mouth? Perform CPR?"

"No. Not required."

"You could have faked a sore jaw. Tell him you bit your tongue and you need him to take care of it. You need to think of these things on the spot."

"I'll try to remember that."

"I would have faked a groin injury."

I snorted. "I'm not that bold."

"So he caught you, held you tight in all the right places. And then what did he do?"

"He asked me twenty times if I was okay, if I needed to see the doctor. I told him I was fine. He handed me my coffee, asked me if I was okay another dozen times. He stoked up the fire for me and left."

"That's an awful lot of fussing."

"And he called me an hour later."

Jayden raised an eyebrow. "Please tell me you have a date with him."

I shook my head and sipped my drink. "No. He just wanted to make sure I was still okay."

"Do you want him to ask you out?"

"No."

He locked eyes with me. "Do you really not want that? Answer me honestly, Gunter. Not what you think you *should* say. Not what common sense is telling you or your recently wounded heart, but what you really want."

My eyes cut to his and I couldn't answer, because . . . well, because maybe I did?

Jayden grinned victoriously. "I knew it."

"I don't know what I want," I replied, trying not to smile. "I don't know what I'm ready for. But it's . . . exciting?"

"It is exciting! And even if it's no more than coffee or dinner occasionally, that's still exciting too. Meeting up with a big gorgeous man for a dinner and a movie should be fun. Even if it never becomes anything more, isn't it still a valuable friendship? There aren't many of us queer men in these mountains, so we should befriend each other. It's what we do. And . . ." A wicked gleam shined in his eye. "Even if you're not interested in anything else, friends with benefits could be fun."

My cheeks burned. "Maybe."

"Do you know if he's queer?" he asked, but before I could answer, before I had to lie, he shook his head. "Don't worry. I've seen how he looked at you. That man is definitely interested."

I shrugged and sipped my coffee.

Jayden watched me for a few seconds. "You're picturing it right now, aren't you? That big strong body that you said was *all man* . . . I bet—"

"Jayden," Cass said as he walked in. "Are you speaking inappropriately with our guest?"

Cass definitely spoke with a hint of warning, but Jayden just laughed and nudged me with his elbow. "Believe me, it's very appropriate. And how are you showered so fast? We weren't done gossiping. Though you do smell good."

Cass sighed and offered me an apologetic smile. "I do apologize for him." Then he poked Jayden in the side with his finger. "Perhaps we could organize dinner so poor Gunter can enjoy his evening in peace."

"I'm not bothering him," Jayden said. "He had a rom-com movie moment today and we need to encapsulate every detail."

Cass raised one eyebrow. "Encapsulate?"

Jayden nodded. "Yep. It means—"

"I know what it means—"

"Well, we need to do that. To every detail. Cass, my love, you've seen rom-coms. I make you suffer through them. You know how they work."

I put my empty coffee cup in the sink and I gave Jayden a wink. "I should go clean up before dinner. And we can finish gossiping later. And encapsulate."

Cass chuckled. "How am I the one outnumbered here?"

"Oh shush," Jayden said, sliding his arm around him. "You can encapsulate me later."

Cass put his hand over Jayden's mouth, clearly shocked that he'd say that in front of me, but I just laughed as I left them in the kitchen. I could hear Jayden laugh as I walked down the hall. It sounded like he was being tickled. And while it made me smile, another pang of jealousy left its mark too.

No, it wasn't jealousy. It was longing and wishful thinking. It was sadness that my marriage was over and regret that I hadn't ended it years before Scott had left me.

All those wasted years . . .

I still loved love. I wasn't bitter. I wasn't sworn to a life of loneliness because Scott walked out on me. If anything, it made me want to fall in love every day with every little thing, to never waste another day.

Love was a beautiful thing.

I refused to believe otherwise.

So maybe I shouldn't be so quick to dismiss a possible thing with Clay. Not that I knew if he was interested in that, but if the opportunity did present itself, maybe I should take the chance.

Thinking about how he'd caught me, how he'd held me, his face so close to mine. He was a big guy: six foot four, 240 pounds. He was an actual lumberjack. His hands were huge, and to feel them on me . . .

To be manhandled by someone almost twice my size was, well, it was hot. I wasn't a big guy. Never had been. Never athletic, never did weights at the gym. I was five foot ten in boots and 170 pounds wringing wet.

And the way he looked at me, our noses almost touching . . . there was definitely interest in his eyes. In those greenish-blue beautiful eyes . . .

And what Jayden had said was right. So what if it led nowhere if we decided it wasn't for us? Having dinner or coffee with a guy was fun. Maybe even being friends with benefits could be an option.

It had been far too long since a man had touched me. Since I'd wanted a man to touch me. And the way Clay's hands held me, large and strong. God, I bet he could do some magical things.

Thinking about that while having a shower wasn't optimal either.

I sighed and shut the water off. I was forty-four years old. I had better self-control than that.

Cleaned up and dressed, I went back out to the kitchen just as Jayden was dishing up dinner. There was no more talk about me and Clay, and at the end of the day, I was kind of glad.

Jayden was excited because the Hartbridge tree-lighting ceremony was coming up, as it was held every year on December first. It wasn't the big light festival night, but apparently, from the first of December, Hartbridge became like a Christmas movie set with festive decorations starting with the lighting of the town's huge Christmas tree.

It was hard not to be excited. I couldn't wait to experience my first Christmas here, but the calendar check was also a sharp reminder that I had three weeks to get my house in order. Things were going well, but it didn't leave much time for possible dates or distractions.

I didn't need the house finished in three weeks. I just needed a working bathroom and kitchen and adequate heating. The rest I could work around.

By the end of the night, I crawled into bed a little sore in the back and across the shoulders. Not from my epic fall into Clay's arms, but from sanding, cleaning walls, scrubbing bathroom tiles and cleaning the kitchen area. And of course, in the quiet dark of my room, my thoughts turned to him. How he'd treated me, cared for me, and fussed over me after he'd caught me, but also how he'd worried enough to call me a few hours after.

I wasn't going to text him, although maybe it wouldn't hurt to lob the ball back onto his side of the court to see how this game played out. So, somewhat reluctantly but mostly excitedly, I reached for my phone and sent him a text.

> Thanks again for checking on me today.
> Just wanted you to know that I'm
> absolutely fine.

His reply came through a moment later.

> Glad to hear that.

Then I thought about this new me. The old me would have left the conversation at that, but this new me was a little bolder. This new me had nothing to lose and wanted to take risks and not miss opportunities out of fear. I didn't want to waste any more time.

So I sent him another text.

> If you ever want to grab coffee or dinner, let
> me know. My treat. I owe you for breaking
> my fall today.

The text bubble appeared, then disappeared. And it stayed gone. I gave him a few minutes, and when he still hadn't replied, I took that as my answer and put my phone down.

No coffee or dinner date then.

And that was fine. He didn't *have* to. It was just an offer and he was allowed to say no.

But it did sting a little, and I tried to ignore the disappointment that burned in my belly. I rolled onto my side, pulled the blankets up, and closed my eyes.

❄

"HE DIDN'T REPLY?" Hamish asked.

I shook my head quickly. "Nope." We were in the hardware store. I had to pick up some gear, and we'd lined up to order coffee. "Two days ago."

"Two days?"

He kind of yelled that, loud enough that a man toward the end of the aisle looked up.

"No reply in two days," I replied, much quieter than him. "Which is answer enough in itself, right?"

He frowned and sighed. "Jayden said he thought Clay liked you." Thankfully that was a whisper. "I wonder what went wrong? Was there an accident? Is he in the hospital? A sawmill accident? A bear?"

I chuckled. "Highly unlikely. More of a thanks but no-thanks kind of reply."

"Then he could have at least had the decency to say that."

I sighed. "Maybe." I picked up a box of screws and read the label. "Are these for tiles?"

Hamish shook his head. "You need a carbide-tipped tile bit." Then his gaze shot to mine and he gasped with his hand to his mouth. "Oh my god, I'm turning butch."

I heard warm laughter behind us and turned around to see Ren grinning. "I don't think you need to worry, Hame."

He looked duly horrified. "I said the words 'carbide-tipped tile bit' because he needs to drill into tiles. Reynold Brooks, what have you turned me into?" Then Hamish turned back to me. "I could start my own home repairs show." Then he leaned in and whispered, "I could get paid to talk about getting drilled and railed."

"Oh my god, no." Ren physically pulled Hamish away, his eyes wide. "I'm sorry."

I laughed. "I can see why he's friends with Jayden." I showed him the screws I was holding. "Will these work?"

He gave a nod. "You'll just need some drilling oil and plugs."

Hamish snorted. "Don't we all."

Ren turned to him. "Are you here to help? Because that's not helping."

"Don't be silly, my love. I'm here for Gunter. We're having coffee across the road. Jayden's working at the diner today."

I nodded. "I just needed to pick up a few things here first."

Ren's eyes met mine. "You are a brave man."

Hamish gave him a gentle prod. "Husbands are supposed to be nice."

Ren laughed, and they joked about Hamish bringing him lunch. They were clearly very much in love, and just like watching Jayden and Cass, it was lovely to see, but I'd be lying if it also didn't hurt a little.

That sense of longing, longing for what they had, for what I'd never had, burned a little warmer around my heart.

"Hey, Gunter, you okay?" Hamish put his hand on my arm. "We lost you there for a sec."

I tried not to startle. "Oh yeah. I'm fine."

Hamish nodded, his lips pursed. "Yeah, okay. Fine is code for in desperate need of caffeine and cake."

He took my items, handing them directly to Ren. I paid, and a few minutes later we were walking out onto Main Street. Crisp white snow clumped along the sidewalk. The sky was blue, too pretty to care about the bite in the breeze.

It really was such a pretty town.

I put my purchases in my car and fixed my beanie, and Hamish took me by the elbow and led me across the street.

The diner was warm and cozy, and Jayden quickly got us squared away with coffee and, at Hamish's insistence, very large servings of warmed chocolate cake.

"Tell me all about the house reno," Hamish said between forkfuls of cake. "How's it coming along?"

I sipped my coffee. "Better than I'd hoped, actually," I replied. "The built-in closets are in. The walls cleaned up and dried nicely, even with this weather. Painting starts tomorrow. Well, all the taping and cutting-in starts first."

"And you? How are you doing?"

"I'm good," I answered on reflex. And I was. That wasn't a lie. "Moving here will be good for me."

"And Clay?"

"There's nothing to tell. He's a nice guy. I asked him if he wanted to meet up sometime and he . . ."

"He never replied."

I sighed. "He's entitled to say no."

"Then he should have said no. But to not answer is a bit rude."

I shook my head. "He's . . . Well, this is all so very new to him. And I was being all up in my head about it. Listening to Jayden talk about the magic of Hartbridge at Christmas and—" I rolled my eyes and laughed at myself. "It's perfectly fine for Clay not to be ready for anything, and I don't even know if *I'm* ready. It's not his fault. I shouldn't have pushed him." Then I remembered that this was Clay's secret. "Maybe he's not even . . . inclined. And even so, I don't know what I'm ready for."

"He sure sounded inclined." He leaned in and whispered, as if it were some huge secret, "Christmas in Hartbridge is kinda magic." He ate some more cake. "But I get it. If you're not ready, then it's best not to rush."

I sighed. "It's a seesaw of not wanting to rush into

anything and not wanting to waste another minute. I've wasted enough of my life. Though I'm kinda leaning toward the taking-chances side of the fence rather than wondering-what-if side."

"Good for you. I had the same lightbulb moment when I decided to move here. I packed up my life and moved halfway across the planet, drove into a snowbank, and was saved by a very handsome hardware store owner in what was, perhaps, more Hallmark movie than an actual Hallmark movie."

I chuckled. "Ah, the Hartbridge Christmas magic."

He grinned and I noticed him subconsciously playing with his wedding ring. I thumbed the empty space on my ring finger and it was funny because I never missed wearing it. I never felt naked without it. I never once felt lost without it.

For me, it was no different than taking off a shirt at the end of a long day. There was no symbolic removal, no ceremony to signify the end of our relationship or that our vows of forever were null and void. I just felt . . . nothing.

I think my indifference said more about how I really felt than words ever could.

Hamish and I finished our cake and coffee. He talked about what he had to do that day; I spoke of the same. Jayden was busy so we didn't get to chat with him much, but sitting there, talking and laughing in the cozy diner with new friends was really freaking nice.

It reminded me that I'd done the right thing in moving here. Even if the big sexy lumberjack guy didn't want me, I was still in the right place. I was sure of it.

Hamish, Jayden, and I, and Ren and Cass, of course, were planning on meeting up again at the tree-lighting ceremony tonight. It wasn't a big deal, just a nice township thing. Apparently the mayor welcomed the holiday period and lit the huge town tree down by the river on Bridge Street.

"I'll buy us pizza afterwards," I said. "It's the least I can do. After all the help you've all given me. And Jayden won't want to think about cooking after working all day."

"Correct," Jayden said as he took empty plates from the table near ours.

"Then pizza it is," I said.

"Sounds great," Hamish said. "Jayden, we'll see you tonight."

"Will do," he replied with a wave from the kitchen.

Hamish and I pulled on our coats and beanies and went outside. The wind was still blustering down Main Street and I shoved my hands into my pockets. "Okay, Hamish, thank you so much for catching up. I need to go do some work to burn off about two thousand calories."

When he didn't reply, I glanced up to see him looking past me, over my shoulder. "Don't look now, but Clay's behind you. Next store up. Looking very sexy in his overalls and plaid—" He turned abruptly. "And he's seen you."

I turned then, and sure enough, there was Clay, in his blue overalls and red-and-blue plaid jacket, staring right at me. He mumbled something to the guy he was with and walked toward me.

"Hey," he said quietly. He swallowed hard, looking nervous and apologetic. "Look, I, uh . . ."

"It's okay," I said. "You don't need to explain."

"It's, um . . ." His gaze went from me to Hamish, back to me.

"I have to go see Ren," Hamish said quickly. "Nice to see you again, Clay. Gunter, I will see you tonight." And with that, he crossed the street and was gone.

"Sorry, I didn't mean to interrupt," Clay said. He scrubbed his gloved hand over his beanie. "God, I'm so bad at this. I've been busy." He glanced over at the red dump truck, which I hadn't even noticed.

I also hadn't noticed the guy he was with, also wearing overalls and plaid, hauling a small Christmas tree off the back of the truck on his own. And I hadn't noticed the line of Christmas trees now in planters up the side of Main Street.

"You're dropping off all these trees?"

He nodded. "Every year. We harvest and net them, then install them. It's a pretty big job."

God, he *had* been busy. There must have been fifty of them. "That's great—"

"Will you be home this afternoon?"

His question was so abrupt, it surprised me.

"Yes. I'm getting ready for painting, so I'll be there until about six."

He nodded. "Can I stop by? I . . . I'd like to talk, if that's okay?"

I gave him a smile. "Sure. Any time."

"See you then," he said, turning back and, without a word, hauled another tree off the back of his truck. He never looked at me again, but his cheeks were red. Now, maybe it was the wind and the cold, but the smile on his friend's face told me he didn't think it was either.

CHAPTER SIX

CLAY

I WAS A FOOL.

I was also confused and experiencing a whole storm of mixed feelings, but mostly I was a fool.

When Gunter took a fall from his top step and landed right in my arms, I was sure. I was one hundred percent certain that I wanted him.

I wanted to be with him.

I dang near almost kissed him.

Then I panicked.

And this was where the fool part comes into it. Because I'd realized something. I wanted to be with him. Physically, I wanted to do all the things I had never done with a man before.

But more than that. I wanted to be with him. I wanted to spend time with him, have dinner with him. I wanted to date him, romance him. See him smile and be the reason he laughed.

I wanted him to look at me the way he did when I caught him from falling down the steps.

And that, without one iota of a doubt, meant coming out.

And that's when the panicking started.

Sure, I made sure he was okay. I even called him later on to see if he wasn't having any of that slow-response muscle trauma, or whatever it was we had to learn about in our work safety classes.

Then he texted me and asked me out for coffee or dinner.

Hell yes, that's what I wanted.

But we couldn't have dinner at his place because he had no kitchen. Or furniture. Or anything. And we couldn't have dinner at the bed and breakfast without Cass and Jayden knowing. We couldn't go back to my place without my dad knowing.

And no place in town was safe from prying eyes and the rumor mill.

How could we go out for dinner without me effectively outing myself?

So yeah. I panicked.

And I ignored his text.

Having two crazy-busy days at work sure helped, and I'd just about convinced myself to go back to my lonely half-bi life.

Until I saw him.

Gunter.

In his red coat, red shoes and blue beanie and red-rimmed glasses.

My stomach swooped, my heart skipped all the beats, my brain stopped working.

God, I was a fool.

There was no denying my full-body reaction. Seeing

him on the sidewalk just made all that foolish panicking seem like nothing at all.

I needed to make things right with him.

Which was why, just after three o'clock in the afternoon, I pulled the truck into his driveway.

Nerves and excitement, anticipation and a healthy dash of fear just about made me puke.

I cut the engine, and before I got to the house, Gunter met me on the porch. "You gotta watch that top step," he said with a smile. "It's a killer."

"I'll keep that in mind." I tried to kick as much of the snow off my boots as I could.

Gunter was holding the door open. "Never mind about that. I'm still not worried about the floors yet. Come in out of the cold."

"At least the wind's died down," I said, walking inside. And the first thing I noticed was the warmth. "Wow. That fire really works, huh?"

"Oh, it's perfect. I'd be lost without it. Thank you for helping me get it set up."

"You're welcome."

"Can I get you a drink?" He waved his hand to where the kitchen should be, where a foldable camping table now stood. "I have a five-gallon dispenser of water, some juice boxes, and some bottles of iced tea."

"Juice boxes?"

"Don't judge," he said with a smile. "Hartbridge Home Mart had limited options, and I don't have a refrigerator. If you'd like the iced tea cold, may I suggest putting it outside for a minute."

That made me laugh. "I'm fine, but thanks."

Then we stood there, staring at each other, and my

nerves were back. It was kind of awkward, and I wasn't sure where to start.

"Look, can I just say something?" he began. "I didn't mean to pressure you or make you feel uncomfortable. You'd barely stuck your head out of the closet for a hot minute and you needed someone you could talk to, not someone asking you out to dinner. I'm really sorry, Clay."

I let out a nervous breath and pulled my beanie off. Then I realized that my hair would be a mess, so I tried to comb it with my fingers somewhat.

"I need to apologize too," I said. "I shoulda replied. It was poor manners not to. And I could lie to you and tell you that work was busy or I was tired or out of town, but the truth was, I panicked."

He put his hand on my arm. "See? And that's my fault, because I asked you before you were ready. I should've known better."

"No, it ain't your fault. Because I wanted to. I wanted to say yes so bad. But I couldn't. I got to thinking, which was my first mistake. I didn't know where we could go . . . If the folks in town saw me on a date with you, then they'd know."

"Oh."

"And I panicked, because I ain't ready for that. I'd have to tell my dad and the guys at work, and it scares me. And all you did was ask if I wanted coffee or dinner, and I . . . I just . . ."

Gunter's face softened. "Oh, Clay. I'm sorry."

"Me too." My mouth was dry and I tried to swallow. "So I spent yesterday being a grumpy bastard at work, my insides all churned up, because it didn't feel right. I felt so bad. And confused. I convinced myself I didn't want to see you. Or have coffee, or dinner, or whatever. That it would just be best if I was . . . back to just being fifty percent of the real me and not attracted to you."

His smile was sad.

"Until I saw you this morning. And right there on Main Street, I realized I didn't much care about all those worries I'd torn myself up about. Or what people might think. Because you . . . you were just standing there in your coat and beanie, the wind made your cheeks pink, and my god, Gunter, you were the most attractive person I think I've ever seen."

He put his hand to his heart. "Oh."

"So I'm here to apologize, and maybe ask if the offer still stands." Before he could answer, I added, "I dunno what it means for me, or us. Or even what you want, but if telling folks I'm having dinner with a man has to happen, then so be it." I puffed out my cheeks. "God, it makes me feel kinda ill just thinking about it."

"Hey," he said, taking my hand. "You don't have to do anything you're not ready to do. I know coming out is hard. It's the hardest thing you might ever have to do. I'd never make you do that." He inhaled and his eyes locked with mine. "I would be happy with take-out coffee or a juice box by the fire, sitting in camping chairs in my half-renovated house."

I squeezed his fingers in mine, not oblivious to how a man's hand felt so different to a woman's. "You came here to finally be the real you. I can't be expecting you to be hiding who you are. That just don't sit right with me. And I meant what I said. I was set on saying no. I was fully prepared to be miserably straight forever." I shrugged. "Until I saw you today."

Gunter smiled and his eyes did some soft-shining thing

I was certain I wanted to see more of. "I was happy to see you too."

"Am I too late?" I asked. "Did I fuck up too bad?"

He chuckled and shook his head. "You didn't fuck up too bad. You're forgiven. This time. Promise me you won't ghost me again. If you don't want to see me, just say so. And I promise I won't rush you into anything you're not ready for."

"Sounds good."

"So we've established that we might want to see each other every so often for take-out coffee."

"Or juice boxes."

"Right." He laughed. "Which is absolutely no pressure. As long as we're both happy with that arrangement, that's fine. And if you wanted to progress to more of a physical thing, then we can. When you're ready."

My heart was hammering hard. "I'd—" My voice hardly worked, so I tried again. "I think I'd like that."

He smiled again. Was he standing this close before? Our bodies almost touching? His face so close to mine?

His gaze went from my eyes to my lips and back up again, slowly, sexy. "I *know* I'd like that."

"Yeah, about that . . ."

"About what?"

"What I'm ready for."

He cocked his head. "Oh?"

"I've never . . . with a man. Done nothing. As you know. Pretty sure we've covered this already. I just don't want you to be disappointed."

He fought a smile. "Well, just so you know, I wouldn't ever be disappointed. So how about we start with the basics first? And you can see if it's something you want to do more of. Before you tell your dad and your friends that you're bi, maybe get used to it yourself first. Who knows, you might not like it."

He was so close. His body heat, his smell; it was intoxicating. "Oh, I really think I'm gonna."

He chuckled, his tongue slipping out to wet his bottom lip. His eyes locked onto mine. "Would you like to kiss me, Clay?"

I was still stuck on the sight of his tongue, that it took a second for his words to register. I drew my eyes up to his. "Yes."

"I haven't ever kissed a man with a beard before," he said, his eyes doing that soft-shining thing again. He brought his hand up to my face, feeling my beard, smiling, before he wrapped his hand around the back of my neck and pulled me in for a kiss.

I was a little stunned at first, for half a second. Until it hit me. Soft lips, rough hand, stubbled jaw.

Man.

I was kissing a man.

And it felt so fucking good.

I opened his lips with mine, teased his tongue a little, and pulled his body flush against me, deepening the kiss. He was shorter and smaller, but every single person I'd ever kissed was. But he wasn't soft like a woman.

He was all fucking man, and it was so—

He pulled back, breaking the kiss, gasping for air. I was dazed and kiss-drunk. Had I done something wrong? "Are you okay? Sorry, I think I got a little carried away."

He laughed and took a step back, letting out a long breath. "Wow. I think we both got carried away. That was so much hotter than I was expecting. Not that I was expecting anything," he said, running his hand through his hair. "It's just been a long time since I've felt . . . that kind of heat."

"So it wasn't terrible?"

"Terrible? Not at all. Oh my god, was it terrible for you?"

I laughed. "Terrible? Hell no. It was . . . it was amazing. I'm definitely one hundred percent bisexual."

He burst out laughing and seemed to take a second to catch his breath. "I'm glad."

"If you were worried I wouldn't like it, I did. Very much."

"So did I. The beard? Hot as hell."

I automatically pulled on my beard, trying not to smile too big. "I was fully expecting to come here and for you to tell me to just keep on driving. I certainly wasn't expecting . . . well, expecting anything, to be honest. If I'd known, I woulda dressed up or something."

He was still smiling. "What you're wearing is fine. More than fine, actually. It's practical and warm and a little bit sexy."

"Sexy?" I looked down at my old coat and dirty overalls. "Well, if this floats your boat, I got a whole wardrobe that'll blow your mind."

Gunter laughed. "I'm serious. You know, people have always talked about the sexy lumberjack look, somehow I've never stopped to appreciate it. And I'm not talking about the California boys who wear skinny jeans with a flannel with three-day growth. I'm talking about actual Montanan mountain men." He looked me up and down. Just checked me out right in front of me. "I like it."

Okay, wow. "So is just saying this outright, direct to someone's face, a gay man thing?"

He chuckled. "No. Well, maybe. It's more of a forty-four-years-old thing. I'm way past mind games and miscommunication and all that childish crap."

"New you, huh?"

Nodding, his eyes met mine. "I'm not going to be an asshole. That's not who I am. But if I want something, I'm going to ask for it."

Oh jeez. The way he was looking at me, the way he spoke in that soft, low tone.

I was a goner.

He stepped in closer. "Would you like to kiss me again, Clay?"

My blood dang near boiled. I barely managed to nod. He didn't move though. He just stood there. Waiting for me to make the first move.

I slid my hand along his jaw, the stubble sparked lightning in my veins, and I cradled the back of his head. With my other hand, I tilted his chin up and pressed my lips to his.

Holding his head, his face, I deepened the kiss. I slid my hand to his neck and he groaned, taking my tongue deep. He leaned into me, giving me full control of his body and his mouth, and I wanted to take him to the floor and—

And a buzzing noise came from his pocket.

I broke the kiss, still holding his head and his neck. His lips were red and wet, his eyes were unfocused, his glasses a little crooked.

"Is that your phone?" I asked.

"What?"

I chuckled and let my hands drop. "Your phone's ringing."

He straightened up and fixed his glasses. "Oh shit. Yes, my phone." He pulled it out and read the screen. "My kitchen people," he said, and cleared his throat before answering. "Hello, Phil. Please tell me you have good news for me."

He turned to me, his cheeks still pink, his smile wide before it slowly faded. "Oh. So what does that mean?"

Ah, shoot. Something to do with the kitchen wasn't going as planned, by the sounds of it.

"Well, no . . . it has to go in next week before the floor goes down, and I've got the plumber lined up . . ." He ran his hand through his hair and sighed, listening. "Yes, please . . . We'll have to, and yeah, okay. That'd be great. Then I can select something else in the meantime . . . Okay, thanks. Bye."

"Not good news?" I said.

"The kitchen countertop. It was a special stone order and they did warn me that there could be delays. He's thinking it won't be here now until late January."

"Oh man. That really sucks. I'm sorry."

He sighed. "I guess something had to go wrong, didn't it? But I told him to still go ahead with the cabinet installation. At least that way the flooring can go down. And the plumber can do his thing." He turned toward the kitchen space and put his hand to his forehead. "I can just get an old door or something to use as a counter top in the meantime. Pretty sure there's an old door or two in the shed. I could just sit it on top, couldn't I?"

I shrugged. "Can't see why not?"

"He's going to email some brochures, though I think I have the actual physical copies somewhere . . ." He sighed. "I'm kinda bummed. What I picked was from a local quarry. I wanted it to be from these mountains . . . Sounds stupid, I know."

"No, it doesn't. It sounds amazing that you want your house to reflect where it stands. That's pretty cool."

"Well, it's not to be." He gave me a sad smile. "I'm sure I can find something that looks just fine, but it won't be the same. If the kitchen's delayed, then the floor's delayed, then moving in is delayed, and Cass and Jayden need me out by the twenty-second at the latest. Which is three weeks away. God. What was I thinking?"

I rubbed his arm. "You'll be fine. You've already done a lot of work." It was true. All the windows, cornices, and moldings were taped and ready for painting. He'd already cleaned the walls, stripped the bathroom of fixtures and fittings, demolished the old kitchen, and cleaned every single thing.

"I'm sorry. I killed the mood." He smiled at me, one eyebrow flicking up. "That was one helluva kiss before."

"Oh." I ignored the way my cheeks burned.

"No, really, Clay. That was some very good kissing. I'll happily volunteer for more of that."

I tipped my beanie. "Happy to oblige."

He chuckled. "And that was your first time kissing a man?"

"It was. Why? Could you tell?"

He stepped in close again. "Clay, you kissed me so well that I'm certain if you weren't holding me up, with your hands around my neck like that, my knees would have given out."

Oh. I found myself smiling, staring at his lips again. "I liked it. Better than kissing a woman. Still soft but also not?" I let out an embarrassed laugh and pulled on my beard. My cheeks must have been bright red. "Can I say that kinda stuff?"

"Oh yes," Gunter replied. "If you feel it or think it, you should absolutely say it." He lightly touched the buttons on my shirt, right at my chest. "Thank you for sharing your first kiss with me."

I laughed, more embarrassed than I was before. The heat from my cheeks was making its way down to my belly. "Thank you for helping me out with that."

His eyes drilled into mine. All fire and promise that sent the heat in my belly a little lower. "And if there's anything else you'd like help with, just let me know."

I tried to swallow and nod, because there was a whole lot that he could help me with, just as his phone rang again. He sighed and I didn't know if I was annoyed or grateful for the distraction.

He answered the call. "Phil . . . oh sure . . . I see . . . Five o'clock *today*? . . . Okay, thanks."

He disconnected the call and groaned in frustration.

"Well, that didn't sound good," I tried.

"He's emailing the *one* brochure with a select few options that I need to choose from if I want to have it installed before Christmas. Oh, and he needs the decision by close of business today."

That really did suck and I could see he was clearly deflated, so I tried to help. "Well then. Let's look at the brochure."

He opened the email and scrolled through the photos of various kitchens. They all looked super fancy to me, and I'd have been stoked with any of them, but Gunter could only shake his head. He didn't love any of them. "I mean, they're all nice," he said, frowning. "But I don't want stone from Utah or even anywhere else in Montana. I wanted it from here."

He really was sold on keeping it local.

"Well, what about timber?" I asked. "I got some slabs

that were sourced from just up the road, maybe a mile or two from here."

His eyes went to mine. "Timber?"

"Hickory." I shrugged. "We've done a kitchen before. Turned out real good." I took out my phone and started scrolling. "Got some photos somewhere. Gimme a sec."

"What do you mean by slabs?"

"Oh, sorry. Where we take the whole log and slice it lengthways. Like two inches thick by five feet wide, fifteen feet long. The ones we got there now've been there a couple years. Aged-up real nice."

I found the pictures and turned my phone around so he could see. It was an L-shaped kitchen counter with an island. "This is the Chen job we did two years ago, out on Ponderosa Road. They went with the teak. Looked great."

Gunter looked at the photos, surprised. "Wow. You did this?"

I nodded.

"I hadn't considered timber before," he said, still looking at the photos. "I just had stone in my head . . . Clay, these are beautiful."

"Thanks."

"And you can cut out the holes and everything?"

I chuckled. "Ah, yeah. What kind of sink are you having? One of those under-mounted ones?"

He nodded.

"Hickory's your perfect choice. We'd need to seal it with a marine grade stuff, but it'd come up real nice. What are you doing for flooring?"

"Vinyl planks, light gray wood texture. Kitchen cabinets are all white."

"So it won't clash."

He was smiling, excited. "What color is hickory, exactly?"

"Well, these pieces are an aged hickory, so they're darker brown. Not as dark as walnut, but not as light as an ash. Probably more similar to Western Hemlock. It's tawny."

He laughed. "I don't know what any of those look like. You're gonna have to show me pictures."

"I can do you one better," I said. "I can show you the actual slabs."

His whole face brightened. "You can?"

"Sure." I checked my watch. Everyone would be gone by now, and even if they weren't, this was a work-related thing.

You weren't going to hide anymore, Clay. Remember?

Okay, so maybe this was a good test. Small steps, but a step forward anyhow.

"Plenty o'time," I added. "I can drive you there and drop you back off. It ain't a problem. If you don't mind riding in the truck, that is."

He grinned. "The truck sounds fun."

"Dunno if fun's the word I'd use."

He grabbed his coat and beanie, then he grabbed two juice boxes, and after making sure the fire was fine and locking up his house, we went out to my truck.

I opened his door for him. "Oh, a gentleman," he murmured. "Thank you."

Well, it was only because the door stuck sometimes, but I'd take it. "You're welcome."

I went to the drivers' side, trying not to smile too big but it was crazy how excited I was. I turned the key and the engine rumbled to life. I wondered if Gunter would think it was too old, too dusty, too old-school, but when I glanced over at him, he was grinning.

"Oh my god, it has a push button AM radio. My dad's old car had one of these."

"She's old, but she ain't quit on us yet," I said, cranked it into first gear, and headed out of his drive.

Gunter took one of the juice boxes, peeled off the straw, and popped it into the seal before he handed it to me. "For you."

I laughed. "Thanks."

He opened his and took a sip. "Hm, not sure why there aren't juice boxes for adults because this is good."

"There are. We just call it wine."

He laughed and looked out at the passing scenery. Snow dusted the trees and covered most of the ground, but there hadn't been huge falls yet. It gave the place a quietness like no other time of the year.

"It sure is pretty," he said quietly.

"I was just thinking the same thing. Peaceful, like the woods are sleeping."

Gunter stared at me. "You just say the prettiest things."

I ignored the bloom of warmth he gave me and sipped my juice box instead. Soon enough, we turned onto Oxen Road and wound our way out to the mill where the trees were tall along the roadside, snaking its way around the mountain.

"Oh my god, it's so beautiful out this way," he said, looking out and upward to the sky.

"Yeah, it is." I pulled into the drive and past the large red-and-yellow sign—Henderson's Sawmill—and drove into the yard. After convincing myself that I wasn't hiding, I wasn't sure if I was thankful or disappointed that all the workers' trucks were gone.

I stopped by the main shed instead of parking in the barn for the night. I knew this would bring my old man out, wondering what I was doing, and sure enough, by the time Gunter and I got out of the truck, Dad was walking out.

He was about to say something when he noticed I wasn't alone. "Oh," he said. "We got company?"

Here goes nothing.

"Dad, this is Gunter Zuniga. Gunter, this is my dad."

Gunter was quick with a handshake and a smile. "Mr. Henderson. Nice to meet you."

"Same." Dad looked at me, then back to Gunter. "What brings you out this way?"

"He's run into a kitchen countertop problem and needs to have a look at those old hickory slabs," I explained.

"Ah." Dad nodded. "Well, I'll leave you to it. I was just waitin' for the kiln to finish. Just about ten minutes to go."

"Okay. I won't be long, Dad. I'll help you lock up before we do dinner and then decorate the trees," I said.

"Oh good, thought you mighta forgot."

"Never."

Dad gave Gunter a wink and walked back into the shed. He winked at him. He actually winked at him? What the hell?

Stunned, I gestured for Gunter to follow me. "This way."

"Your dad is the cutest thing I've ever seen," he whispered. "Well, if cute's a six-foot-three Santa look-alike."

That made me laugh. "I'll tell him you said that."

I walked him through rows of stacked lumber to the end where the slabs were.

"This place is huge! And it smells amazing," Gunter said.

I grinned at him. "Smells like home to me."

We got to the end wall and I patted my hand on the top slab. "Here it is. There's more than enough to do your countertops and your island."

Gunter's eyes were wide, his mouth open. "Oh my god, this?"

I looked at it. It was still rough, but it was a fine piece of lumber. "Well, yeah, if you don't like it or don't think it's right for you, that's fine. I was only suggesting an alternative."

He shook his head quickly. "No, I mean it's gorgeous. It's amazing. I can't believe you have this!" He ran his hand along the grain. "And the edges?"

"Well, that's called a live edge. It's the outside contour of the tree. We can cut that off, put a smooth edge on it, no problem."

"Oh, can I not have it like this? With the natural edges?"

"They'd have to be sanded down some, but the effect would be the same. It'd still have to be treated and finished. Lemme just grab some water." I went back to grab a tin of water, and when I came back to Gunter, he was at the other end of the slab inspecting it, grinning.

"A bit of water will let you see the real color, the grain," I explained and poured a splash of water over the surface. The colors deepened, a rich brown with hints of gray.

Gunter put his hand to his mouth but still managed to squeal and do a little jumpy dance. "Oh my god, it's perfect! And it's from Hartbridge?"

I nodded. "Up past your place."

He squealed again. "Argh! I have to call my kitchen people."

"Uh, Gunter? Should I get you a price first? These aren't cheap."

He already had his phone to his ear. "It doesn't matter what it costs." He leaned up on his toes and gave me a quick peck on the lips, sending electric butterflies through me, just as his call picked up.

"Hello, Phil? It's Gunter Zuniga. I've found my kitchen countertops."

I DROVE Gunter home and he was still buzzing about his new kitchen countertops. I'd explained the upkeep and maintenance he'd need to do, but he wasn't fazed at all.

And after he leaned across and kissed me goodbye, it was me who was buzzing all the way home.

I knew my dad would be curious. Like why I gave Gunter a personal tour after hours? Or why he arrived in the truck with me and why I drove him home?

But after I'd locked the gates and made sure everything was in its place, I bypassed my place and went straight into Dad's. And I was sure he was gonna ask me something, or even look at me sideways. He simply finished stirring the pot on the stove. "Chili sound good?" he asked.

"Perfect."

He nodded to the box on the old sofa. "Got them decorations down already."

"I said I'd get 'em for ya."

He waved his hand at me. "M'arms and legs still work just fine. I was climbin' ladders long before you were alive."

"Yeah, I know. It ain't the ladders that bother me. It's how fast the ground comes up at ya. Like there ain't much difference between falling off the barn or outta bed—the fallings much the same, but the landing is what gets ya."

He chuckled. "Well, if I ever need gettin' up on the

barn, I'll leave it to you."

"Good."

Dad put the box of decorations on the table by the tree and opened it, and just like every year since my mom died, he'd hand the first ornament to me.

The one my mom gave to me.

I'd hang it, right in the middle at the front. Then he'd do the same with the one she'd given him.

Then we'd do the tinsel and lights and add the rest of the ornaments. We were *never* gonna be winning any tree decoration awards. I mean, the tree itself was beautiful but we lacked any flair for artistry with decorating it.

Still, it's what we did.

Every year on December first, just me and Dad. We did his tree first, then we walked the few yards to my place and decorated mine. Then we'd have dinner, sitting in front of the TV watching his favorite show.

He never asked me about Gunter.

Not a word.

Not even about the job we'd be doing for him.

And, for selfish reasons, I was kinda glad. Would I tell him I was bi? Yeah, I was pretty sure at some point I would. But tonight, this December first, we did our traditional Christmas thing. Unmarred by any possible arguments about my sexuality.

It would be my last December first before I told him, and I didn't know what would change after that. So I gave myself tonight. Of good chili and a beer or two with Dad watching reruns of Family Feud, laughing and just being us.

It kinda felt important to have that with him one last time.

Because I kinda got the feeling that things would be different soon enough.

CHAPTER SEVEN

GUNTER

"YOU WENT TO HIS HOUSE?" Jayden asked around a mouthful of pizza.

Hartbridge Pizzeria was a small darkly lit restaurant. I could only guess it was modeled after Pizza Hut in the 1980s and never updated. The booths even had red padding and the pans the pizzas came out in were easily thirty years old. I had to admit . . . I freaking loved it. The pizza was amazing too.

I nodded. "I went to the sawmill, not his house, exactly. And I met his dad. And I picked out a new kitchen counter-top. He showed me the slab of timber and how the colors would come up. I called my kitchen people and they said it was fine. They'll be sending through the specs to Clay in the morning. They've worked together before, so it was all very easy."

Hamish smirked at me. "And? What else happened? Because I saw the way that man was looking at you in the street today. I know something had to have happened."

I laughed and hoped they thought the color of my cheeks was from the red lighting.

"We might have kissed," I said. They stared at me. "Twice. Wait, no, three times if you include in the truck. No, four. I kissed him in the lumber shed."

Hamish put his hand to his heart. "I left you at midday, and it's not even eight. I'm a little proud."

I laughed, and Jayden gave me his serious eyes. "You. Are going. To tell me. Everything."

I snorted and gave Ren and Cass an apologetic smile. "I'm sorry. I sound like a teenager. It's ridiculous."

"It's fine. We get it," Ren replied. He pointed his thumb at Hamish and Jayden. "We know how these two are."

Hamish pretended to be offended, but Jayden reached over and patted my hand. "Don't you listen to them. You haven't had any romance in your life for a long time. You enjoy every minute of it."

"Well," I mumbled. "I don't know about romance, but it's fun. And no, I haven't had any . . . thing in my life for a long time. It does make me feel young again. Even though I'm old enough to be Jayden's father."

Jayden's eyes lit up. "Oooh, can I call you Daddy?"

"No!" both me and Cass yelled at the same time.

Hamish almost fell out of the booth laughing so hard.

Ren smiled around his mouthful of pizza. "So, tell me about your new kitchen countertop."

THEY WEREN'T LYING when they said Hartbridge would turn into a Christmas wonderland after the lighting of the town tree. The lighting ceremony hadn't been anything special, truth be told. The mayor gave a speech about how the people of Hartbridge were what made the giving season so special. They lit the tree, the crowd stood there and watched, ooh'd and aah'd, then dispersed.

But when I drove into town the next morning, I was stunned by what I saw.

Almost every Christmas tree that Clay had delivered to Main Street was now decorated with tinsel and ornaments. Decorations filled windows and people were up ladders installing Christmas lights.

And with the snow on the ground and the mountains as a backdrop, well, I'd never seen a town as pretty as this.

Not just the town, but also the people.

They smiled, they helped each other. They said hello and they waved.

It was adorable.

I grabbed my coffee and bagel from Carl's and drove to the house. I was expecting a few contractors today but I was also excited to start working on the bathroom.

Painting the tiles really was a better option. I was short on time, and ripping out the bathroom on such a time crunch just didn't make sense.

So now all I had to do was fix up some grout before painting the tiles and installing all the things like towel racks and faucets. The plumber had to do most of it, but I wanted to do what I could.

Like the painting. Sure, I could pay someone to do it, but I wanted to put my touch on it. I wanted to be part of the renovation, not just hire people to do it all for me.

Would I be absolutely terrible at it?

Probably.

But it was mine to be terrible at. And if I hated it so much, I could redo it any time. I didn't have someone telling me to leave it alone, to not spend money on it, or to leave it before I made it worse and just call someone in to do the work.

I didn't have anyone to belittle my choices, or to warn me not to overcapitalize, or to tell me to do . . . anything.

If I wanted to paint the bathroom or the inside walls, I damn well could.

Any color I wanted. Any design, any damn thing.

It made me happy, giddy almost. So I hit up my favorite playlist on my phone and got to work.

JUST AFTER THREE o'clock in the afternoon, I heard the familiar rumble of a truck pull into the drive.

Smiling at the sound, I walked out onto the front porch just as Clay pulled to a stop. The cab of his truck was dark, but I could see him smiling too. I felt like laughing.

It was ridiculous.

He climbed down from his truck, some white papers in his hand.

"To what do I owe this pleasure?" I asked.

He chuckled as he came up the steps, knocking snow off with each tread. He held up the papers. "I have kitchen plans."

"You do?"

He produced a measuring tape from his overall pockets. "I'm technically here for work," he said. "But it was honestly just an excuse to come see you."

I did laugh then, and held the door open for him. "Then you better come in out of the cold."

He took two steps through the door. "I smell paint."

"Bathroom." I grabbed the sleeve on his forearm. "Come and have a look!"

I all but dragged him down the hall and into the bathroom. There was blue painter's tape on all the edges and on the window sill, but two walls of tiles were now white instead of that godawful brown.

"Wow!"

"They'll definitely need a second coat, and don't mind the messy grouting job on that wall, which I need to fix. But it's made a difference already, hasn't it?"

"It sure has. It looks bigger already."

"And cleaner."

He laughed. "That too."

"The plumber has to install the new cabinet and mirror, and he's fitting a glass shower door for me. But the shower is a decent size. And like you said before, even if it only gets me through a year or two, then I can rip it out and remodel. But I'm pleasantly surprised, and I'm so glad you suggested it. And the plumber is too, I can assure you."

He chuckled. "Is that Trevor Shortly?"

"It is! How did you guess?"

"You said you were using local contractors. The Shortly's are Hartbridge's only plumbers."

"Oh." Then I remembered. "Oh, and come have a look at this."

I walked into the main bedroom across the hall and gestured to the window. "See?"

"What am I looking for?"

"The bottom left panel of glass is fixed. It was cracked. And the one in the other bedroom . . . fixed today."

He touched the wood strip and glazing putty. "Nice.

"He was actually really excited," I explained. "Antique double-hung windows are his drug of choice, apparently."

Clay laughed. "Was it old Mr. Sidler?"

"Yes!" I had to stop being surprised that he knew. It was Hartbridge, after all.

"He's been the local glazier for fifty years. Loves his work. Does a mighty fine job too."

"He was the sweetest man. I offered him a drink. He chose the juice box. I'm beginning to think they could be a new trend."

Clay chuckled, then he noticed the new closets. "You *have* been busy."

"Well, I didn't build them. I'm not that clever," I said. "I just sent the guy the measurements when the house contracts went through, so a few weeks ago now. He pre-fabricated them and basically just had to install them and add the molding. No doors yet. I had to order some to match the originals." I waved my hand at the bedroom door. "I'll paint it all when I do the room to make it all look like they were always here."

"It's a decent size."

"Well, storage room." I shrugged. "And I'm gay. I have quite a lot of clothes. And shoes. So it's mostly for storage. And there's the same in the other bedroom as well."

Clay gestured down his legs to his feet. "My closet is work coveralls, plaid, and steel-toed boots."

"Very practical. And sexy."

His cheeks went red. "Well, I dunno if that's the word I'd use."

I chuckled because it absolutely was the word I'd use, but I didn't want to embarrass him too much. "So, the kitchen plans?"

"Oh, right. Yeah." He looked at the papers as if he'd forgotten he was holding them. "Phil called me today. I've worked with him a time or two for kitchen stuff. He wanted to touch base, that's all. Just to make sure we're both working off the same plan."

"Perfect. I can help you measure it out if you'd like."

"Sure."

He followed me back to the kitchen, and he diligently used his measuring tape to double check all the measurements on the plans to make sure his work on my new countertop would be perfect.

"Is it all up to scratch, Mr. Henderson?" I asked with a smile.

He put the plans on the camping table. "Well, yeah, but . . ."

"But what?"

"I didn't really need to remeasure anything. Phil's good at what he does, and sure, double checking never hurt no one, but honestly," he shrugged, embarrassed. "I just needed an excuse to see you again."

My belly did a full swoop. "You don't need an excuse, Clay."

"I know. You said so before. I just . . . having another reason to stop by makes me feel less desperate."

I laughed. "Desperate?"

His cheeks were rosy red and he pulled down on his beard, that nervous-embarrassed trait of his, but he didn't say anything.

So I reached out and took his hand. "Then we need to come up with more excuses. One for each day."

His smile really was something else. "The kitchen is a good one. We may have to meet regularly about that."

"We just may."

We'd somehow drawn closer to each other, our chests almost touching. I was still holding his hand. I was about to ask him if he'd like to kiss me again when he lifted my chin, took hold of my face, and pressed his lips to mine.

Gentle, warm, soft scruffy beard.

Perfect.

He never moved to deepen the kiss, and neither did I, and there was something sweet about that. Something lovely.

He pulled back, smiling. "I've been thinking 'bout doing that all day."

"You think about me all day? Or about kissing me all day?"

His cheeks reddened. "Well, without embarrassing myself too much. Both?"

I slid my hand along his forearm and squeezed. "Don't be embarrassed. You just made my day. Telling someone you thought about them is very sweet. I'm flattered."

"Oh."

"And honestly, you're a great kisser. You can kiss me any time you want."

He chuckled. "That's good to know."

It was mind-boggling that just a kiss could turn my insides to goo. How long had it been since I'd experienced that? Twenty-five years? There was an innocent sweetness to just being kissed without it being a precursor to sex.

Or just even being wanted was a head rush.

A heart rush.

Not to mention what it was doing to other certain parts of my body.

I considered pointing out that it was probably a good thing there was no furniture in my house, nothing to lean against, nothing for him to push me up against, nothing to have sex on . . . well, there was the floor . . .

"You okay?"

I straightened up. "Oh yes, just thinking," I said quickly. "Thinking about you kissing me again, not gonna lie, and how I would not be opposed. At all. But also thinking about how exciting it is to start something new. The getting-to-know-someone stage, when a simple kiss can give me butter-flies. Just a kiss. I feel like a teenager again. It's crazy." I palmed my forehead. "Ignore me. It's just been a long time since I've had this, and it's all new for you, so yeah, just ignore me."

His eyes met mine, shining, happy, and he peeled my hand from my forehead and took it in his. "It is new for me, and yeah, it's crazy. But I like it. I've never had this before, not with any of the girls I've dated. I mean, it was nice and fun, but this . . ." He squeezed my hand and sighed. "It's different. And it makes me want this. I dunno what *this* even is. What we are. If that's what this even is, I dunno. And yeah, I want it. With you. A man. And I get a buzz just thinking about it, but then I remember that it's a whole thing, and if it's gonna be a thing, then I have some things to sort out first."

Oh, Clay.

"You don't have to do that alone," I whispered. "Regard-less of what we are or what we become, you're not alone. Okay?"

He nodded. "But I have to tell my dad alone. I need to do that, just him and me. He deserves to have me dump that on him without an audience. I know him. It'll be better if it's just him and me."

"Then I'll be on standby. Just a phone call away. When-ever you want to do it. Whenever you're ready." I leaned up on my tiptoes and kissed him softly.

"Thank you."

I smiled at him. "Did you get your Christmas trees decorated?"

"Yeah." He chewed on his bottom lip. "I, uh, I almost told him. I almost told him I was bi or that I was maybe interested in seeing a guy." He shook his head. "But I chickened out. I wasn't . . . well, I dunno if I wasn't ready. I just didn't want to spoil the night, ya know? It was December first. We decorate our trees, eat my dad's chili, and have a beer. I didn't want to mar that. If it was my last December first with him, I didn't want to take that away. Is that selfish?"

"Not at all. It's perfectly reasonable."

"But not exactly brave."

"Hey. There's no bravery or courage parameter to coming out. You do it when it's right for you."

"I wanted to tell him. I almost did."

"And you might have a dozen times like that, where you almost tell him. No one can judge or blame you if you do or don't."

He almost smiled. "Thanks."

"Do you think it would be your last Christmas with him if you told him? Would he react like that?"

Clay sighed. "I dunno. Honestly, I think he'd be okay. Maybe shocked. Maybe mad or disappointed. I know things'd be different after I tell him. It's a bell you can't unring, ya know?"

I nodded. "Yeah. I know."

"Figured you would."

"And some people might react like that. But that's on them. You can't control their reaction. It sucks. And it's not easy. There will be people who choose not to be in your life anymore. That just goes to show that they're not real friends. True friends don't put disclaimers on friendships, right?"

He shrugged.

"How do you think your friends would react?"

He shrugged again. "I dunno. Rusty's cool with a lotta stuff. But how can you ever know for sure until you do it? And it ain't just our friendship, I work with him. And Dad too. If things go to shit, it affects the business too."

I took his hand, and holding it in both of mine, I lifted it to my lips and kissed his knuckles. "You'll be okay, Clay. And you and me, we'll be okay. No pressure, okay?"

He thumbed my jaw. "Thank you. You understand what I'm trying to get my head around."

I had no idea how his huge calloused, oil-stained fingers could be so gentle. "No rush."

Clay's eyes searched mine. "I should be on my way," he murmured. He didn't look like he wanted to leave, more that he felt he should.

"Yeah, of course." I walked him to the door but before I opened it, I stopped. "For what it's worth, Clay, I don't know what *we* are either, or what this is, but I'm liking the direction this is headed. I like you. I like spending time with you. And I'd like to ask you out on a date. An official date. Not tomorrow night, because I already told Jayden I'd help him, but I'm free the night after. Here, at the house. Just you and me."

"An official date?"

"Yes! I'll bring dinner. It'll be just you and me. No prying eyes, no curious townsfolk wondering what we're doing having dinner together. It'll be fun. And no pressure."

I was suddenly nervous that he'd say no. He panicked about a date before . . . jeez.

"Only if you want to," I added quickly. "I just said I

wouldn't rush you and I mean that. If you're not comfortable with it, you can say no, it's fine. I don't mind either way. I don't want to push you into something you're not ready for, but I think talking about what you're dealing with might help you. I should have asked if—"

In one fast and forthright move, Clay tilted my face upwards and kissed me, pushing me against the wall. His mouth demanding, his body big and strong. I opened my lips and his tongue met mine, my knees almost buckling as sparks shot through me.

This was no sweet kiss.

This was heat and desire, want and passion, and my god, he could kiss.

Then it was over as quick as it began. Clay pulled away and took a step back, his hand on the door handle, a smug smile on his handsome face. "I might be confused about a lotta things, but I know what I like," he said.

My brain was completely offline.

"I really should go," he said. "Yes, by the way. To the date. Thank you for asking. Saves me tryna find the words."

I put my fingers to my lips. "Oh, you found them," I mumbled.

"You okay?"

I managed a nod.

He smiled and opened the door. "Don't be too late leaving. Looks like a storm blowing in." He ducked his head and went out, closing the door behind him.

I wanted to slide down the wall. My mind was still spinning from that kiss. No one had ever kissed me with such fire. My blood was still running hot.

A buzzing sound cut through my brain haze. My phone . . . I pulled it out to see Jayden's name on the screen.

"Hello?"

"Hey, it's Jayden," he said. "You okay? You sound weird."

I laughed. "Oh, I'm fine. Never better, actually."

He snorted. "You can tell me all about it when you get here. Cass said there's a storm coming and that you should probably think about heading back."

My heart felt almost too big for my chest. First with Clay, and now with Jayden and Cass looking out for me. I had to wonder if this was what true happiness felt like.

"Sure thing," I replied, my brain finally kicking into gear. "Need me to pick anything up on the way?"

CHAPTER EIGHT

CLAY

I WASN'T KIDDING about the storm. She blew in low and heavy, blustering with a decent dumping of snow.

I made sure the mill and all the sheds were locked down, made sure Dad was settled and had his dinner simmering away on the stove, then I went to fix mine.

My place was only small. Barely a studio, really, with just a tiny living room with a small kitchenette at one end, one bedroom and a bathroom at the other end. I had a book-case and a Christmas tree that took up considerable space by the TV. That was about all that'd fit.

Small, yes, but easy to keep warm with a small stove fire.

And it was private.

So my dad didn't see me grinning like a fool when I was texting Gunter. I was just making sure he got home okay, and the banter back and forth until bedtime just topped off a real good day.

That kiss by his front door gave me some real pleasant dreams too.

Kissing him was something I could get used to.

And we had ourselves an official date coming up. He

said he liked me. He said he wanted to spend time with me and maybe kiss some more.

Yep.

Pleasant dreams, indeed.

BY THE TIME I was done opening up the yard and trudging through the snow, Dad handed me a steaming cup of coffee. "Might wanna call ahead of time on the Overly job today," he said. "See if the snow drifted into their driveway."

The turn into that drive had always been tight for the truck, and a fresh snowfall certainly didn't help it none. "Good idea."

Dad sipped his coffee. "So, wanna tell me who's got you smiling?"

I had to make myself not smile. "I'm not smiling."

"You were whistlin' a tune walking knee deep in snow just now," he replied. "And you been smiling all morning. And when you got home last night. Wanna tell me about that?"

Shit.

Was now a good time?

Was there ever a good time?

Dad eyed me. "Dunno why you're bein' so secretive about it. Unless they're married. Christ, they're not married, are they?"

I snorted. "No, Dad. I mean, they were."

"So there *is* someone!"

Right on cue, Rusty and Eddie came into the shed, heading straight toward us. Well, toward the coffee. They were grumbling about the cold and the snow.

I looked at Dad, hoping he could read between the lines. "I'll tell you about it later, Dad," I murmured quickly. "Not now."

"Not now, what?" Rusty asked as he collected his coffee mug.

Of course he had to hear it. "Oh, just a job today. Haven't heard how much snow they've had out on East Pine Gap Road, have ya?"

Conversation quickly went to the weather report on the radio, and Dad gave me a nod, telling me that yes, we would be continuing our little conversation later.

I almost wished I'd blurted it out before Rusty and Eddie came in because it would be over by now. It would've been a shitty way to tell him, just to dump it on him like that, but at least it'd be over and done with.

The anticipation, the buildup, and the dread hung over me all day. We were up to our ears with work and there wasn't much time for talking. The weather just slowed us down, making an already busy day even busier. And I kind of got the impression that Rusty wanted to catch me alone too, no doubt to ask me where I went yesterday afternoon and why I wasn't back before quitting time.

I wasn't ready to tell him yet. I needed to tell my dad first.

And it was kind of fitting that I would be working on Gunter's kitchen countertops when Dad found me at the end of the day. I knew he'd come to find me so we could finish our little chat about just who I might be seeing.

God, I ain't ready to have this conversation . . .

"Oh, they've come up so nice," he said, then ran his hand along the still-rough edge. "Look at that grain."

"Yeah, it's beautiful." I checked my watch. "Jeez. I didn't realize the time. All the guys gone home already?"

"Yep. You been in here fussin' over these slabs for hours."

"Need to make sure they're perfect, Dad."

He nodded real slow. "Not avoiding me, are ya?"

I shot him a glance. "What?" Of course I was. "Of course I'm not."

"Look, I don't care who it is you're seeing," he said. "You don't gotta tell me nothin' till you're ready. Just as long as one"—he counted off his fingers—"you're happy. Two, it ain't hurting no one, and three, ain't no one cheating."

Oh god.

"No one's cheating on anyone, Dad," I said. "And I want to tell you. I do. It's just new, and it might turn into nothing."

"And you don't want to jinx it."

I don't wanna make any announcements and possibly upend my entire life if it turns into nothing.

"Something like that."

He clapped a hand on my shoulder. "Well, I'm just glad you're gettin' out there, son. Being happy is the only thing me and your mom ever wanted for ya."

"I know."

Tell him.

Tell him now.

"Dad—"

The business phone rang, and Dad took the cordless handset out of his pocket. "Henderson Sawmill." He turned to walk back toward the office, no doubt to have the delivery schedule at the ready. He took a few steps and stopped. "Deputy Price." Dad's eyes cut to mine, and he gave a nod. "We're on our way."

Trees coming down after a heavy snowfall wasn't uncommon. Sometimes they fell where no one ever saw

them. Sometimes they fell onto fences. And sometimes—
like now—they fell across a road.

There were plenty of folks in Hartbridge with chainsaws that could help, and oftentimes they did. But if it was
on our side of town or if it was a big job, the local police
department or sheriff's office would call us.

I was already grabbing my coat and beanie. "Where
is it?"

"Mossley Road."

Shit.

The main road down the mountain. Well, mountain on
one side. Sheer fucking drop on the other.

"Anyone hurt?"

"He didn't say. Just that it's blocking traffic in both
directions."

Jesus.

We grabbed our gear, and I called Rusty on the way.
He'd meet us at the bridge in town and we'd all go down in
the truck.

I tried not to think about anyone being hurt. Oh god.
Had Gunter said what he and Jayden were doing tonight?
Did they have to go to Mossley? It was where Gunter was
from, after all.

I gripped the wheel a little tighter.

It was ridiculous. And the odds of Gunter being
anywhere near it were slim to none, but . . . but I guess I
never really had anyone to worry about before.

I was getting way ahead of myself and thinking
nonsense.

"You okay?" Dad asked.

"Yeah, sure. Just hope no one's hurt." It was already
dark and flurries of snow were falling.

We drove into town, and sure enough, before the bridge,

Deputy Price's cruiser was blocking the road, red-and-blue lights flashing. There were curious townsfolk, of course, but he stood there diverting traffic, and as soon as he saw us, he waved me through.

I stopped the truck by his cruiser and rolled my window down. "Evening," I said.

"Thanks for coming," he said. "It's about half a mile down. You won't miss it. The captain's down there, and Mossley Fire Department are on their way up too."

Just then, Rusty's truck pulled off onto the shoulder and he ran over to the truck. Dad shuffled over to the middle and Rusty climbed in.

I gave the deputy a nod. "Anyone hurt down there?"

"No, thankfully."

Relief flooded through me, which was stupid. I mean, I didn't want anyone to be hurt. Not a single person. But I was especially glad it wasn't Gunter.

So ridiculous.

With a wave, I rolled my window back up and we rumbled over the bridge, around the corner and down the hill.

More flashing police lights lit up the dark, and Sherrif Ronny Harper greeted us as we got out of the truck. The tree was a big one, at least a hundred feet tall, its roots now skyward.

I left Dad to complain to Ronny about the road construction done on the embankment in the summer, leaving trees dangerously unstable, and Rusty and I got to work.

It was a big job, no two ways about it. But we soon got the top end cleared away so they could at least open up one narrow lane of traffic. And with the fire department guys soon on the job, we made pretty quick work of it.

And by quick, I mean hours of hard work under industrial spotlights, on the side of the mountain in the freezing cold and falling snow.

It was awesome.

And it was almost midnight by the time we were done, and the huge sections of tree were winched into our truck. We were tired, wet, hungry, and covered in sawdust and sap. I told Rusty to take tomorrow morning off, knowing dang well he wouldn't anyway. And I heated up some leftovers for me and Dad before I called it a day.

I'd had no time to think about almost telling Dad I was maybe-dating a guy.

I'd had no time to think about texting or calling Gunter, and I only saw I had a message from him when I plugged my phone in to charge as I crawled into bed.

> I heard you were the town hero, clearing a
> fallen tree. Looking forward to tomorrow
> night. See you around six-ish.

It was too late to reply. I didn't want to wake him.

But boy, I sure did fall asleep exhausted, sore . . . and smiling.

I WAS GETTING office work done when Rusty found me. People tended to leave me be when I had my nose in the accounts; it was the sole reason I was doing them. I'd already cleaned the chainsaws and rotated one whole row of the drying racks.

I hadn't meant to avoid him. And it wasn't exactly *him* I was avoiding. It was his questions, his curiosity, and maybe his concerns.

I didn't want to lie to him.

"Hey there, big guy," he said cheerfully. "Got all the lodgepole split and sorted. And the cottonwood's good to go. Ready for the next deliveries."

"Sweet. Thanks."

"I can get 'em out if you're busy here."

"Nah, man. I got it. I need to get out for a bit. Going cross-eyed here. But thanks. And thanks again for helping out last night."

"No problem at all." He smiled and it was followed by the awkward silence I'd been trying to avoid. "So," he hedged.

"So . . . ?"

"Any more news on the secret dates?" With his goofy grin and his hair sticking out from under his beanie, it was hard not to smile at him.

I turned in my chair and gave him my full attention. "I will tell you, I promise. When the time's right. You'll be the first to know . . . Well, second. Dad'll be first, but then you. I promise."

Confusion crossed his face like it was a joke. "It's no big deal, Clay."

"Well, it kinda is. For me, anyway. I just . . ." I sighed. "I need to figure some shit out first, is all."

The confusion was now concern. "Okay. I didn't mean to pressure ya or to make a joke out of it or nothing. I just thought . . ." His words trailed off with a shrug. Then he thumbed outside. "We gotta load up that delivery to the Percy's, if you wanna do that now?"

I nodded as I stood up. "Sounds good."

He never brought up my dating anyone for the rest of the day, and I was glad. I was kinda bummed that I didn't tell him the truth. Kinda glad too.

God, this was all so confusing.

I told myself, not for the first time, that tonight—my first official date with Gunter—would be the test. I'd told myself that before, I was well aware. But this felt different. Like a litmus test of sorts, to determine if I was really set on doing this.

In my heart, I already kinda knew the answer.

Or maybe that was hope.

I wanted this to be the real deal, and while that should have been answer enough, I was kinda hinging my decision on this date. And on Gunter.

Which wasn't strictly fair to him. I knew that. It was just a little easier to tell myself that while I got myself showered and dressed. Heaven help me, I even trimmed my beard a bit.

Thankfully, it was dark when I left. I pulled my coat collar up, pulled my beanie down, and crossed the yard, heading for the truck.

Of course, Dad was standing on his porch, like he was waiting for me. "Clay?" he hollered out.

Cussing that I wasn't quick enough, I turned. "Wassup?"

He grinned and held two thumbs up. "Good luck!"

Oh god.

Because that wasn't embarrassing at all.

I returned one thumb up. "Thanks, Dad." I was thankful he couldn't see my trimmed beard from that far away and thankful he never noticed I was wearing my good jeans.

Then his brow furrowed. "You gonna take some wine or flowers or something? You can't be turning up empty-handed, son."

Well, shit.

I hadn't thought of that.

"Yep. Getting it on the way," I yelled back. I tapped my watch. "Gotta go. Don't wait up."

His grin widened and I got another two thumbs up.

Lord.

I waved him off and wondered what the heck I should bring on a date. With a man. I'd never had to think of that shit before . . .

Wine and flowers were a sensible choice, so I made a quick stop at the Home Mart in town. Rosie was getting ready to close the shop for the day.

"Will be real quick," I said as a greeting.

"You're fine, Clay," she said. Then she noticed my clean clothes, my new jeans. She smiled all conspiratorially at me. "All dressed up there, Mr. Henderson. Impressing someone I know?"

"I don't know what you're talking about," I said and quickly made my way to the back of the store.

Now, I loved Hartbridge. I really did. But was nothing a secret here?

I found a bottle of wine, but then I got to thinking . . . we both had to drive at the end of the night. We could have one glass each—wait, did Gunter even have wine glasses at the house? He didn't even have chairs . . .

I put the wine back.

Chocolates seemed like a good idea. Maybe I shoulda asked if he wanted me to bring chairs.

I stopped at the candy aisle. Gunter really didn't seem like a chocolate guy. Well, not the ones the Home Mart sold anyway.

Ugh.

This was now a disaster.

I couldn't bring him a house gift because his house was

under construction. Not even a houseplant for a windowsill because they were all taped up, ready for painting.

I turned around and scanned the aisle, trying not to panic, when I saw them.

The most perfect gifts.

I put the six-pack of juice boxes and a Hershey's Advent Calendar on the service counter. Rosie looked at them, then looked at me. "Not what I was expecting you to get, Clay, seeing that you're all dressed up."

I grinned at her and added a pack of mints for her to ring up. "And those too."

"You know," she said, "that new fellow in town bought these same juice boxes. Isn't that funny?"

Oh god help me.

My heart stopped.

Breathe, Clay.

"Did he?"

"He seems nice. He bought the old Nolan house. So good to see someone buy it who wants to live here and not just knock it down for some big development."

I tried not to smile. "Very true."

She handed me my purchases. "Well, you have a good night. Say hello to your dad for me."

"Will do."

Now I didn't know what to expect on a date with a man, but I was getting all kinds of nervous on the drive out to Gunter's place. I never felt this when I'd gone on dates with women. Sure, it had been all nice and fun, but this was different. This was a rush, a thrill.

I wanted it to go well—because I really did like him a lot —and I hoped he wouldn't think my two gifts were stupid. Hell, maybe they were stupid, but they weren't meant to be serious.

Oh hell, what if he thinks they're stupid?
Stop overthinking it, Clay.

"Too late now," I grumbled to myself as I pulled up and shut off the engine. I took the juice and calendar, climbed out of the truck, and made my way to the front porch. Lights were on inside, but the porch was in darkness.

Gunter opened the door as I was navigating the steps, shedding some light for me. "There's no porch light, sorry," he said with a wide smile. He was wearing dark jeans and a green sweater and looking incredibly handsome. "Come in, come in."

I took one step inside and stopped, because . . . wow.

In front of the fire, laid out on the floor, was a picnic blanket with a whole bunch of plates and baskets and what looked like different foods. The lights were low. The fire was flickering an orange glow over the room.

"Wow."

"Do you like it?" Gunter asked.

"It's amazing. I didn't know what to expect but this is perfect."

His smile was something else until he realized I was holding something. "What have you got there?"

"Oh." God. "Well, I had to bring something. And of course I forgot, so I had to go to the Home Mart. I was going to get wine, but we have to drive, so . . ." I handed over the juice boxes. "I got you these."

He burst out laughing. "Oh my god, I love them. Thank you."

Then I handed over the calendar. "And this. I didn't think you were much of a chocolate guy, but this is Christmassy and you didn't have anything very Christmassy here at the house, and I figured you were coming here every day, so now you can open one every day when you get here. It's probably stupid."

"Are you kidding? It's perfect." He leaned up on his toes and lightly kissed my cheek. "Thank you, Clay."

He put them by the blanket and I took off my coat and beanie, and I tried to fix my hair but Gunter didn't seem to mind. He just took my hand and led me toward the picnic blanket.

CHAPTER NINE

GUNTER

"I HOPE YOU'RE HUNGRY," I said as we sat down on the blanket. "I spent most of today with Jayden. He was testing all kinds of recipes for his Christmas menu, which I'd like to say that I helped with, but he did all the hard work while I mostly got in his way and sampled stuff. But," I gestured to the food spread out on the blanket. "We basically have a buffet of samples."

I hadn't really taken into account his size. Clay was a big man, and watching him trying to figure out what to do with his legs while sitting on a picnic blanket shouldn't have been so funny. "Oh my god, let me get you a chair."

"No, no I'm fine," he said quickly. He stretched his legs out and leaned back on one arm. "Just not sure about the getting back up part."

"Oh shush. I'm forty-four. If anyone needs help getting back up, it'll be me."

He chuckled. "This is fun. And the food looks great."

"Jayden's a really good cook. I've been spoiled staying with them. I'm going to move into this place with my brand-new gorgeous kitchen and not want to cook a single thing."

"Oh. That reminds me." Clay pulled out his phone. "Photo updates."

He found the photos he was after and handed me his phone. It took me a second to realize what I was looking at. "Oh my god, is this my countertop?"

He nodded. "Dried, cut, and treated," he said. "And all sanded by hand myself."

I couldn't believe what I was seeing. "It's beautiful."

"Wait till we oil and seal it. It's gonna be amazing."

"And you'll do it by hand?"

He gave a nod. "It's a special piece."

I waited for his gaze to meet mine. "It really is."

He smiled, and it was hard to tell if he blushed or if it was the firelight playing tricks on my eyes.

"Come on, let's eat. We need to tell Jayden what we think." I handed Clay a small plate. "This is the slow-cooked turkey brisket with a spiced walnut and cranberry relish."

"Sounds fancy." As soon as he put it in his mouth and chewed, his eyes cut to mine. "Holy shit, that's good."

I laughed. "I know! And here's some of the turkey with an apricot Dijon sauce."

He chewed it, nodding. "That's amazing too."

"Which do you prefer?"

"He's gotta make both."

I laughed. "I'll let him know."

Then we tried the next one. "He called it winter holiday roast. Because the sauce has berries and thyme. It looks like Christmas, apparently."

Of course it was amazing. Clay groaned when he tasted it, and the sound warmed my blood.

The bread was baked fresh, and the honeyed carrots

were divine, as were the mustard greens, and the little pastry parcels of mushroom and cheese.

"Does he cook like this all the time? Because wow."

"Crazy, huh? I'm going to need lessons."

There was more picking, more eating, more moaning. And this little picnic idea was turning into one of my best plans ever. The food, the firelight, the company . . .

I opened the six-pack of juice boxes and handed Clay one. "From our cellars, the finest selection of—" I read the box. "—twenty-five percent reconstituted fruit juices."

Clay laughed again. "Perfect selection."

We sipped our juices and I could see it in Clay's eyes that he was trying to figure out how to word something.

"Is everything okay?"

"It's perfect. It's just . . . Jayden knows about this date?"

Ah.

"Yes. But I promise you he won't say anything. Not to anyone. But he knows, yes. And he's absolutely certain we're destined to be together. That good ol' Hartbridge Christmas magic romance he and Hamish keep talking about." I rolled my eyes. "But Clay, he knows what it means to keep secrets. And he knows more than anyone else that someone else's secret isn't his to tell. It's an unwritten gay rule: you don't out anyone. Not ever. He's not telling a soul, I promise. And I never said if you were bi or just curious. I haven't mentioned any of that."

He nodded quickly, his smile a sad one. "I almost told my dad yesterday." He held up his fingers close together. "This close."

"But you didn't?"

He shook his head. "Nah. We got called to clear that tree from Mossley Road."

"Oh yes, I heard that the local strapping lumberjacks were on the job. Is there like a bat signal for that?"

He snorted. "Just a boring old phone call."

"Shame."

He smirked. "And I didn't get your message until I got home. It was around midnight, so I didn't want to wake you."

"Oh my god, it took you hours. Does the town or the county pay you for that?"

"Nope. It's just what you do in a small town. You help out. And we did get to keep the timber."

I smiled with a sigh. "I love that."

"Then I almost told Rusty today. He wanted to know who it was I was seeing and I wanted to tell him, but it's only right that I tell my dad first."

I reached over and squeezed his hand. "Only when it's right."

"Can I be totally honest?"

Oh dear . . .

"Of course."

"I wanted to get through this date. Like a kind of test, I guess. To see if it was really what I wanted, ya know? Before I go telling folks I'm not as straight as they think and ringing bells that can't be unrung."

My heart skidded to a stop. "And? How's it looking so far? This test date?"

He laughed, a gentle warm rumble. "Well, it's perfect, so I'm thinking it's a pass. A perfect score, even. So far, anyway."

I laughed with pure relief. "Wow, perfect so far. That's a lot of pressure on the rest of the date."

"Well, it's not over yet," he said, his tone full of innuendo, of promise.

It gave me butterflies. "I hope I don't disappoint."

His eyes fixed on mine. "I'm sure you won't."

The room felt instantly hotter, the air between us thick and electric. I could remember how he'd kissed me the day before, how it felt, how it made my knees weak.

How I wanted to do it again.

Then I remembered that this was the new me. That I was done wasting time and not getting what I wanted. So I leaned forward, almost crawling across the blanket, laughing at how utterly absurd this was, and kissed him.

He was smiling too, but he soon deepened the kiss with his hand to my cheek. He sat up straighter, as if he wanted to bring me closer, and I ached to feel his body against mine. I wanted to crawl into his lap, straddle him, and kiss him for hours, with his tongue in my mouth and his . . .

The fire crackled and sparked, startling us. We both looked at the fireplace and I had to straighten my glasses, and Clay chuckled. "Is it trying to tell us something?"

"Yeah. That we were conducting too much heat?"

He laughed at that. "You're not losing any points on the perfect-date test, lemme put it that way."

I sat back down, closer to him this time. I nudged my shoulder to his. "You're doing pretty good too, just so you know. Granted, it's been a long time since I went on any kind of date."

"You didn't have date nights with your ex?"

I snorted. "Uh, no. We didn't do anything together. Which says a lot."

Clay's eyes met mine. "How about I put more wood on the fire and you crack us another juice box? Then you can tell me all about you."

Another juice box . . . It made me smile. This whole date was making me smile. Watching the giant bear of a man on his knees stoking up my fire wasn't exactly a chore either.

I popped us a juice box each and took the advent calendar he'd brought for me. We were five days into December already, so I popped those doors and shared the chocolates with Clay.

He honestly couldn't have bought me two more perfect gifts. Not expensive or cliché, just fun and thoughtful.

He popped the chocolate in his mouth, and looking at the fire, he nudged me gently. "Tell me, what's the Gunter Zuniga story?"

Ugh. Where to start?

"I was born and raised in Spokane. Went to college there but moved to Mossley about twenty years ago. I got an entry-level job at the town hall, straight out of college, so I took it. I was only ever going to stay for a year or two, but I worked my way up. I was assistant to the finance director on the town council for almost ten years."

"Finance director? That's pretty cool."

"Pretty boring, too."

He chuckled. "Have you got a job lined up here?"

I shook my head. "My dad left me and my brother enough. I might look at something later, something remote maybe, just to keep me busy, but for now I want to concentrate on the house and on me."

He smiled. "Good for you."

Then I figured I'd get straight to the point. "I met Scott at work. He was one of the town planners at city hall. We were together for twelve years, married for the last six of those. In hindsight, I can see that getting married was a last-ditch effort to save our relationship. We'd been together so long it was almost assumed that we'd tie the knot. Maybe he thought it would rekindle the spark, you know? And maybe it did for a few months . . . There was no romance in the proposal or in our marriage. He just thought it made financial sense, for tax and insurance purposes."

"Jesus."

"I don't hate him. In fact, I'm glad he left. I mean, his timing was terrible, but that in itself showed me who he really was. There was no doubt in my mind that we were finished. And the divorce was surprisingly easy. No kids, no contesting finances. He had his own money, so if he wanted any of my inheritance, then I could argue for half the money his grandfather left him, so we just kept our own. It was all rather amicable."

"I'm glad."

"Me too. Our relationship had been over for a long time, and I'd spent years pretending it wasn't. But he wasn't a bad person. And I did love him . . . In the beginning. We were in love, but somewhere along the way, we just stopped trying. I censored myself to keep the peace."

"Did you fight?"

"No. That's just it. We didn't argue. If I disagreed or if I felt as if I'd been treated unfairly, I just didn't say anything. In hindsight, I think it was because I just didn't care enough. If I'd truly cared, I would've fought for it, don't you think?"

Clay nodded.

"When he left, I was stunned. Not surprised, as such, just blindsided that he chose to do it the day after my father's funeral. I was dealing with everything else, my brother was in town, there were lawyers and estate matters to deal with. And the grief. I loved my father very much. I'd been his caregiver for the last year or so."

"That can't have been easy."

"No, it wasn't. His passing wasn't unexpected, but it

didn't make it any easier. So when Scott left, I was stunned. For the days following, I was just in a daze. One foot in front of the other, complete autopilot." I smiled at the fire. "I remember very distinctly, it was about a week after the funeral when we'd finalized my father's will and my brother left to go back to Texas. Scott had been to collect his things, and when he said goodbye, I was in the house alone for the first time in what had been a helluva week. I fully expected the wheels to fall off. I expected to have a meltdown, for reality to come crashing down and to realize that I was really alone. But it never came."

"Because you were so used to being alone already?"

I nodded. "Yep. I remember walking through our house into each room trying to find the hole that Scott had left in my life, but there wasn't one." I let out a long sigh. "And in the weeks that followed, I came to realize the funniest thing. I actually felt freer than I had in a long time. I wasn't walking on eggshells. I didn't have to pretend. I didn't have to fake a smile. I didn't have to agree with something just to make life easier. Or try and think of things to say. I hadn't realized just how much smaller I'd tried to make myself. How passive and compliant I'd become. And I don't even know why. Not really. I'd just lost who I was. But that was over. And I felt happy and relieved."

"And now you're here. A new life for the real you."

That made me smile. "Exactly. I know I'm only newly single. The ink on my divorce is barely dry. But I've been alone for a long time. Single in every way except on paper. Scott and I had not shared a bed in a very long time. That part of our marriage died very early on. God, in hindsight, it all just sounds so hopeless, but he was a terrible snorer and every night, at some ungodly hour, I'd end up in the spare room just to get some sleep. In the end I just started sleeping in there . . ." I sighed again. "In the end, we were barely even friends. I don't blame him for leaving."

"A *friend* wouldn't have left you the day after your father's funeral."

"No, though he did me a favor. He did us both a favor. Funerals have that effect on people; they're a very stark reminder of the brevity of life, and he obviously didn't want to wait another day."

"It wouldn't have hurt him to wait a week."

That made me laugh. "No, it probably wouldn't have. But no more wasted days. It's my new motto."

"It's a good rule to live by. But I'm still sorry you had to go through all that."

I tapped my juice box to his. "Me too. But it brought me here, so it can't be all bad."

"True. Maybe I should send your ex a thank-you card."

I burst out laughing. "I'm sure he'd love that."

Clay chewed on his bottom lip. "I'm glad you're here, Gunter."

"I am too."

This time he leaned over and kissed me, a soft and slow kiss, a nudge of his nose and his hand along my jaw. I was doing just fine until he pulled my bottom lip in between his teeth.

I groaned like a B-grade porn star.

I couldn't help it.

He deepened the kiss, holding my face in both hands, tilting my head so he could explore my mouth with his tongue.

He just knew every button to push, and so help me god, he knew how to push them well.

I pulled him closer by his shirt collar and kept pulling

until I was lying down and he was on top of me. He stared at me, stunned.

"Is this okay?" I asked.

He snorted and slid his knee out to widen my legs before crashing his mouth to mine and lowering his body-weight onto me.

So this was very okay.

I wanted to strip naked. I wanted to have him naked between my legs. I wanted him inside me.

But that was too fast and too soon . . .

My god, this man could kiss.

He was so much bigger than me, taller, wider, stronger. He outweighed me easily, and he could certainly best me if he'd wanted to. And I had no idea how much that turned me on until now.

Until Clay.

Then he slid upward, forcing my chin up as he kissed me, and for a brief moment, I wondered why . . .

Until I felt it.

His erection.

And holy shit.

He was big.

I groaned as he pressed against me, lifting my hips automatically, desperate to feel more. I ran my hands down his back, over his ass, and he moaned into my mouth.

And then he stopped.

He broke the kiss, put his forehead to mine, his eyes dark and heavy lidded.

Sexy as hell.

"You okay?" I whispered.

He smiled, his lips swollen red. Then he rolled off me so we were both on our backs, catching our breaths, and he laughed. "I'm very okay. You?"

"Oh yeah. I'm very okay too."

He put his hand to his forehead. "Just trying to cool it a bit."

I was going to say he didn't have to cool it if he didn't want to. I was more than willing to participate, but I had to keep reminding myself that this was so new to him.

"I didn't mean to lead you on and then just stop," he said.

I quickly grabbed his hand. "No apology required." Both of us were quiet then, still staring at the ceiling, still holding hands. "Is that a cobweb up there? Oh my god!"

Clay chuckled. "He's just getting outta the cold."

"Well, he's just gonna have to find somewhere else. And wow, I really need to paint the ceiling."

He laughed then and I laughed too, his fingers threaded with mine. "I've had a really good time tonight, thank you. I didn't know what to expect. I've never been on any date with a man before."

"So I passed? The date test?"

He chuckled, his eyes shining. "Oh yeah. You definitely passed. Except I might have to deduct a point for there being no furniture to sit on."

"Oh."

"I'm kidding!"

"Just as well," I joked right back. "We should probably be glad there's no furniture, so we couldn't get too comfortable, if you know what I mean. There's no rushing anything explicitly sexual because there's no bed. Or couch. Or shower. Or kitchen counter, or dining table you could bend me over. Or—"

His eyes widened. "Oh my god."

I laughed. "I'm just kidding. Kind of. I mean, it's kind of true." His eyes were still comically wide. *Oh shit*. "Well, the sex conversation is one we can have, only if that's something you might want to consider. At some point. No pressure."

He blinked a few times and stared at the ceiling for a few seconds before looking at me again. "Well, yeah. Probably. Uh, yes? But I dunno . . ."

I squeezed his hand. "Hey, no pressure."

"Is that something you'd want? If we were dating or seeing each other."

Be truthful, Gunter. No more hiding. No more not saying what you want.

"Sure. I like sex. But it's not a simple answer, and it's not a deal breaker. If the person I was seeing didn't want sex or couldn't have sex, I wouldn't *not* be with them. I wouldn't dump someone because of that—"

"I like sex. A lot," he blurted out. Then he cringed. "But I have exactly zero experience. With a guy. As I'm sure you could tell. This is my first date with a man and I wasn't even sure what to expect. Or what gift to bring. Having sex is a whole other . . . complicated thing."

"I don't know if I could tell you had no experience just now, Clay. Because, holy hell, you were doing every single thing right. A few minutes longer and I'd have been trying to get us both naked."

He chuckled. "I didn't want to stop."

"I didn't want you to stop," I added, smiling at him. "But I know why you did. And I get it. I'm glad we can talk about this."

"Me too."

"And we can take it slow. See what you like and don't like. And who knows, I might even have some furniture by then."

He laughed again. "Yeah, honestly, I dunno how I'm gonna get up."

"Same." We both laughed and eventually got up. We cleared away the picnic and folded the blanket. I showed Clay the finished painted bathroom and the spare bedroom. I'd done the trim in my room and would start in the kitchen and mudroom tomorrow.

But it was getting late, and after Clay helped me lock up the house and carry the picnic basket to the car, he kissed me goodnight.

"Thank you, Gunter," he said, pulling my beanie down over my ears. "Best official first date ever."

"You can plan the next one."

He snorted. "No pressure to beat the best date ever then."

"No pressure at all," I replied with a laugh. But a second date begged another question. "So do you think you'll be telling your dad?"

A flurry of snow danced around us, but his eyes met mine and he nodded. "Yeah. Tomorrow, if the timing's right."

"Need me to come with you?"

He shook his head. "Nah. I got it. But knowing I can talk to you about it afterwards is good."

"Any time. Day or night."

He booped a gloved finger on my nose. "Thank you. We should get out of this cold. I'll text ya. Or call. Depends how it goes."

I nodded. "Of course."

With a smile and a nod, he walked to his truck and I got into my car. Tonight had been better than I could have imagined, and I tried to act cool and nonchalant when I got back to the bed and breakfast.

I carried the basket of plates and containers into the kitchen so I could unload them into the sink, and of course

Jayden was waiting for me. He took one look at me. "Well, I don't even have to ask how it went."

I faced him, trying not to grin or laugh and failing a little at both. "It went so well. The food was amazing, just so you know. All of it. Thank you, again, for making it all perfect. Clay said he couldn't choose which was his favorite and you need to cook them all. And he's amazing too, and sweet, and . . ." I lowered my voice. "When I tell you that man knows how to kiss . . . The man has skills, I'm telling you. Like, heaven help me, he has skills."

Jayden clapped his hands and laughed. "That Christmas elf who becomes Cupid every year in this town has incredible aim."

I laughed and began to fill the sink with hot, soapy water. I knew Jayden and Hamish often joked about the Hartbridge Christmas romance nonsense . . .

Now I was starting to think it really might be true.

CHAPTER TEN

CLAY

BY THE TIME I had the front gate open and the work sheds open, Dad had the coffee machine going. I knew he was going to ask me about my date last night and I knew this conversation had to happen. I wanted it to happen. It just didn't make it any easier.

When I walked into the breakroom, he handed me my mug. "You were home early last night," he said. "Everything go okay?"

"Yeah, everything was great. I wasn't expecting to be out late."

"I thought you might have been driving to work after breakfast, if you know what I mean."

Oh god.

"Yeah, I know what you mean."

It was bad enough we had to have this conversation without getting into the physical aspect of it. I just about died when Gunter and I spoke about it. I certainly wasn't ready to have that conversation with my father.

He sipped his coffee. "I'm glad it went well."

I put my mug down on the table. We had a good few

minutes before the others should be arriving, so now was a good time.

"Look, Dad . . ."

His eyes met mine, excited to hear about my big secret dating life. Because he was assuming it was a woman. He had no idea what I was about to drop on him.

I let out a slow breath and tried to swallow, but my mouth was too dry. "What I'm about to tell you, well, I don't know how you're gonna take it. I'd really rather you not say anything just yet. Maybe take the day to think about it. Then you and I can talk over dinner. If that's still okay."

I was starting to feel a little queasy and like my lungs couldn't take in enough air.

"Jesus, Clay," Dad whispered. "You're starting to worry me now. Who are you seeing? Are they on death row for murder?"

"What? No!"

"Then what's got you so nervous? You look about ready to puke."

"Because the person I'm seeing is a man, Dad. A guy. I'm bisexual. Always have been. I just hid that part of me away for so long that I . . . God. Growing up, I liked girls just fine, and the women I dated were all okay, but I met a guy who's better than just okay, Dad, and it reminded me that part of me still exists. I tried to fight it, and I tried to tell myself to ignore it, but it's who I am. I'm sorry. I haven't told anyone else, and I don't know what this means for us. I'm just sorry. I'm sorry I didn't tell you sooner. I'm sorry if it's not what you want."

We both turned to the sound of Eddie's truck pulling in.

But Dad still hadn't said anything, and he looked like he'd been punched in the gut.

I stood up. "I got a lot to do today."

"Clay."

"We can talk about it at dinner," I said as I walked out. I figured between now and then it'd give him time to think, and maybe—hopefully—he wouldn't say something we both might regret.

It seemed fair to give him a few hours for him to gather his thoughts and distance his reaction from his emotions.

So I put on some ear protection and went straight to the sawmill. We had a nice cherry log all ready to go, so I tensioned up the blades, double checked the specs were right for the job order, kicked over the motor, and got to sawing.

It was one of my favorite things to do, not gonna lie.

But it didn't hurt none that no one would interrupt me for a good hour or so.

Not including Rusty who, every time the blade stopped for just a minute, appeared and cleared away the dust and offcuts. Never had to ask him, never had to say a word. He'd just be there doing his job and making mine easier.

I'd look outside every so often and see him zip past on the tractor with the power claw, lifting some logs to move to a different place for drying or milling. Then he'd zip past on the front loader for another job. He just never stopped, and I'd known and worked with him since I was a kid. He was like a big brother to me.

And I had to tell him too. I promised I'd tell him, which meant I had to come out to him, put it all on the line, and hope like hell he didn't think any less of me.

Hoping like hell I still had a friend at the end of this.

I pulled out my phone, about to text Gunter, when a hand touched my shoulder.

I spun around, pulling my hearing protection off.

"Whoa," Dad said, putting his hands up. "Didn't mean to scare ya."

My heart was hammering. "Shit."

"You good?"

I still had my hand to my heart. "Yeah. I'm good. Look, Dad—"

"No, you've said your bit. Now you can listen to me, Clay. I know you said to wait till dinner time, but I don't need to wait. And maybe you wanted me to wait until dinnertime so *you* can avoid it or whatever your reasons, son. But what I gotta say needs sayin' now."

He hadn't looked this mad since he found out Rusty gave me my first beer at sixteen.

I felt a little nauseous.

He shook his head. "It's been just you and me for a while now, ain't it? And we did okay, didn't we?"

"Dad—"

He put his hand up. "Lemme speak, please." He let out a frustrated breath. "Now why on earth did you think I would make a fuss over something like who you were seeing? I get that it's a big deal and you finally sayin' that shit out loud is scary or whatever, but I ain't ever seen you actually scared, Clay, like you could be thinkin' I was gonna be pissed at you? Or disappointed?" He shook his head again. "You listen to me, son. I don't give one single damn who you spend time with."

Oh.

God, was he actually okay with it?

The back of my nose burned and I got choked up.

His face softened along with his tone. "As long as they treat you right, I don't mind one bit. I just want you to be happy, Clay. That's all me and your mom ever wanted."

I let out a long breath and blinked back tears. "I didn't

know how to tell you," I admitted. "It was something about myself I just pushed aside for so long."

"Since your crush on David Bowie, probably."

"Since my what?"

"Your crush on David Bowie. You had more posters of him than was probably normal." He laughed at my expression. "What? Your mom and me wondered."

They what?

"You what?"

He chuckled. "It's true."

"I had posters of hockey players, and Annie Lennox, and Axl Rose."

He raised an eyebrow. "You're not helping your argument there."

"Oh, and I had *The Terminator* poster with Linda Hamilton. She was so hot in that."

"And so was Arnold, right?"

"Dad!"

He laughed and leaned against the stack of lumber. "Look, I'm gonna tell you something I don't want you repeating. Especially not to your Aunt Janette."

Mom's sister?

"Your mom was bi," he whispered.

I stared at him. I couldn't believe it. "She was?"

"I can't tell you of all the things we did with other women—"

"Oh my god!"

"What? It was the 1970s. It was a crazy time. And it was before we were married and long before you came along. Don't act like such a prude."

"A prude? Jesus, Dad."

He just shrugged. "And if seeing two women together

weren't no problem, then I'd be a hypocrite if I said two men bothered me."

I tried to get my head around everything he'd just told me. "You really don't mind?"

"Not at all. I thought you were gonna say they were married or in prison for murder or something."

"Not sure those two criteria are the same." I snorted. "But no, he's not married. He was." God, was I really going to tell him this? "He's just a really good person, and he's smart and funny. And I wasn't even looking but there was just something about him I couldn't get past."

"Does the man have a name?"

"Gunter. Gunter Zuniga. He bought the old Nolan house."

"Ah. I wondered if it was the guy with the kitchen countertops. It's not real often you give clients a personal tour of the lumberyard."

I rolled my eyes. "He needed to see the slabs."

Dad's grin widened. "I bet he did."

Oh god. "Yeah, I'm glad you can joke about it, but I dunno if I'm ready for that yet. It's all real new and you're the first person I've told. I gotta tell Rusty yet, and . . ." I groaned. "It's just a lot, ya know?"

He nodded with a frown. "You'll be all right, Clay."

"I don't even know how things with Gunter will pan out. This thing with him could all be over next week and I'll have told Rusty for nothing."

"It's not nothing, Clay." He was quiet for a second. "But you like this guy enough to tell *me* about him."

I nodded. "I do, yeah. He's kinda great. But it's just new."

"I think Rusty'll be fine with it, son. We've known him a

lot of years. He wouldn't still be here if he weren't a decent person."

I sighed. "I know. But you just can't ever tell how someone'll react." I met his eyes. "I'm so relieved you're cool about it. I probably coulda done without knowing about yours and Mom's extra-curricular activities. But thanks, Dad. Knowing you support me, it means a lot."

He put his hand on top of my shoulder. "You can tell me anything, you know that."

I nodded. "Me doubting how you mighta taken it wasn't a reflection on you. I hope you know that."

"Oh, I know that." He squeezed my shoulder, giving me a gentle shake. "You gotta stop doubting yourself. Finding someone who makes you happy in this town doesn't come along real often. Just enjoy the ride, son." He paused for a second. "Speakin' of enjoying the ride, while we're having this conversation, you gotta be safe. If you know what I mean."

Enjoying the ride.

Be safe.

Oh my god, was he . . . was he having the sex talk with me? The *gay sex* talk with me?

"Oh my god, Dad, please don't."

He laughed. "You gotta be puttin' the little party hat on the birthday boy, if you get my drift."

"Jesus Herbert Christ, Dad, please stop."

Rusty laughed behind me. "Stop what?"

"This whole conversation," I replied.

Rusty snorted, and when Dad and I didn't explain or tell him what we were talking about, his smile kinda faltered. "Got the truck loaded up for ya. You got two deliveries this afternoon."

I checked my watch. Shit. I hadn't realized the time. I was now officially late. "Thanks, man."

"I put the logbook next to yer coat," Rusty said. "Keys are in the truck."

I clapped his arm. "Dunno what I'd do without ya."

"Be later than you already are, I'm guessin'."

I headed for the office, and Dad called out, "Will you be around for dinner?"

"Yep. Should be," I yelled back.

"Don't forget to pick up some party hats!"

Oh, he did not just say that . . .

I shoved my arms into my coat, grabbed the logbook, and got my ass outta there before anyone could ask whose party it was.

I'd hoped my dad would be okay with me being bisexual, and in my heart I knew he'd accept it eventually, if not right away. But for him to be this cool with it and making sex jokes?

I wasn't prepared for that.

No sooner had I pulled the truck out of the yard and onto the road that I put my phone on speaker and called Gunter. He picked up right away. "Hello?"

"Hey," I said, grinning like a fool. "I'm in the truck, driving, and I got you on speaker if you're wondering why it's loud."

"Is everything okay?"

I chuckled. "Yes. I told my dad. About me. About us."

"Oh my god, you did? How did he take it? Are you okay?"

"Yeah, I'm fine. Great, actually. He took it really well. I told him and went and did some jobs to give him some time to process, but he came and found me after a while. Said he didn't need time. He said it didn't matter to him at all who I brought home."

"Oh, Clay, I'm so happy for you! That's amazing!"

"He told me my mom was bisexual."

"Oh my god."

"And that they'd had some threesomes with other women, or something. I dunno."

"Oh my god! Clay!" He laughed. "*What?*"

"I know! I'm still trying to get my head around that. Or maybe I need some of that brain bleach I heard about."

"It's called tequila."

I laughed. "It's been a crazy day, not gonna lie."

He sighed. "Clay, I'm so happy for you. And I'm proud of you."

I was smiling so hard it hurt. I felt like laughing and maybe a little bit of crying at the same time. "Me too. Sorry if I interrupted your work. I just had to tell you."

"Are you kidding? That's the perfect interruption. I'm painting the kitchen. Well, where the kitchen will be going. Installation date is next week."

"I know. I have one very fine-looking countertop I'm working on for it. I won't let anyone else touch it, 'cause I want it to be perfect. I gotta treat it when everyone goes home this afternoon."

"You're working on it after hours?"

"Yeah."

"Oh, I'm sorry. I didn't mean to be a hassle. I know you said you were busy."

"It's no problem. The guy I'm doing it for is kinda cute, so I don't mind."

He laughed. "Cute, huh?"

"Yeah, I suppose."

"Well, Mr. Henderson, just so you know, flattery will get you a second date."

"Is that right?"

"Oh, as it so happens, and this might be a little bold."

"I'm okay with bold."

"On Wednesday, Jayden and Cass are taking Cass's kids Christmas shopping in Mossley and they were going out for dinner with Cass's parents, so they won't be home till late. They asked if I'd be okay to get myself some dinner and keep the fires burning, so to speak. Their last guests just left today, and they won't have anyone else staying until the weekend."

I was pretty sure I knew where he was going with this . . .

"So I'll have the whole place to myself," he said quietly. "I can pick up some takeout, we can watch something on Netflix . . ."

My face was now hurting from all the smiling. "I thought I was supposed to plan the next date."

"Well . . . you can. I just thought . . . we were presented with an opportunity. My father used to say to 'make hay while the sun shines' which probably doesn't apply here."

"Will there be actual haymaking?"

"Literally, no. Metaphorically, maybe."

I laughed. "Well, it would seem we've been presented with an opportunity. And they do have furniture? No picnics on the floor this time?"

"Hey, my picnic idea was great."

"Your picnic idea was amazing. I'll have to think of something to better it."

"So you don't want to come around on Wednesday night?"

"Oh, I absolutely do. I was talking about date number

three." I drove onto Main Street and turned down Bridge Street. "And you know, we do have my place. But no doubt my Dad would invite himself over. And after today, when he already tried to have the safe-sex talk with me, maybe somewhere else would be better."

"Oh my god. He did not."

"He absolutely did. Well, he started to. I begged him to stop. I'm thirty-five years old, for fuck's sake."

Gunter laughed and laughed. "Your dad's awesome. And if you want to have dinner with me *and* your dad, I'd be more than okay with that. I've already met him, so it's no big deal."

That made me smile. I knew Gunter missed his dad, and I really liked that he appreciated my dad being a big part of my life. "Thanks. How about we keep the first few dates just between us?"

"Deal."

I slowed the truck down at the address on my list. "Well, I gotta go. Just got to a job. Text me tonight. Or call." Hearing his voice was so much better than a text.

"Will do."

I clicked off the call, smiling, and got out of the truck.

The client, Cordelia Gray, a woman in her sixties with a striking resemblance—in looks and personality—to Blanche from the *Golden Girls* came bustling out to greet me, but her smile died when she saw me.

"Oh, Clay," she said, clearly disappointed. "I was expecting Cliff."

I wasn't sure what to say to that. "Well, I can go get him if you prefer." I was kinda joking, but she looked like she just might say yes.

After a pause, she laughed me off. "Never mind that. How is he anyway?"

"Oh, he's just fine. Fit as an ox."

She hummed. "I bet he is."

Okay, wow. All righty then. "I've got a load of wood . . . *fire*wood," I specified, not realizing how it sounded until I'd said it out loud. "I got a load of firewood for you. It's bundled already. Where would you like it?"

"Around the back," she said, and I hauled it down and followed her. She watched, delighted. "Ooh, you're big and strong like your father. The apple doesn't fall far, now does it."

I thought about what my dad had said about me and Mom being bi. It made me smile. "No, I suppose it doesn't."

"Well, thank you so much. That should see me through a week or two."

I gave her a nod and tipped my beanie. "You call when you need a delivery and I'll make a note that Dad be the one to make it."

She gave me a pouty, sly smile. "Only if it's no trouble."

"No trouble at all."

I said goodbye and made my other deliveries, and Dad was closing up the office when I got back. "The others just left," he said.

"Yeah, I passed them on the way in." I hung my coat up. "Say, I had a delivery for Cordelia Gray earlier."

Dad stopped and turned slowly to face me. "Is that so?"

"She seems nice."

"She is."

"You been delivering wood to her a lot? Because she was very disappointed when I got out of the truck."

Dad tried not to smile, his cheeks turning pink. "I dunno what you're talking about."

"Hm-mm." I put the logbook down and put the keys to the truck away. "Now if today's a day for being honest, I'd call you out on that bullshit, but because you were so good to me earlier, I'm gonna let it slide."

Dad shoved his hands in his pockets. "I weren't bein' good to ya. I was just bein' your dad."

I smiled at him. "And I told her to call when she needs her next delivery and you'll be the one to bring it."

"Hmm."

I nudged the logbook. "But if you have her number, you could just call her any time and, you know . . . deliver her wood."

He narrowed his eyes. "Speaking of delivering wood, did you get some party hats for your date with your boyfriend?"

I snorted. "Nice try at changing the subject. But I don't have a date tonight and he's not my boyfriend." I cringed. "Yet. I dunno what the criteria or date quota is for that. And we're not up to the party-hats part yet. I told you it was new."

"Well, as long as you're not stoking anyone else's fire is about all you need to worry about. And as long as he's not getting his fire stoked by anyone else—"

"Dad!"

"You gotta talk about that, son. Put all your expectations on the table, then there's no feelings gettin' hurt or hearts getting broken."

I sighed. "Okay, okay."

"And I'd imagine with two men, there are other conversations you need to have. Like whether you stoke the fire or if you get your fire stoked—"

I'm sure he saw the horror on my face. "Oh my god, you and I are not having this conversation!"

"Not you and me. Christ almighty, son. I meant you and him."

I put my hands up in a please-stop manner. "Yeah, I understood. Gunter and I will work that out, *if* that's something we need to work out, Dad. Like I said, we're not up to that yet."

"Okay, calm down. I was just tryin' to be helpful. If it's new to you, you mighta needed some advice."

"I got it all under control." I let out a breath, wondering how the hell this was my life now. "But thanks. I guess."

He nodded. "Good. So . . . dinner?"

"How about we order a pizza? I can pick it up. I just gotta get these countertops treated tonight so I can seal them tomorrow."

"How about you order the pizza, and I'll go pick it up?"

I nodded, a slow smile spreading across my face. "You know Cordelia lives just two blocks down from the pizza place."

"I know where she lives, son."

I raised my eyebrows. "Oh really?"

He grumbled under his breath at me.

"Oh, that reminds me," I added as I got to the door. "I mentioned having dinner here one night to Gunter and he said he'd like you to join us. I dunno when that'll be, but just so you know."

Dad seemed pleased by this. "I like a man with manners."

I smiled right back at him. "Me too."

CHAPTER ELEVEN

GUNTER

I WAS TRYING NOT to be nervous, but I wasn't having much luck. It was a good nervous, though. It wasn't dread and a sinking-feeling kind of nervous. It was excitement and anticipation.

It wasn't the fact I was driving to Clay's place, that I was about to see my kitchen countertop before it was installed tomorrow. And it wasn't that I was meeting his dad again, this time with him knowing Clay and I had a thing going. And I wasn't afraid of meeting the other men that worked there. In particular, Rusty, who Clay was friends with but still hadn't found the right time to tell him about who he was dating.

I'd told Clay there was no rush to tell anyone, and in the grand scheme of things, it had only been a few days since he'd told his dad.

What I was most nervous about?

Jayden and Cass would be gone until late, meaning when Clay came around for dinner, we'd have the whole place to ourselves, and if the lack of furniture at my house was any reason to not get to second or third base, then we had absolutely no excuses now.

I'd even visited the drugstore for supplies.

Confident and presumptuous, maybe. But better than being caught without.

And I'd be lying to myself if I said I wasn't excited about it.

The way he'd kissed me up until now was out of this world. Hell, even if he did nothing but kiss me ever again, I wouldn't complain.

But the idea of physical intimacy? After so long without it? Well, my body was on board with the idea, that was for sure.

But first the countertop. Equally exciting, just in a different way.

I pulled my car into a spot by the other vehicles and got out. Clay knew I was coming, and I wasn't sure exactly where to go, given it was business hours and this was a working lumberyard, and the whole place was huge. There were many sheds, many rows of logs.

I guessed it'd be the main shed where Clay had taken me before, but I didn't want to walk through the big open doors because that was a work area, and I could hear a motor running and the buzz-and-whirr sound of lumber being sawn in there. And off to the right, there was a man on a tractor with a huge claw-like thing carrying a huge log, and it looked like someone else was feeding a wood chipper out back.

A door opened at the side and Clay appeared, and his smile made my heart skip a beat.

I had to remind myself that this was his workplace and he wasn't out to his coworkers, so me launching myself at him was out of the question.

"Hey," he said.

I tried to rein in my smile. "Afternoon."

"Come this way," he said, ushering me into an office. It was all wood paneling with desks and planners on the wall, and it smelled of sawdust and diesel, which was fast becoming my new favorite smell.

His dad was standing there, grinning like the cat who got the cream. He stuck out his hand. "Hello again. Clay here tells me you—"

Clay groaned. "Dad . . ."

I chuckled and shook Cliff's hand. "Nice to meet you again."

"I was just gonna say that Clay was telling me you're here to see your countertops. What did you think I was gonna say, Clay?"

I smiled and Clay rolled his eyes, then looking at me, he opened a door to the work shed. "I'll take you through this way."

I followed Clay past what appeared to be a lunchroom, through a corridor of stacked lumber to another room. This room was warmer and noticeably cleaner. No dust, no sawdust, no stacks of anything. Just three long stands with . . .

I put my hand to my mouth. "Oh my god, are these mine?"

Clay gave a nod. "They came up real nice."

Nice? They were better than that. "These are works of art."

Cliff was there and the man I'd seen helping Clay before, unloading the trees on Main Street. He was about my age, with shaggy hair and a roguish smile. I probably would have placed him on a surfboard before a lumberyard.

"Oh," Clay said. "Gunter, this is Rusty. Rusty, Gunter is the owner of these slabs."

Ah, the best friend who didn't know about me yet.

"Yeah, kinda gathered that," he said, shaking my hand. "Gonna have yourself a beautiful kitchen."

"Did you work on these?" I asked.

He laughed. "Nah. Clay wouldn't let anyone else touch 'em."

"One-of-a-kind lumber," Cliff said, a buffer between them.

I smiled at Clay. "The photos didn't do it justice."

The grain, the rich color, the live edges . . . utter perfection. "And the cutouts? Which are which?"

Clay walked by each piece, careful not to touch them. "Your sink goes here. This one is for your stove. And this is your island. We allowed for a max five percent shrinkage in the finished drying stage, but because of the age of the timber, it wasn't even half that. Then I treated it, sealed with a marine grade finish gloss. That color sure is something, huh?"

"It's beautiful. More so than I could have imagined." I was taken aback by how emotional it made me.

Don't cry, Gunter. Do not cry in front of them.

Clay shoved his hands in his pockets and looked back to his masterpieces. He cleared his throat. "Glad you like 'em. We got the temperature set in here to dry the sealant. We'll get 'em wrapped and ready for transport tomorrow."

Tomorrow . . . *Focus, Gunter.*

"Yes, tomorrow. The big install." I held up my paint-covered hands. "I've been getting everything ready. As you can see."

Cliff put his hand on my shoulder. "Can I get you a cup of coffee?"

Clay's gaze cut to his father's, but Rusty was still there, looking between them, and I had to say something . . .

"Sure!"

Cliff led me out, waving his hand at Clay and Rusty. "Never mind them, they've got work to do."

Back in the lunchroom, I sat with Cliff and a much appreciated cup of coffee. I wondered if he was about to give me some fatherly shake down, but of course, he was just the sweetest. "Clay's been workin' on those kitchen countertops, getting 'em just right."

"Well, he's certainly done that. I can't believe they're mine. My kitchen is going to be amazing."

"Mosta the time we just do lumber or fencing posts or construction lumber, nothin' too special. So it's not too often he gets to make something pretty. I think he inspected every inch of grain in your new countertops, makin' sure they were the best they could be. He's got a real talent, and he's come a long way since the likes of this."

Cliff nudged the table with his boot.

"Clay made this?"

He nodded. "When he was in high school. He was about fifteen, if memory serves."

Oh my . . . "I'm impressed. The only thing I could make at fifteen were awkward conversations and terrible fashion choices."

Cliff laughed, and wow, he sounded just like his son. "Well, Clay did his fair share of that too. But I shouldn't be tellin' stories without him bein' here."

"True. It might not be fair."

"Well, yeah. And all that good embarrassment gone to waste. I'll save it for when he's around."

I chuckled as I sipped my coffee. "It's a great setup you have here."

"Ah. It wasn't always like this. The sawmill we use these days makes everythin' easier. All the equipment, all the tools were nothin' like what my grandpa or my dad used. Even in my early days, it was backbreaking work. It's still hard, still physical, and these young bucks can do it all day. But we got log turners now, splitters, laser cutters, tractors, portable sawmills. Clay dragged us kickin' and screamin' into the twenty-first century, and he's set on rehabilitation and makin' it a sustainable industry. Most of what you see out there is refurbished. Clearing fallen trees, storm clearing, that kinda thing. He reckons it's the only way forward, and he's not wrong."

I was smiling without even realizing it. "He is kinda great."

He clucked his tongue, amused. "Oh Lord, help us. You get the same kinda smile he gets when he talks about you. Did you see how nervous he was in there?" He nodded toward the drying room. "That was pitiful."

I could feel my face burn, and I chose to finish my coffee instead of speaking.

"So, he tells me you have another date tonight," Cliff added casually.

"Ah well, yes. Just dinner."

Truth be told, I had hopes for more than just dinner. But I wasn't saying that out loud. To his father, no less.

"I should be going," I said, putting my empty cup on the table. "But I've enjoyed our chat, and thank you for the coffee."

"My pleasure. I'll tell Clay to take some photos of your new kitchen tomorrow so I can see what it looks like."

"Or you can come and see it yourself?" I said. "And see what I've done to the house."

His eyes lit up. "Oh, I'd really like that. I'll have Clay

bring me up some time. I'm sure he won't mind the excuse for another visit."

He winked, and I laughed. "Sounds good."

I left without seeing Clay again, though by the time I'd gone back to my house and finished some more painting, I'd barely had time to get back to the bed and breakfast, shower, and scrub paint off my hands before I heard a very familiar truck coming up the driveway.

I fixed my sweater and combed my fingers through my still-damp hair, trying to tamp my nerves.

I went out onto the back porch and waved him in. He took his boots off in the mudroom, and as he was bent over, I noticed he'd showered, and boy, he smelled so good.

"Are you sure Cass and Jayden don't mind me being here?"

"Are you kidding? Jayden was so excited he cooked us dinner."

Clay snorted. "A live-in chef, huh?"

"I know. It's gonna suck to move out." I hung his coat up for him. "Come on through this way. I just have to dish up dinner and heat it. It's pasta. I hope that's okay?"

I only got a few steps in the hall when Clay took my hand, pulling me closer. "Are you okay?"

I was confused. "Yeah. Of course. Why?"

"You were upset when I showed you the finished countertops. If you don't like it, you can tell me."

Oh my god. The worry in his eyes hurt my heart.

I put my hand to his cheek. "I was upset because . . . well, I don't even know why. I was overwhelmed with how beautiful they were, that they were mine. For me, in my new house. And that you made them for me. It made me emotional. I don't know why."

"Are you sure that's all?"

"One hundred percent." I leaned up and kissed him softly. "I saw it made you nervous. And in front of your dad and Rusty. I'm sorry."

His hands slid down my waist, firm, strong. "I wanted to touch you so bad, I didn't know what to do with my hands. I wanted to see if you were okay, and then Dad dragged you away. Which was probably a good thing."

I scratched his beard lightly and leaned up on my toes so I could kiss him again. "Your dad is so sweet. I told him to come up to my house with you sometime."

"He told me. He likes you." His gaze kept dropping to my lips. His voice was just a murmur. "And we're definitely alone?"

I leaned into him and he pulled me flush against him. I had to bite back a moan. His strong arms, his huge body, those green eyes full of desire, his lips so close to mine. "Did you want dinner first? Are you hungry?"

"Starving," he whispered, before crashing his mouth to mine. His kiss was desperate and deep, his hands snaking up my back, keeping me pressed to him. His tongue was in my mouth, his fingertips digging in my sweater, his erection hardening against me.

Oh yes, he was hungry, all right.

Not for food.

I broke the kiss, breathing ragged. "Should we take this to my room?"

He gave a nod, so holding his hand, I led him down the hall.

"Jeez, how big is this place?" he mumbled behind me.

I snorted. "My room is the last one."

I opened the door, thankful the room was warm. I turned to him and that fierce desire was now tinged with uncertainty.

"You okay?" I asked.

He nodded. "I've never done anything . . ."

"With a man. I know. But believe me, the way you kiss? I'm pretty sure you'll do just fine. Actually, I think you could probably make me come just by kissing me."

His eyes widened, and I laughed. "I'm not even kidding. But for a first time, how about we just take it slow? No pressure. Kissing on my bed, hand jobs, maybe? If you want to go that far?"

His cheeks were red and he balked. "Oh, wow. You just talk about these things?"

I chuckled. "Well, yeah. But if it helps, if I was a woman, what would you do to me right now?"

He put his hands on my shoulders, his forehead pressed to mine. "I'd put you on that bed, kiss you all over, touch you where you wanted to be touched. Make your body sing."

Christ.

I groaned, leaning into him. "Yes, please."

He tilted my chin up and kissed me, softer and sweeter this time. He walked me backward, laid me down on the bed and kneeled over me, his dark gaze just about setting me on fire.

I pulled the hem of his sweater up and he pulled it over his head, revealing a white T-shirt underneath. His broad chest, huge biceps, and as I raked my eyes down his body . . . my god. The bulge in his jeans.

"Jesus, Clay."

He pulled my sweater up and off me so fast, then kissed me, slowly lowering his body onto mine. The hot press of his erection through his jeans sent bolts of lightning through my veins. I widened my legs to accommodate him and he drove me up the mattress, sinking his tongue into my mouth.

Lord.

I lifted his shirt up, raking my hands up his sides, across his back. His skin warm over tight muscles.

To feel his skin.

Just to feel his skin.

When I slipped my hands under the waistband of his jeans to his ass, he moaned and broke the kiss. His nose to mine, his lips swollen, his eyes heavy lidded. "You're killing me."

"I want to feel you in my hand," I whispered. "Is that okay?"

His eyes rolled back and slowly closed. "Fuck. Yes, Gunter."

I squeezed my hands between us and he gave us some room so I could unbutton his jeans. I unzipped him, slid my hands into his briefs, and sweet mother of god . . .

"You're huge," I gasped. "Christ."

He *was* huge. Which was understandable—there wasn't one small thing about him. But I could barely get my grip around him, and he was rock hard and scorching hot. He hissed when I pumped him. "Fuck, Gunter."

So I did it again, and again, and he thrust into my fist, now slick with his precome.

The sounds he made were going to make me come. The sight of him above me, his weight on me, his cock in my hand.

I couldn't take it anymore. I let go of him so I could unzip myself and get a hand to my dick.

"God, sorry," he said, his voice low and tight. And he went to lean back so he could use his hands.

"No, let me," I said, taking a hold of his erection and

lining it up with mine. I held them together, our shafts sliding in my hand.

"Holy shit," he said, falling onto both hands again, looking down at me, his hips driving the best friction.

I could just imagine him inside me, fucking me like this. How this would feel, filling me completely, with him in me, over me, with that lost-to-pleasure look in his eyes.

I was chasing that high with every thrust, every glide, every groan, until I reached my peak, toppling over the edge.

"Oh fuck, yes," Clay grunted, and with a long, rough moan, he came, his orgasm spilling between us.

He was on his elbows, trying to keep his weight off me, his body trembling. I wrapped my arms around him and pulled him onto me. "Come here."

He snorted. "I just did."

I laughed, and his beard against my neck tickled me, but we were already a mess that needed to be cleaned up. Holding him felt nice. Having him lie on me, his soft kisses under my ear and murmurs of contentedness felt even better.

"You okay?" I asked. "After your first time with a man?"

He laughed and propped his head up on his hand. His eyes searched mine, a gentle smile on his lips. "I am so much better than okay. That was amazing and maybe the hottest thing I've ever done."

I stroked his hair, his cheek, his beard. "I wouldn't say no to a repeat, at any time. You are a sexy man, Clay Henderson."

His cheeks blushed red and he ducked his head a little. "I'm down for repeats."

"Good, because there are a lot of things I'd like to do to

you and have you do to me. And just so you know, I did buy condoms, but I think I may have to get a bigger size."

He huffed out a laugh and covered his eyes with his hand. "Oh god."

"And a lot more lube."

He laughed again and rolled us over so I was on top of him. I leaned down and kissed him softly. "Don't be embarrassed. I was totally imagining how you'd feel inside me."

His cheeks were still pink and he bit his lip. "I did wonder 'bout that," he said. "You said before, on our first date, that there wasn't any furniture for me to bend you over, so I presumed you . . . you know, liked it that way."

I smiled at him and thumbed his bottom lip. "I'm a bottom, yes. Love it, when it's done right."

"Will you teach me? How to do it right?"

I hummed. "Yes."

"I've watched some gay porn recently," he said with a wince. "I get the mechanics of it, and I know it's not real life. But I guess I'm a top?"

I kissed him again, smiling. "When you watched, did you imagine yourself as the top? Or when you think about sex with a man, which are you?" Then I realized that this was probably too much, too soon, because this was all so new to him. "It's okay to not know. It's okay to want to explore, and it's okay to not want to do certain things. I shouldn't have assumed, and I shouldn't have put my expectations on you, sorry—"

"Hold up," he said. "Lemme speak."

"Sorry, I just keep forgetting this is all so new to you."

"Which means I gotta lotta catching up to do. I wanna try anything you want me to do to you. And when I watch porn or when I'm thinking of sex, I'm stoking the fire, not the one getting my fire stoked." He cringed. "Sorry, that's the way my dad put it."

I laughed. "It's a great analogy."

He conceded a smile. "So yeah, if what we did just now is any kinda indication, then I wanna do it all. And if you want your fire stoked, I'll be real happy to oblige."

"Hmm," I kissed him again. "And I'll be really happy to show you how it's done. But for now?" I peeled myself off him. "We need to get cleaned up and fed."

I changed my shirt and offered to clean his. He took it off, revealing a broad, muscular hairy chest.

Damn.

"You okay?"

I laughed, not even embarrassed that I'd been caught ogling him. "You are . . . like no one I've ever been with. What the hell have I been missing out on all these years?" I ran my hand through his chest hair. "I like this very much."

Then I traced my hands over his biceps. "And this."

And then I gently tugged on his beard. "And this."

He slid his hand along my jaw and tilted my face up for a kiss. "And I like this."

Then his stomach growled.

I laughed. "Let's get you fed."

After I found him the biggest shirt I owned and a dinner of beef ragu pasta, courtesy of Jayden, Clay and I sat on the sofa in front of the fire, surrounded by the beautiful Christmas decorations and lights, and we talked. About everything and nothing, and it was easy and effortless. He held my gaze when I spoke, he listened to my answers, and he made me feel important.

Something I hadn't felt in a long time.

I wished he didn't have to leave. I wished he could have

stayed the night. Sure, the dating aspect was nice and sweet, but . . . this felt so natural.

"You okay?" he asked. "You looked sad there for a second."

I really liked that he could read me so well. In the short time we'd spent together, the handful of hours, he read me better than Scott ever did.

"Yeah, I'm fine. I just wished I was in my house already, and we were on my couch and in front of my fire with my Christmas decorations, and I wish that you didn't have to leave. That you were wearing your wool socks and my clothes and looking at me the way you are right now, so comfortable and safe. You make me feel comfortable. And important. Like I matter."

He cupped my cheek. "You do matter," he murmured. "And you are important." His thumb traced a gentle line along my cheek. "And I wish I could stay."

"I know."

"Soon."

As much as I wanted that, as much as I wanted to sleep in his arms, I couldn't rush him. He needed to tell the other important people in his life first, and that was something I understood. "Whenever you're ready."

CHAPTER TWELVE

CLAY

I NEEDED TO TELL RUSTY. I could tell myself that I had to wait for the perfect time, but the truth was, there was no perfect time. But god, being with Gunter last night and seeing the look in his eyes when he wished I coulda stayed . . .

I wanted that too.

I really needed to tell Rusty.

It might not have mattered all that much, but I lived and worked at the lumberyard. Rusty worked there, and he got to work early most days. If Gunter were to stay over at my place, Rusty or one of the guys at work would most likely see. I could stay at Gunter's place when he got it finished and furnished, but then the guys at work would know I was coming home in the morning. Rusty would want answers and I needed to tell him before it came to sneaking around.

And I couldn't rightly stay at the bed and breakfast. It felt wrong to be having an all-nighter in someone else's house.

But if I told Rusty, then it would be out in the open.

Whether he liked it or not was beside the point. I was

done with the lying and the half-truths. If I weren't completely certain about wanting a relationship with Gunter before, then I sure was now.

I hadn't ever been surer.

There was something about him that connected with me, like no one else ever had.

And maybe I was getting way ahead of myself, but if I could take a leaf out of his book and say what I was thinking and feeling—and live like there were no more wasted days—then I could admit I had feelings for him. That I wanted something with him.

"Yo, Clay," Rusty said, snapping his fingers. "You in there, buddy?"

I blinked at him. I was supposed to be making sure the countertops were secure for transport in the back of my truck. Jeez, how long had I been standing there for? "Yeah. Sorry, just . . . thinking."

He smiled slowly. "About anyone in particular?"

Shit.

"Uh, yeah, actually. And maybe after this job you and me can sit down and I can tell you about it."

Rusty shrugged, pulling on the strap to check the tension. "Jeez, Clay. It ain't that big of a deal." His gaze cut to mine. "Unless it's my mom. Clay, are you and my mom—"

"What? No! Christ, Rus."

"Okay then. Good." He squinted at me. "And it's not Briella from the bar?"

"No."

Just tell him, Clay. No more wasted days.

Heaven help me, here goes nothing.

"The person I'm kinda seeing right now is a man."

"A man? Amanda? The preschool teacher?"

"No. Not Aman or Amanda. A man, Rusty. A guy. A dude."

His smile faded. Confusion crossed his face. "A dude?"

I nodded, not able to meet his eyes. God, I shoulda waited . . . "Gunter Zuniga. The guy who we made these for." I tapped the wrapped-up and secured countertop. "I'm seeing him."

"But you're not gay."

"No, I'm not."

"But he's a guy."

"Yes, he is. I'm bisexual. If that helps any."

He squinted at me and shook his head. "Nah. I'm not buyin' it."

I met his eyes. "I needed to tell you, Rusty, 'cause I don't wanna hide it anymore. At first I just thought it'd pass and I could go back to being the old me. You've been like a brother to me all these years, and I don't want that to change. But you don't gotta buy it. It is what it is."

His expression was one I couldn't quite place. Shock, disbelief, anger.

Mostly anger.

The office door banged and Dad came over, trudging through the snow, pulling his gloves on. "We ready to go? The kitchen folks'll be waiting, and we got deliveries to make this afternoon." He clapped his hands. "Time's money. Let's move."

I gave a nod, thankful for the interruption, and walked to the cab of the truck. I climbed in and started it up. The passenger door opened and I thought for a second that maybe Rusty wasn't getting in.

But he did.

He didn't speak a word the whole trip. Feeling the tension between us, Dad did most of the talking. He even tried fixing the radio, knowing dang well it hadn't worked in twenty years.

Pulling into Gunter's place, I just about felt sick.

The kitchen company truck was there, and another truck, and Gunter's car, of course. I pulled up to the front of the house and Gunter met us as soon as we climbed out.

He gave me a smile but spoke to all of us. "I'm trying to stay out of their way," he said. "Let them do their work without being one of those clients who watch everything."

Before I could say anything, Dad walked right up to him. "We'll let them do their thing," Dad said with a hand to his shoulder. "Now show me this house."

Man, I really loved my dad.

That man, one hundred percent, had my back.

Without a word to Rusty, I climbed the porch steps and went inside. The kitchen was all but installed. They were finishing up the white cabinetry, and it surprised me how much it made it look like a house.

It wasn't an empty shell anymore.

I could see all the repairs and paintwork Gunter had done. And he certainly was a perfectionist. All the little details that no one else probably noticed.

To be fair, they'd not seen it the day he got the keys . . .

Phil saw me and came over, his hand outstretched for me to shake. "Hey, Clay. I hear you've got an amazing countertop for us."

I smiled, because clearly Gunter had told him it was amazing. "Sure do. When your boys are ready to give us a hand, we'll get it out of the truck. They're heavy as hell."

Looking out the front window, I could see Rusty already had the back of the truck open and was unfastening the tie-downs. And I could see Dad and Gunter, pointing up to the roof and Dad was laughing.

It made my heart knock against my ribs in ways I wasn't expecting. I coulda watched them all day.

Until I saw Rusty watching them too.

I was pretty good at reading him, and he either didn't like it or didn't understand it. Possibly both.

Two of the kitchen guys came out with me, and along with Rusty, we got each piece inside. We needed to unwrap them, of course, so they could be fit and secured, and as the first piece was exposed, Phil let out a low whistle, clearly pleased with what he saw. They all were.

Except for Dad. He was looking up at the ceiling beam. "Well, would you look at that," he said. "That's hand-hewn. Forty-inch tooth saw, I'd guess. What a beauty. It's the art and craft of timber-frame joinery."

Gunter's eyes met mine and he smiled, because I'd said almost exactly the same thing when I first walked in.

"Come through to the bedrooms," Gunter said, leading Dad down the hall. "I'll show you the old windows."

We got busy with the countertops, fixing and gluing, and thankfully, thankfully, thankfully there were no problems, no mishaps, no catastrophes.

When Phil's crew packed up their gear and left, I was so relieved. I'd have some joints to seal in a day or two, but for now it was a job well done.

Gunter's kitchen looked like a million dollars.

And he was so happy he looked about ready to burst. He took lots of photos before we covered them up again. The house was still a construction site, after all.

"If you got some flattened cardboard boxes," Dad said, "lay 'em out on top. And make sure no contractor puts anything heavy on there."

"Good idea," Gunter said.

Rusty was making himself busy at the truck, folding up

the plastic and blankets we'd used, coiling the tie-downs, getting us ready to leave.

And avoiding being anywhere near me and Gunter.

"Clay, you okay?" Gunter asked me.

I looked at him, fully aware my dad was right there. "Yeah. I told Rusty. About us, and well, he . . ." I nodded out the window to where Rusty was still organizing our gear. "It went that well."

"Oh, Clay, I'm really sorry," Gunter said quickly. His hand flinched as if he were about to reach out for me, but he stopped himself. "I'm sorry."

"He just needs some time," Dad added.

"You didn't," I replied.

"I had thirty-somethin' years to get used to it. I told ya, son, your mom and me kinda wondered. You were way too into David Bowie for a straight kid."

Gunter tried not to laugh, making me look at him. "Sorry." This time he did touch my arm. "I am sorry about your friend. Give him time." He frowned up at me. "Are you okay?"

"Yeah. I am. Just . . . you know." I tried to smile for him. "But you got your new kitchen today! That's exciting, and I'm happy for you."

His eyes softened. "I know you have to go. I'll call you later."

"You can come for dinner," Dad said. "To my place. I'll make my famous chili."

"Dad," I began.

"Zip it, Clay. He ain't your guest. He's mine. But if you're lucky, I'll feed you too."

He winked at Gunter, and I rolled my eyes. Gunter laughed. "What time?"

"Six o'clock." He walked to the door. "Then what you

two do after that is none of my business."

Dad made it down the stairs while telling Rusty to watch his fingers as he closed the tailgate.

Gunter gave me a sad smile, leaned up on his toes, and pecked a soft kiss on my lips. "I'll see you at six."

"THE PLACE IS FINE," Dad grumbled at me. "You move my recliner an inch one way, then move it back five seconds later. Leave my shit alone. You know Gunter won't care."

I was refixing the seating for the tenth time, and he was stirring his chili.

"And what're you nervous for?"

"I'm not nervous. I just want him to . . ."

"To what? You think he's not gonna like it here? Lemme tell ya something, Clay. If this house or your place ain't good enough for him, then show him the door."

"No, I don't think he'll think that."

Didn't I? Was I sure?

"I just want him to . . ." Goddammit. "I want him to like me."

Dad laughed. Honest to god laughed. "Don't think you need to worry about that. Pretty sure he's well past that. Shoulda seen the way he was looking at you when you were liftin' that countertop today." He shook his head. "I ain't ever seen a grown man drool before. Well, not countin' that time your great uncle Ronnie drank too much whiskey."

I laughed. "Gunter wasn't drooling."

"Clay, the man forgot how to blink."

I snorted, and then we heard the sound of car tires on snow. My stomach was a knot, my heart thumping.

I met Gunter outside. He was wearing his red coat, his

boots and beanie, and his red glasses, looking cute as hell. He was grinning, holding a take-out container.

"There's no one here?" he asked, looking around the empty parking lot.

"Nope."

"Then I can do this." He greeted me with a soft kiss.

I chuckled. "Yes, you can." I looked at the container he was holding. "Whatcha got there?"

"Something for your dad."

He brought something for my dad? God, it just made me so stupidly happy. I gestured toward Dad's front door. "This way." We got to the porch and I held the door for him. "You go in. I gotta lock the front gate."

His eyes lit up. "Oh, I could walk up with you."

I didn't have the heart to tell him I was gonna drive up and back. It wasn't far, but the snow was starting to come down, and I didn't want to miss a minute with him—or leave him alone with my dad.

Dad still wouldn't tell me what they talked about when Gunter was showing him the house.

But the idea of taking a walk with Gunter sounded kinda great.

Gunter smiled. "I'll just give these to Cliff."

Like a genie, Dad appeared at the sound of his name. Or like he was standing there listening. "Good evenin'," he said with a bright smile.

"These are for you," Gunter said, opening the take-out container. "From one cook to another. I told Jayden I was coming here for dinner for your famous chili, and he said to bring these for dessert. They're little caramel apple-pie bites, or something like that. He's been cooking non-stop in the lead up for Christmas."

"Oh, he didn't have to do that," I tried.

Dad took the container and looked at me like I was crazy. "But we're not gonna say no. I'll put them inside."

"Quick, count them," I said.

"Oh, you hush," Dad said, disappearing inside. "Don't forget the flashlight."

Yep. He'd totally been listening.

I grabbed the flashlight, my gloves, and Dad's gloves for Gunter and waited for him to put them on. As soon as we were out of the porch light, I turned the torch on. "You okay? You can totally stay inside where it's warm if you want."

Smiling, he slipped his arm through mine, resting his hand on my forearm. "Is this okay?"

It was sweet and romantic, and it made my stomach swoop. "It's perfect."

And so we walked up to the front gate. It was dark, freezing cold. The ground was slushy and gross from the trucks and vehicles all day. But every time Gunter slipped or slid, he'd hold my arm a little bit tighter. And he'd laugh. And steam would billow out of his mouth; his cheeks were rosy red.

And my heart swelled enough for two.

He held the flashlight while I closed the gate, and a light dusting of snow started to fall.

"My god, it's so beautiful here," he said.

"It's pitch black. How can you see anything?"

He pointed the flashlight above my head to the north. "I know the mountain is right there." He swung the flashlight to his left. "And there's a whole pine forest right there." Then he shined the flashlight past the sheds. "And there's heaps of rows of logs that would be creepy if you weren't here with me."

I laughed.

Then he pointed the flashlight straight up. "And the snow." Then he shined it at me. "And the company."

I pulled him close, the flashlight between us, my arms around him. "The only beautiful thing I'm seeing right now is you."

He leaned up on his toes, and standing right there in the driveway, I kissed him. Cold noses, warm mouths, smiling lips. Until he shivered.

"Let's get you inside. Dad's probably wondering what we're doing."

"I have a feeling he might know." This time he slung his arm under my coat and around my waist, fitting perfectly under my arm as we walked. "Oh, you're nice and warm," he said. "Is that you or your coat?"

"It doesn't help any that every time I'm near you my blood runs all hot."

He burst out laughing. "Maybe that's a problem we can take care of after dinner."

I groaned. "Great. Now I'm gonna be thinking about that at the dinner table."

He was still laughing when we got back inside. By the time we got our boots off, Dad had our plates dished up on the table. And so we sat at his small table that had only been set for two people for far too long.

The third mismatched chair felt right somehow.

Just like Gunter felt right somehow. He was rich and sophisticated, yet he fit in with us so utterly perfectly.

The TV was on low for some background noise, the lights were on the Christmas tree. The pot of chili in the center of the table, a side plate of cheesy garlic breads, and a cold beer.

And Dad told stories, and Gunter laughed as he ate,

first the dinner and then dessert, and I'll be damned if we didn't sit there for two hours.

I can't remember if I said much. I just sat there the whole time thinking about how perfect it was, how real and happy it was. How I was already in way over my head.

I wished Rusty understood.

I wished he could see us right now.

"Okay, so serious question time," Dad said.

That sure got me out of my head.

"When we left your house this afternoon, did you or did you not hug your new kitchen countertop?"

Gunter laughed and nodded. "I absolutely did. Very carefully though."

"I thought you were gonna," Dad said.

"Okay, my serious question time," Gunter replied. He looked at me. "Tell me more about this obsession with David Bowie."

I let my head fall back and I groaned. "It wasn't an obsession."

Dad scoffed. "He had posters. That one where he was in a leotard. It didn't leave much to the imagination."

"Ziggy Stardust," I explained.

"Oh." Gunter nodded as if it now made sense.

"There were a few posters," Dad added. "And records and cassette tapes. The movie . . . with the spiky hair."

"*Labyrinth*," me and Gunter answered at the same time.

"But to be fair," I added, "I did have posters of Annie Lennox and Linda Hamilton. And the hockey poster."

Dad snorted. "Son, those hockey players were half naked in the dressing room. You can see why I wasn't too surprised, Clay."

Gunter laughed so hard he almost fell off his chair.

Dad stood up and began clearing the table. "You boys go on. I'll get this squared away and put myself to bed."

Gunter was about to protest, but Dad wasn't having any of it, and to be honest, I was very much looking forward to some privacy.

We said goodnight and headed over to my place. It was a short walk, but boy it was cold out. "This is my place," I said, stating the very obvious. I stoked the fire and added a log. "Did you want coffee or a drink?"

"No, I'm so full," he said, rubbing his stomach. "I've had the best night. Your dad is so great."

I finished with the fire and joined him on the couch, but not close enough apparently, because he half climbed onto my lap. Legs and arms tangled, his head on my shoulder.

"Tell me what happened with Rusty," he said quietly. "Did he say anything to you in the afternoon?"

"No. When we got back, there was another call about a fallen tree. So he and Wayne went to that job and I had deliveries. It happens sometimes that we don't see each other all day, so it wasn't like he was deliberately avoiding me or anything."

I hoped.

"He might just need time," he offered. "Let him get his head around it. I know today has been kinda shit for you, and I'm sorry about that. You were brave and honest with him. And I know you and him go back thirty years and I've only known you for two weeks, and that sounds kinda lame when I say it out loud like that, but I'm here for you."

I lifted his chin and looked him right in the eye. "Yeah, I have known him for a long time. But you know what? I sat at my dad's dining table with you tonight, just blown away by how right it felt." I ran my thumb along his jaw. "It ain't ever felt that right before. So I just can't regret telling him.

And if he don't want what's right for me, then he's not the friend I thought he was."

"Am I what's right for you?"

I put my forehead to his. I knew what he was asking. And it was both the hardest thing and easiest thing I had to answer. "I think you might be, yeah."

He kissed me then, his hand on my cheek. Soft at first, quickly turning into something else. And as he deepened the kiss, he climbed on top of me, straddling me. My head pushed onto the back of the sofa, his tongue in my mouth, and him grinding on me.

Jesus.

And just when I was thinking it couldn't get any hotter, he peeled himself off me, kneeled on the floor between my legs, undid my pants, and gave me the best blow job of my life.

CHAPTER THIRTEEN

GUNTER

THE WALK down Main Street was magical. Christmas decorations adorned every shop window, the awnings, the street lights. White snow lined the sidewalks, Christmas music drifted out of every store, and people with their winter coats and gift bags smiled at every one they saw.

I really loved this town.

The door of Carl's Diner chimed above my head as I walked in, and Jayden and Hamish waved me over to their booth. I'd no sooner sat down than Christa had put a cup of coffee in front of me. Just how I liked it, without having to order.

"What else can I get you boys?" she asked.

"The spiced apple cake," Jayden said, holding up three fingers. "Three, please."

"Oh god, I'll have put on ten pounds in my first month here." I pulled my scarf and beanie off and held them up. "The only things in my wardrobe that will fit me soon are these."

"You look amazing," Hamish said. "And happy."

"Oh my god, yes," I said. "The plumber's been there. I

have a dishwasher and new outlets in the mudroom for my washer, and all the fittings in the bathroom, a new toilet, and running water."

"I'm not talking about the house," he said, leaning in. "I'm talking about that big hunk of a man you got yourself. You look *happy*, if you know what I mean."

I laughed and might have even swooned a little. "He's . . . he's kinda great."

"I want details. All of them," Hamish said.

"Even the dirty details?" Jayden asked.

He squinted at him. "Especially the dirty details. My god, Jay, how long have you known me?"

I laughed and sipped my coffee. "Well, things in that department have been steady. And amazing," I said. "It's all kind of new to him, so we're not rushing too much. But there's been—" I looked around to make sure no one could hear, and still spoke in a whisper. "Hand jobs and a BJ." I rubbed my jaw. "Though I think I'm going to have to learn how to unhinge my jaw like a snake because when I say that man is—"

Christa put our plates of cake on the table. "I do not want to know," she said with a shake of her head and a smile. "I do not want to know."

We waited until she'd gone before the three of us laughed.

Jayden gave me a nudge. "What else do you expect from a bear that's six foot four?"

Hamish ate a spoonful of cake. "Ooh, a bear. Does that make you Goldilocks?"

I snorted. "That depends if he can be both too big *and* just right." They both laughed.

I ate some of my cake and hummed. *Definitely going to put on ten pounds . . .*

"That Christmas Cupid got you good," Hamish said, shaking his head at me.

I couldn't even deny it because I was starting to think it was true.

I sipped my coffee. "On the downside? He told his best friend and didn't get the best response."

Jayden was clearly surprised to hear this. "He still hasn't said anything to him?"

I shook my head. "It's been a week. And I know they've been so busy they've hardly had a minute. I've only seen Clay twice since then. I had dinner with him and his dad a week ago, and he'd just told his friend that day. They've been friends a long time, like brothers, really. And I know it's been hectic at the lumberyard. Clay and his dad have barely stopped all week. He's only been to my house once 'cause he was passing by, and I've been to his place two nights ago and he was exhausted. Even then, he and Rusty still hadn't talked. He says he's okay, but I think he's pretty hurt. Which is understandable. And they work together so it's more complicated. It just sucks."

Jayden frowned and he put down his fork. "The poor guy. God, I hate that for him."

"His dad was okay though, right?" Hamish asked.

"Yeah. His dad is great. Thank god."

"But things between you are getting serious?" Hamish asked.

I shrugged but my smile gave me away. "I think so? Nothing official, but we talk or text every night, and he told me I was right for him. And it gives me butterflies to think about him." I rolled my eyes at myself. "Which is crazy."

"No it's not," they both said at the same time.

"I've been divorced for a hot minute," I said.

"You were married, yes, but you've been alone a long time," Jayden offered gently.

That was true.

"Fate brought you here," Hamish added. "The way fate brought us all here."

"I've only been here for three weeks!"

Hamish snorted. "I crashed my car in front of Ren's place three days before Christmas, and by Christmas Day, I knew he was the one." He held up three fingers. "Days, my friend."

Jayden laughed. "And I met Cass one week before Christmas." He shrugged. "He was technically my boss, and I'm pretty sure he was dicking me by day three."

Hamish nodded. "So technically, Gunter, you're behind schedule."

I laughed because, oh my god, these two cracked me up. But I didn't want to explain that while they were in their twenties, I was middle-aged, divorced, and starting over. I didn't have the excuse of youth and frivolity on my side.

But still, no more wasted days . . .

If this thing with me and Clay tanked eventually, then I'd enjoy it for what it was, for as long as it lasted. Regardless of what my heart wanted.

And my heart *was* already in this . . .

"Gunter?" Jayden nudged me.

"Yes, yes," I replied. "Sorry, I was a million miles away."

"I was just talking about the new coat and matching doggie boots I'm getting Chutney for Christmas," Hamish said. "Honey, are you okay?"

"Yeah, I'm fine, honestly." Then it occurred to me that they were talking about Christmas gifts. "Oh, holy shit." I stared at them. How could I have not thought of this before?

I'd been so busy with the house, I hadn't even considered it . . .

"What the hell am I going to get Clay for Christmas?"

They both stared at me. "You haven't got him anything yet?" Hamish asked.

"No! I haven't even thought about Christmas. I mean, I have. I love the main street and all the decorations: it's really magical. The bed and breakfast is something straight out of a magazine. But my house is a construction zone. All my furniture is in storage. I haven't thought about Christmas for me." I put my hand to my chest. Then I sighed. "Ah, jeez. That reminds me, I have to send my brother a gift."

Jayden patted my arm. "What does he like?"

"My brother?"

"No." Jayden shook his head. "Your dreamy lumberjack bear of a man."

Oh.

"Well, I'd say he likes working with timber but he owns a whole lumberyard, so he has that covered." I sighed because I didn't really know. "He has a bookcase full of his mom's old poetry, which he loves."

"Oh my god, he's a Hallmark Christmas movie character," Hamish said. "A big sexy lumberjack who loves poetry finds real love for the first time." He fake-swooned.

I laughed. "He could be." But was it sad that I didn't know what he liked? What he needed? "He was obsessed with David Bowie when he was younger. And the woman from *The Terminator*, and Annie Lennox, and half-naked hockey players."

They both stared again. "And angsty poetry? Honestly, no one picked up that he was bi?" Hamish asked. "That's like a bisexual starter pack."

Jayden laughed. "Oh shush. No stereotypes allowed."

I smiled into my coffee. "His dad guessed as much."

"Well," Jayden said. "Sounds like you have yourself a mission."

"And what's that?"

Jayden nudged me. "Operation twenty questions. Maybe instead of unhinging your jaw like a python, you could engage in conversation."

I nudged him right back. "Oh, fuck off."

They both laughed, and Hamish tapped his half-eaten cake with his fork. "Jay, did you make this? It's really good."

CLAY'S big truck rumbled down to the house and he jogged up the steps. "Knock knock."

"Come in," I said, getting to the door just as he came through it, holding a paint brush in my hand.

"Hey." He smiled as soon as he saw me. "Got your text message. Everything okay?"

"Yes, of course."

"Just that you said you really wanted to see me when I finished work. I know I've been busy; the days leading up to Christmas is always the busiest. I haven't been avoiding you, I promise." He took my free hand. "I'm sorry."

"No, I just meant that I really wanted to see you," I said, leaning up and waiting for him to kiss me. He did. "I didn't mean to make you worry."

"I thought you were mad."

Smiling, I tugged on his beard and kissed him again. "If I was mad, you'd know. I just missed you, that's all."

His eyes widened, along with his smile. "You did?"

"Come through here," I said, taking his hand and dragging him into the dining area where the paint tray was on the floor. "Let me put this down," I said, laying the paint-brush on the edge of the tray. "So I can do this."

I put both my arms around his neck and gave him a true kiss. He wrapped his arms around me, kissing me just as eagerly. His huge hands palmed my back and slid down to my ass.

Of course I groaned, and it made him smile.

"It'd be so dang easy to get carried away right now," he murmured, his voice low and gravelly.

"I still don't have any furniture," I said. I eyed the brand-new, still-covered kitchen countertops. "Well . . ."

He pulled my chin around so I looked at him instead. "We're not doing that."

I laughed, and I might have pouted a bit. "Do you have to go back to work? Are you working late?"

"I'll have a bit to do. Mostly catch-up stuff, get ready for the morning. But no jobs."

"Then I'll bring you dinner. And your dad. How does some stroganoff sound? It was a daily special at the diner today. I'll pick it up on the way."

"You'd do that?"

"Of course I would. Then we cuddle on your couch, and talk, and kiss and maybe indulge in an orgasm or two."

He chuckled. "Never saying no to that." He kissed me again, then hugged me so hard, he lifted my feet off the floor. "I've missed you too."

Then he set me down and looked around. "What are you painting? The other day on the phone, I thought you said this was done."

"I'm just touching up the trim. Oh, come and have a look at my bathroom!"

Taking his hand again, I dragged him down the hall and stopped. "You can't go in. The floor's still drying. But look!"

All the new fixtures were in. The faucets, the towel bars, the cabinet and mirror. It looked brand spanking new. "I did the floor in a charcoal gray. I wasn't sure about painting it, but you can literally get a paint for any surface now." I was one hundred percent sure he knew that already, but he smiled at me like he was hearing it for the first time. "And I watched about fifty YouTube tutorials on how to do it. I even had to fix some grout."

Clay put his arm around my shoulder. "It looks amazing."

"And look! The brown monstrosity toilet is gone forever. Behold brand-new sparkling white porcelain."

He laughed and kissed the side of my head. "You should be proud. You've done a lot of work all by yourself."

"Well, I had professionals for the main things. And Ren at the hardware store knew every product I'd need. I mostly just painted."

"And sanded, and stripped, and cleaned, and primed, and painted," he corrected. "Be proud, Gunter."

I smiled up at him, warmth flooding my whole chest and belly. "I am proud."

He pulled my chin between his thumb and forefinger. "I'm proud of you too."

I threw my arms around him, not realizing just how hard those words would hit me.

No one had said those words to me in so long.

He held me like he knew.

I ARRIVED at Clay's with a bag full of take-out containers, among other goodies, and he met me on his little front porch.

"Hey, you," I said. "I bought enough for the three of us. Are we eating at your place or your dad's tonight?"

He stared at me for a long second, then skipped down the steps and walked over to his dad's. "You know what?" he said as he knocked on his door. "I have a much better idea."

Cliff opened the door. "Since when did you knock?"

"Dad, Gunter bought you dinner like I said. But I've barely seen him all week, so I'm sure you understand." He reached into the bag and pulled out one container. "One stroganoff for you."

"There's garlic bread—" I began to say.

Clay reached in, took out a white paper bag, and thrust it at his dad. "Don't mean to be rude, Dad, but he's all mine tonight."

Then Clay led me by the arm to his place, took the whole bag out of my arms, and slid it on the table before taking hold of my face and kissing me. He walked me backward until my ass hit the back of the sofa and he pushed me against it, his tongue in my mouth, his erection pressed between us.

Jesus. The desire, the urgency.

So hot.

"All I could think about," he mumbled, pulling my coat off. "Your body, and mine." He crashed his mouth back to mine while fumbling with my belt. "Need. This. Off."

From zero to scorching hot in two seconds. It took my brain a second to catch up with my body.

I pulled at the buttons on his shirt while I kissed his neck and he popped the button on my jeans. "I wanna taste you," he murmured.

I groaned.

There was a knock on his door. "Clay? Sorry to interrupt."

Clay froze, then he sighed, his breathing ragged. "Dad. Is there an emergency?"

"I didn't get the garlic bread."

Clay closed his eyes and sighed. "Sure that's not an emergency."

Oh no . . .

"I got a bag of condoms and personal lubricant. The lube is kinda cylindrical. I can see why you thought it was garlic bread, but the bread won't help you in the bedroom, son."

I gasped back a breath, covered my face with both hands, and laughed and laughed and laughed . . .

I heard the rustle of the take-out bag and dared to look. Clay was peeking into a white paper bag. "This one is the garlic bread," he mumbled and opened the door.

His shirt was undone, his hair was a mess. Cliff took one look at him. "Jesus, Clay. Where are your manners? Let the man eat his dinner first."

I was trying to, Cliff.

I tried to hide the fact my jeans were undone and manage a wave at the same time. "I'm fine, Cliff."

They exchanged white paper bags.

"Enjoy your dinner!" I called out as Clay went to shut the door.

"I'd say the same to you, but I think that's a given."

"Night, Dad." Clay closed the door and locked it, letting his forehead fall against the wood.

I burst out laughing again. "Oh my god. I went via the drugstore and popped that bag on top of the takeout so I could carry it all. You pulled me in here so quick and began ravaging me, I didn't have time to stop and think."

Clay slowly turned to look at me. The urgency was gone, but the desire was still there. "Ravaging?"

"Mauling. Consuming. Devouring."

He stalked over to me. "Devouring? I don't think—"

I put my fingers to his lips. "Pretty sure you said you wanted to taste me."

"I don't remember that."

I gently pulled on his beard to bring his lips to mine. "Get on your knees."

His eyes went wide, pupils blown. "I can do one better," he said. Then, before I knew what was happening, he threw me over his shoulder, took me into his room, and tossed me onto the bed.

I laughed . . . until he pulled me down the bed by my ankle, spread my legs wide, pressed his erection against me, and kissed me so hard my eyes rolled back in my head.

He devoured my mouth, and when I needed air, he kissed my neck, grating his teeth on my skin, sucking, biting, tasting.

He pulled off my shirt and sucked each nipple, his fingers digging into my sides. He trailed his tongue over my sternum, then went lower and lower until he nuzzled my happy trail.

Holy shit.

I fisted his hair and he smiled up at me, eyes dark, lips wet.

He'd jerked me off before, and I'd given him head, but he hadn't tried it yet . . . I wondered how far he'd go. What he was ready for. I wasn't about to push him. I wanted him to want this.

My jeans were open as far as they could go, and I was trying not to writhe, desperate for touch. His fingers dipped under my briefs and he pulled the front down, freeing my cock.

He studied me, wrapped his hand around me, and gave

me a long slow slide of his fist. Then he licked me, testing himself and tasting me.

He did it again, and again, flattening his tongue and tasting the tip.

"Holy fuck, Clay," I breathed, gripping the comforter instead of his hair.

He took me into his mouth. Hot, wet, slick, and sliding, he pumped me and sucked me. He consumed me as if he were a starving man.

It had been so long since anyone had done this to me.

So good. So, so good.

I could just imagine him flipping me over and burying that huge cock in me to the hilt, every inch of him filling me with every drop.

"Fuck. Clay, I'm gonna come."

He pulled off and continued to pump me, his lips wet and swollen. My back arched, and I held onto the covers as my orgasm hit me like a freight train.

I came in spurts across my stomach and he hummed. "Fuck yes."

I was too lost in my own pleasure to realize he was now kneeling between my legs, his monster cock in his huge hand. Pumping himself, stroking and sliding his hand over his cockhead.

"Bring it up here," I urged.

He looked uncertain, so I licked my lips. "Feed it to me."

Then he was straddling my chest, his cock near my mouth. I ran my hands up his thighs to his hips and brought him closer. I took him into my mouth and rocked his hips back and forth until he took over.

I tongued his slit, his frenulum, and sucked and sucked

until he grew impossibly hard, swollen, and the sounds he made—

"Gonna come," he gasped.

So, holding his hips, I pulled him deeper and took his load into my throat.

He shook, trembled, and groaned as I swallowed what he gave me.

When he collapsed beside me, his chest heaving, he stared at the ceiling for a long while. I think he was stunned.

I chuckled. "You okay?"

He turned to face me. "Sweet mercy."

I liked that I could render this huge man to a trembling mess. "You were on edge when I got here."

He snorted. "You mentioned orgasms when I saw you this afternoon. I haven't been able to think of anything else."

That made me laugh and I almost put my hand in my jizz. "Well, I'm gonna need a towel or tissue."

"Oh shoot. Sorry." He got off the bed, his heavy dick swinging out of his jeans before he tucked himself away.

Fucking hell.

I ached with the need to feel that inside me.

"See something you like?" he asked with a smile.

I groaned, forcing my gaze up to his eyes. "Yes. God yes." I was just about to offer to roll over, offer my ass and his first lesson in anal sex, but then I remembered my mission. "But first a wet washcloth. Then dinner and conversation. Then maybe more orgasms."

He nodded. "Definitely more orgasms."

CHAPTER FOURTEEN

CLAY

HAVING dinner and conversation with Gunter was as easy as breathing. We talked about movies, TV shows, and books. We talked about music. We traded a whole bunch of "what's your favorite" questions, and it was fun to learn things about each other.

I learned he liked peanut butter sandwiches, lemon meringue pie, the color red, panda bears, Billy Joel, the smell of rain.

Silly, trivial things that I wish I'd thought of asking long before now.

As the night wore on, I made us some hot cocoa and we sat on the couch. He asked me about logging sustainability, and it wasn't just to be polite. He was interested, and if he didn't understand something, he asked more questions. He talked of environmental significance and importance, and I swear something warm and pleasant settled inside me.

Gunter understood me.

We clicked in ways I wasn't expecting at all.

It wasn't just a physical thing. It wasn't just my body that reacted to him. My mind and my heart did too.

Things got quiet between us, just staring at each other, like he could read my mind.

I had my arm along the back of the sofa and I traced my thumb along his cheek. "I'm so glad you're here," I whispered. "And I think back to when I was a fool who tried to ignore what I was feeling."

He smiled, and taking my hand, he kissed my palm. "Clay, I'd really like to stay tonight. You can say no, and I'll understand. No hard feelings. And I don't expect sex. That's not why I'm asking. I just want to fall asleep in your arms. I want to kiss you until we both fall asleep. I want to be naked with you—"

I leaned over and kissed him. "Yes."

I dumped everything in the sink while he sent off a quick text to Jayden to say he wouldn't be back at the bed and breakfast tonight. I stoked up the fire, turned off all the lights and took Gunter to my room.

We undressed each other, one slow button at a time, a kiss to newly revealed skin, sure hands and light fingers. And when we climbed into bed, every touch, every kiss was gentle and slow.

And being in bed fully naked with a man didn't feel weird at all. It felt just as right as being with a woman. Maybe even more so, because I had feelings for him.

We'd been on our sides, facing each other, kissing and stroking, unhurried and sensual. But then he pulled me on top of him, widened his legs, and wrapped his arms around me.

I could so easily be inside him like this. I could push in, my cock was hard and ready, right there near his hole, and he was rocking us, and . . .

The condoms and lube were in the next room.

I stopped and pulled back, resting on my hand, trying to get my body and mind together.

"What's wrong?" Gunter asked. His eyes were so uncertain, so concerned. "We can stop if you want."

I laughed. "Just the opposite. I don't want to stop. I want to . . ."

He bit his bottom lip, and I felt his cock twitch. "Oh."

"But it's late and this is perfect and I don't know what I want more." I put my forehead to his. "I want to do it all."

He put his hand to my cheek, his eyes searched mine. "I want that too. So bad. But it is late and there are certain preparations I'd need to take care of first."

Oh god.

"Oh."

"Next time. I'll be ready and you can bury yourself inside me all night long. And we won't be rushed or out of time." He rolled his hips. "But right now, why don't you take both of us in your hand and make us come?"

I leaned down and kissed him. "I can do that."

And he was right. Right about not being rushed, right about it being late. He was right about wanting to fall asleep wrapped around each other, because I never, ever slept so well.

"HAVE A GOOD DAY," Gunter said, leaning up on his toes and kissing me. His eyes were serene. Probably had something to do with the shower we'd had together this morning.

I put half a piece of peanut butter toast in his mouth. "You too."

He laughed as he chewed it, and as he got to the door,

he put his hand to my chest. "I hope things with Rusty improve. I'm sorry he reacted the way he did."

I covered his hand with mine. "His silence is pretty telling. I was thinking of telling the other guys that work here, but now I dunno if I will. I mean, it ain't their business. I just want to be honest with them. I've never lied to 'em before."

"You're not lying to them," he said gently. "You don't need to tell them anything. Do they tell you who they sleep with?"

"Well, no, but most of them are married." I shrugged because I understood his point. "I just think I need to do this. I don't want them hearing it from anybody else."

Gunter smiled. "Okay, then I'll support you no matter what."

Just like that.

So easy.

He drove me up to the gate, which I unlocked for him, and I walked back down to the office, knowing I'd find Dad in there.

He held out a steaming cup of coffee for me and smirked behind his own. "Morning."

I sipped my coffee, waiting for him to mention last night. "Morning."

"Logging truck'll be here this morning," he said. "Just as well. Snow storm expected later today."

"Yep." Gunter was expecting his flooring installation today and I didn't like his chances. "Gives us a chance to get some yard work done until the truck gets here."

"So . . ."

Oh boy. Here it comes.

"Stroganoff was good," he said. "Garlic bread was a bit rubbery though."

I almost inhaled an entire cup of coffee and choked on it, but all he could do was laugh. I was still coughing when the first worker pulled in.

Of course it was Rusty.

Dad watched me for a second. "Want me to talk to him?"

I shook my head. "Nah. I will."

He came into the breakroom, pulling his beanie off, and he stopped when he saw me. Dad had vanished like a freaking magician, which meant it was probably now or never.

"Hey," I said.

He gave a nod. "Hey."

"Haven't really had much of a chance to talk this week, have we?"

He licked his lips like his mouth was dry. "Look, Clay, I don't really have much to say about it."

"Well, I do."

His eyes cut to mine. "I'm sorry, but I . . ."

"Wanna know what I'm sorry for?" I put my cup in the sink. "I'm sorry for being honest with you. I'm sorry for the way you reacted and I'm sorry for thinking of you like a brother. But I ain't sorry for who I am. Rusty, this silence bullshit gotta end. I won't be walking around here on eggshells. That's not who we are. So you either deal with it and get over it and we get back to work." I stared at him. "Or you can go."

Okay, so I hadn't intended to basically give him an ultimatum like that, and from the look on his face, neither had he, but fuck it.

"I don't wanna see you go, Rus," I added, softer this time. "I've always thought of you as a brother, and you're by far the best worker here. But I will bust my ass twenty hours a day to do your job on top o'mine rather than have anyone here treating me like shit just because of who I fell in love with." I got to the door. "I got work to do. Have your coffee, and if you wanna join me, great. If you'd rather not, take your cup with you when you go. S'up to you."

I walked out and got stuck straight into splitting logs. The firewood processor made the whole job easier, but it was in the last shed, it was loud, and when I had head-phones on, people usually left me alone—and I had to be using my brain, which left no time for overthinking.

But it wasn't cutting the logs and holding pressure like it should and they were getting caught up, so I changed the chain out, and once I got it back up and running, it still wasn't much better. I was only on my second log when I noticed a leak under the engine block.

Goddammit.

I shut it all down and took a closer look. Sure enough, hydraulic fluid was dripping out of one of the hose seals.

I wanted to kick the shit out of it but knew I'd come out worse for wear. "God fucking dammit!"

"What's the problem with it?"

I turned to find Rusty standing at the door. He was kinda smiling, kinda sheepish. But still here. And he didn't look about ready to quit.

Couldn't begin to admit how happy it made me to see his stupid face.

"We got a leak."

He grumbled and came back with a wrench and slid underneath the splitting tray. "Grab me an empty drum. Clean one if you've got it."

We emptied out the hydraulic fluid, catching nearly all of it, and once the lines were clear, Rusty unscrewed the hose clamp, pulled out the connection joint and found the culprit. "Busted O-ring."

"Thank god that's all it is. I'll go get a new one."

"Get three. I'll do 'em all while we got her stopped."

And so that's what we did. Me and Rusty working side by side, like we had for twenty-something years. We didn't talk much, we never did. But we worked together like a left and right hand.

We always had.

Once we had the machine going again, I fed the splitter and Rusty sorted and stacked, and we got way more done than I ever could on my own.

It reminded me of what I'd said to him earlier.

But dang, if guilt wasn't standing right there with me. Knowing the logging truck'd be rolling in soon, I shut the machine down again and picked up a shovel and cleared away the debris into the sawdust bin while Rusty finished up the stacks.

Then it was quiet again.

"Rus, I'm sorry about what I said before," I began.

He put his hand up. "It's okay. I probably deserved it." He let out a sigh. "I'll be honest with ya, Clay. I was shocked when you told me. I thought you were jokin'. I was like, no way. I've known you since you were a kid, and you dated women, and . . . and I thought you were pulling my leg." He sighed. "But you weren't."

"Nope."

"And I didn't know what to say. All week. I just didn't know what to think. And I'll be lying if I said it didn't sting . . . why you didn't tell me sooner? And seein' your dad and him laughing together, I had to wonder just how long you hadn't told me for. Then I realized after my reaction, it was no wonder."

"I didn't tell you because I didn't know." I winced. "No, that's not true. I've always known. I just did nothing about it. I liked girls just fine, and the women I dated were all super nice, and we had a good time. The part of me that liked guys, well, I just pushed it to the side, for twenty-something years. I ignored it. There was no need to go disrupting my entire life, risk losing people I cared about, because the chances of me finding any guy here in Hartbridge were slim to none. So I just ignored that part of me. Pretended it doesn't exist."

"Until you did find one."

I shook my head. "God, I tried to deny it. I tried to push it away again. But he's . . . he's worth the risk."

Rusty nodded and toed the sawdust with his boot. "You're really serious about him. I can see that now. And if you really are serious and it's what you want, then it's okay by me. Hell, you said before that you fell in love with him."

"No I didn't."

"Yeah you did. You said you didn't want anyone here treatin' you like shit just because of who you fell in love with."

Oh.

He laughed and nudged me. "Ah, Jesus. Look at your face. You do love him."

I let out a slow breath and gave a nod. "I think I could, yeah. He ain't like anyone I've ever met."

"I shoulda known, you know," he said with a sigh. "When we were delivering the trees down Main Street and you ran into him by the diner . . . the look on your face. I just thought it was funny. I wondered what that was about. Guess I ain't ever seen your stupid face in love before."

I must've turned five shades of red. "That was the day I knew I had to stop fighting it. We'd met up a few times and it was all going far too well, and I panicked. Told him I couldn't do it. I was more worried about what other people might think." I shook my head. "And then I saw him in the street that day, and I just knew. I don't give one fuck what the gossipers in this town think. I care what he thinks."

"Your dad was okay with it?"

"Yep. Pretty sure he likes Gunter more than he likes me."

Rusty snorted just as Neil yelled out that the truck was here. "Work time," I said, giving him a smile. "Thank you. For being okay with it, and for not quitting."

He clucked his tongue. "That was when I knew you were serious. Well, that and you sayin' you loved him. It was a bit of a wake-up call. And for what it's worth, you're like a brother to me too." Then he shoved me. "An annoying little brother."

I shoved him back. "Shut up."

"Do you really think you could do my job?"

I laughed as we walked out. "Fuck no. Regretted saying that as soon as I said it."

LATE FALL and winter were always the best time to log the timber and mill the lumber. It certainly was our busiest time of the year. The fact that it was freezing cold and snowing hard didn't mean much to us.

Logging truck deliveries meant all hands on deck, grading, measuring, and sorting the logs into inventory, then stacking them into their rightful groups by species and quality. Guys on the ground, guys on the tractors, with their coat hoods pulled up against the snow, beanies pulled low.

No one complained. No one ever did. We just did what was needed.

So once the delivery was done and we'd got it all squared away, we put all the machinery to bed and came into the breakroom to find Dad had put on a huge pot of tomato soup.

And looking around at the men who'd worked for us for most of my life, at their smiles and red noses, and as they warmed their hands on their mugs, I was tempted to tell them.

So tempted.

But what Gunter had said was true. Had I ever discussed their sex lives with them?

Absolutely not.

Not even their dating or married lives. Sure, I knew if they were married or single, but not the intimate details. It wasn't any of my business.

Like mine was none of theirs.

Rusty was different, of course.

And if the time ever came where it was necessary to tell them, then I would. But not until then. Not now.

When soup time was over, everyone went back to their post in the mill like there wasn't a dang near blizzard outside: Eddie on the headsaw, Neil on the planer, Derek on the edger, Juan on the resaw, Darrell and Bobby sorted and graded, Wade did the banding and stacking. Rusty kept an eye on every chain, every cog, every conveyor belt, every blade, never standing still for a minute.

I was fooling myself to think I could do his job and mine. And at the end of the day, I was just grateful I still had him as an employee, but more than that, as a friend.

Of course he was the last to leave at quitting time.

"Thanks, Rus," I said. "For sticking by me, and for not leaving when I had my head up my ass this morning."

He laughed. "So, suppose I should meet this guy. Officially, I mean."

I grinned at him. "Suppose you should. Dunno when though. He's busy getting his house finished, and I was supposed to plan some kinda date. What the hell do I know about that stuff? I haven't got a clue."

"For a guy?" He thought about it for a second and counted on his fingers. "Buffalo wings and beer. Can't go wrong."

"Sounds good to me, but it ain't too romantic."

He held up a third finger. "And sex. That's the three main food groups right there."

I rolled my eyes. "I want him to know that I put actual thought into it."

He sighed. "Wanna know what I did for Trina before we got married? She said it was the most romantic date ever."

"Does it involve your three food groups? Because I'm not sure . . ."

He laughed at that. "Shut up, dumbass. Want me to tell ya or not?"

CHAPTER FIFTEEN

GUNTER

CLAY WAS MAKING good on his promise of a date, and I was excited. He told me to wear layers, and to bring a coat and gloves. Whatever he had planned sounded very outdoors, which was not typically my thing, but he said it should be fun and I trusted him.

And it was a beautiful day for it. The sun was shining, but after the snowstorm on Friday, it seemed the whole country was covered by a thick blanket of snow.

And if Hartbridge was pretty before, it really was magical now.

Clay picked me up from the bed and breakfast, we picked up fresh coffee and pastries from the diner, and I asked Clay to go past my house before we set off for whatever he had planned.

"I want to show you my new flooring," I said. "We can't walk on it yet because of the glue. They wanted two days with their special heaters."

"Because of how cold it's been?"

I nodded. "Apparently. But it's fine. The movers aren't coming until next week anyway, so it's not like it puts me behind. I'm just glad they could get it down. And it looks really good."

He smiled at me. "I love how you get when you talk about your house. Your eyes light up, and if you have a setback, you just roll with it."

"I'm not the epic meltdown type. Well, I'm sure if a herd of moose went through my house and trashed every single thing, then an epic meltdown would probably ensue. But until then."

Clay laughed. "Just as well we don't get too many moose in these parts."

"Just as well."

We got to the house and peered in through the front window into the living room. The gray planks looked amazing against the kitchen cabinets.

"Oh wow, Gunter," Clay said. "It looks amazing. And you got the walls painted in the living room too?"

"While you were busy all week, so was I." I went down to my bedroom window. "Look in here. You can see the floor into the hall."

He rubbed his glove along the cracked paint on the window sill. "So . . . when are you gonna do the outside?"

I whacked his arm. "Oh shush. I am but one man."

He laughed. And slinging his arm around my shoulder, he pulled me into his side so we could look in the window together. "It looks amazing. And those heaters are okay in there unsupervised?"

"Sure. They just need to maintain an even temperature that isn't below fifty-five." I gestured to the snow on the ground, literally everywhere. "Old houses get cold when they're empty. Especially with no window coverings, and especially when it's absolutely freezing outside."

"Speaking of which," he said with a kiss to the side of my head. "Are you ready to go?"

We walked back to his truck. "Should I be worried about where you're taking me?"

"I hope not. It's supposed to be fun," he said, opening my door for me and holding it. "And romantic."

"Oh, thank you, kind sir," I said, climbing in. "Fun and romantic are two of my favorite things."

Except I was starting to question his idea of either of those things when we drove out on some road along the mountain and he pulled into what looked like a small parking lot, although it was hard to tell because of the snow. There was also a trail sign. At least I think it was. Again, it was hard to tell because of the build up of snow.

"Ah, Clay?"

He laughed. "You ready?"

"For what, exactly."

"This is part of the national park. There are walking trails that go up into the mountain. The view is incredible."

Walking trails.

The view.

"And I'm sure they're lovely," I said. "In spring, summer, or fall. But unless you packed snow shoes." My eyes widened. "Oh my god, did you pack snow shoes?"

He laughed again. "Not exactly. Do you trust me?"

"Yes. Well, I did until the mention of walking trails in winter and snow shoes."

He grinned at me. "God, you're so cute. Come on. Let's go."

He got out, and with a roll of my eyes and a leap of faith, I did the same. "I'm only getting out of the truck because you said I was cute."

He grabbed a duffel bag from the back, slung it over his shoulder. "This way."

I could see now that "this way" was a path that had been somewhat shoveled. Not particularly well, but good enough for us to trudge along in single file.

"Oh my god, who cleared this?" I asked about thirty yards in.

"I did."

"You what?"

"I did. Yesterday and this morning."

"You what?"

He laughed. "Well, not just me. Rusty helped."

"I'm glad you and he worked everything out, but conspiring like serial killers to make me hike up a snowy mountainside before you kill me is just mean."

He stopped and turned around, half amused, half horrified. "Kill you?"

I ignored the way I was panting, out of breath, and he was not. "And if you think I'm spending my last moments alive digging my own grave, I have news for you."

"What are you talking about?"

"I'm trying to think of any other reason why you would want me to hike into the snow in this remote part of the mountains."

He laughed so loud it startled the birds from the trees farther up. "You're so stinking cute. Keep walking and I'll show you."

He could walk faster than me, given his legs were twice as long as mine, but he climbed up a bit of a rise and waited for me to join him.

"This is why. Ain't it beautiful?"

Oh my word.

It was a small lake. A pond, really. There were snow-covered park benches on the other side, the tree line beyond it, and the rise of the mountain was a magnificent sight. And clearly the pond would be a lovely picnic spot in warmer weather.

Now it was frozen solid and shoveled clear. Perfect for ice skating . . .

"I brought some skates and some other stuff . . . uh, Gunter?" I'd obviously been silent for too long. "What do you think?"

"It looks like a dream," I whispered. I had to drag my eyes away from every perfect snow-covered detail to look at Clay. "And you did this?"

"Well, nature did most of it. Rusty and me just shoveled it."

"You did that?" I swallowed down the lump in my throat. "For me?"

He nodded. "Full disclosure, and I'll be perfectly honest with you. This was Rusty's idea. I told him I needed to think of an idea for a date. Because I'd never planned a date with a guy before. And at first he said Buffalo wings, beer, and sex is all most men ever want."

I laughed.

"But I said it needed to be more romantic than that."

"I love wings, beer, and sex."

"You mean we did all this for nothing?"

"Oh no, we're going to do this too."

He grinned. "Anyway, he said he did this for Trina back when they were dating. They've been married sixteen years, so clearly it worked. I woulda liked to set up some of those pretty fairy lights but there's no point in the middle of the day. And it'd be a bit dangerous to cut along the path at night."

"Clay, it's absolutely perfect." I squeezed his gloved hand. "This is the best date ever."

He dumped the bag and pulled out one of those water-proof blankets and set the skates down. "One more thing," he said, holding up a pack of juice boxes. "Couldn't forget these."

I kissed his cheek. "Now it's the best date ever."

We sat on the blanket and put the skates on. Clay had borrowed the pair for me from Rusty. Which was sweet, and I was so happy that he and Clay had talked it out. Clay was certainly happier too.

Pretty sure he knew not everyone in his life would be so accepting that he was dating a guy, but with his dad and now Rusty in his corner, he'd be okay.

"My turn for full disclosure," I said, trying to stand up. "I haven't skated in a long time."

He took my hands and pulled me to my feet, and we drifted slowly out to the middle of the "rink."

"The surface is a bit uneven, so be careful," he said, watching me intently. "You good?"

His smile was so contagious. "I think so."

Clay let go of my hands, and while I wobbled a little, he skated like a pro. Actually, he skated like a hockey player. "Did you play hockey?"

"A bit," he replied as he did a lap. He came to a stop in front of me, grinning now, and took my hand. We did a lap hand in hand, much slower of course, but it was so much fun, and Rusty's wife was absolutely correct.

It was so romantic.

After another lap and when I was steadier on my feet, he dropped my hand and stole a kiss before he zoomed off. I was getting braver with my strides and, of course, mistook this short-lived confidence for actual ability and ended up on my ass.

He laughed and came over, helping me back on my feet. And holding both my hands, he skated backward, facing me. He leaned in and kissed me, and I fell on my ass again.

He pulled me up again, more concerned than humored now. "Oh my god, are you okay?"

I nodded. "Yep." My body was going to hate me tomorrow, and I was certain I had Advil in my future, but this was so much fun.

We did another lap together holding hands, and then another, and I was getting better. It was kinda like riding a bike. It wasn't a skill you forgot, but I was never a strong skater and I certainly wasn't the athletic type. Not to mention I hadn't put a pair of skates on in almost thirty years.

But the sun was shining, it was a beautiful day. Sure, it was freezing cold and my pants now had a wet ass, but all that aside, spending this day with Clay, knowing he'd put such effort in to impress me, well, it was all kinds of wonderful.

I managed a few laps on my own, and we laughed and caught each other, and of course I fell on my ass again with an oof. "Ow!"

He rushed over to help me, pulling me to my feet. Then we heard a man's voice call out.

"Clay?"

We turned just as a man climbed up over the embankment. It was an officer.

Oh my god. "Are we in trouble?" I asked.

"Oh no," the officer said. "Saw Clay's truck and the pathway in the snow up to here. Was coming to see if everything was all right and heard someone yelp and wondered if you were in trouble."

"Deputy Price, we're all good," Clay said. "Gunter here just fell over. That's all."

Clay was still holding my hands and he only seemed to realize that very second. He dropped them, taking my elbow instead. "You okay?"

It was a quick reminder that Clay wasn't used to this.

I waved him off and gingerly headed toward the blanket and, unfortunately, the deputy. "My skating ability is probably a criminal offense," I said. "And if you do arrest me, in lieu of my one phone call, I'd like to request a hot bath and some Advil."

Clay laughed behind me and the deputy even smiled. I slowly lowered myself onto the blanket, trying not to groan. *My poor ass.*

"Anyway," Deputy Price said. I noticed him holding eye contact with Clay for a long beat before tipping his deputy hat. "I'll be on my way. You two gentlemen have a good day. See you at the Christmas lights festival."

We watched him leave, and Clay, now standing by the blanket, could see over the embankment. I heard the faint engine of the cruiser and Clay frowned. "That was weird."

Hmm.

Or not.

"Have you known him long?" I asked.

Clay shrugged. "Think he's been in town for a few years or so. Not too sure. He's from Billings. That's all I know."

"I think he might like you?" I offered.

Clay whipped his head around. "What? That's ridiculous."

I sighed and gestured to all six-foot-four inches of him. "What's not to like?"

"He's not . . . he's never . . ."

"And before I got here, neither had you."

Clay blinked his surprise away. "I guess." He plonked himself beside me. "Are you okay? You hit the ice pretty hard that last time."

"I think it was one too many falls for my forty-four-year-old body."

He chuckled and nudged me. "It's a fine body."

I opened the pack of juice boxes and handed him one. I popped my own and sipped it. It was stupidly good. "Are you okay?" I nodded to where our friendly county deputy sheriff had disappeared. "It's very likely he's assumed that you're . . . in my company. You're alone here with me, the new gay guy in town, and you were holding my hands, helping me skate. And he's a cop; he has deductive reasoning skills."

Clay sipped his juice box, squinting out over the pond, through the trees. "Yeah, I'm okay with it," he said quietly. "And if we're doing the official thing, then people are gonna know."

The official thing.

His eyes met mine. "Are we, Gunter?" he asked, nervous, a little scared. "Official?"

Oh wow.

"As in boyfriends?"

"Well, yeah. I guess. I dunno what to call it. Dating? It's been a coupla weeks and I don't wanna see anyone else. Do you?"

"No, god no. I don't want to see anyone else." I couldn't imagine dating anyone else, possibly ever. Clay was everything I didn't know I needed. I grinned at him, nudging my shoulder into his. "Really? Boyfriends?"

He shrugged. "If you want. It's okay if you don't think

so. I just don't want to go telling the whole world that we're a thing if you don't think we're up to that."

"I'm okay with that." I sighed happily. "I mean, we're kind of doing the boyfriend thing anyway, aren't we? Dinner dates, sleepovers. Giving your dad the bag of condoms instead of garlic bread. The usual."

He chuckled. "Don't remind me."

"So do boyfriends take off each other's skates and help them stand up? Because I don't know if I can bend my legs."

He laughed then sprang up with more agility than his size should have allowed. He kneeled on the blanket at my feet and undid my skates and helped me into my boots.

It was sweet.

Boyfriends . . . wow.

Clay packed up the bag and helped me to my feet, wrapping the blanket around me instead of folding it up. "Your pants are wet," he noted. "We better get you warm and dry before you freeze to death."

The walk back to the truck wasn't so bad, but oh boy, climbing into the truck . . . my ass and thighs. "You know, for all the physical work I've done on my house these last few weeks, I expected more resilience to exercise out of my body."

Clay got in behind the wheel and cranked the heat up. He frowned at me. "Are you honestly okay?"

"I'm fine. Nothing a change of clothes won't fix."

And maybe a hot shower and definitely those Advil . . .

So he drove me to the bed and breakfast, and by then my muscles had seized up and I all but fell onto Clay as he helped me out. He caught me easily, letting me slide down his body.

"Oh," I murmured. "I should let you catch me more often."

He laughed. "I feel bad."

"Don't be silly. It was the most perfect date, and if I could go back to this morning, I'd do it all over again."

He gave me a shy smile and warm eyes. "Me too."

I looked over at the house. "I think both Jayden and Cass are here. If you don't want to—"

"I want to," he said. "They're your friends, and if anyone in this town is gonna be cool about us being together, I'd hope it's them."

"Of course they are." I started to walk to the back patio. "I need to get out of these wet clothes or I will freeze to death."

I only got to the first step when Jayden came out the back door. "What on earth happened?"

I groaned with each step up. "I broke my ass."

Jayden's concern became a grin. "Oooh, was it worth it?"

I snorted. "Get your mind out of the gutter. It's from ice skating."

"Well, that's nowhere near as much fun," he said, holding the door for me. He winked at Clay. "Can I get you guys anything? A late lunch, hot coffee?"

"Maybe later, thanks," I replied as we took our boots off. I tried not to groan. "I need a hot shower."

"Well," Jayden said. "I'm sure Clay can help you with that."

I turned to see poor Clay's cheeks a bright pink. "Happy to oblige," he mumbled.

Jayden was so happy he looked about ready to burst. "It's good to see you here, Clay," he said kindly, tapping his hand on Clay's arm. He obviously felt the muscle. "Oh my."

"Hands off, Jay," I said with a laugh.

Cass appeared in the mudroom with a basket of laundry. "Is he accosting the guests again?" He gave a nod to Clay. "Nice to see you."

"Likewise."

"Will you both be staying for dinner?" Cass asked. "Jay's been cooking non-stop, getting ready for Christmas and the weekend guests, of course, so I thought I'd cook dinner."

"You're not making a mess in my kitchen," Jayden said. "I have six different things cooking right now."

Cass ignored him. "We have a bunch of leftovers, that vegetable—"

Jayden gasped. "You cannot serve guests leftovers!"

I laughed. "Leftovers are perfect." I looked up at Clay, and he nodded.

"Sounds great."

We took our coats off and that was when Jayden noticed my pants. He ushered us out into the hall. "Okay, shower and dry clothes right now. I'll make fresh coffee."

In my room, I stripped naked and had the best hot shower of my life. Clay laid on the bed and waited, eyeing me approvingly when I came back out with just a towel around my waist.

"How're you feeling?" he asked.

I rolled my shoulders and back. "Muscles feel much better. I think the cold made me freeze up. But my ass . . ."

"Is hot?" he added.

I pulled a shirt over my head. "My ass is sore." Then I tried to step into some underwear. "Ah, yep. Right there." I somehow managed to pull my underpants on and rubbed my left butt cheek. I turned around to show him. "I think it might need massaging later."

Clay's smile became a smirk. "I'll see what I can arrange."

I leaned down and kissed him. "Thank you for today. Are you sure you want to stay for dinner?"

"Yeah, I'm sure."

"What about your dad?"

"He had plans anyway, and you're here. Happy to be anywhere you are."

"You say the best things," I murmured, then I stupidly tried to straddle him, regretting it immediately. "Ow, ow."

God, my ass.

"You poor thing," Clay said, frowning. "Let's get you dressed and warm."

I pulled on some sweatpants, a sweater, and Clay helped with my socks. I probably could have done them on my own, but he insisted, and I'd be lying if I said it wasn't the sweetest thing.

He pulled me to my feet and took hold of my face so he could kiss me. And the way his eyes met mine, I thought for one second he was about to confess his feelings. Not that it would have been a bad thing, but was it too soon?

It made me wonder, in that split second, what my real feelings for him were.

And I wasn't one hundred percent sure, but maybe he saw the same in my eyes staring back at him.

I was pretty sure he did.

Instead, he kissed me again. On the mouth, and on the forehead before he pulled me in for a hug. And then, as if he was trying to stop himself from saying something out loud, he kissed the side of my head.

It felt different to be held by him. Not just the physical protection in his size or his strong arms, but I felt safe with him. A different kind of safe. An emotional well-being, a safe-harbor-for-my-heart type of protection.

Something I certainly never felt with my ex.

It warmed me all the way through.

We sat by the fire and drank coffee while Jayden finished his preparations and Cass puttered about. Clay kept his hands to himself at first—clearly still acclimating to physical touch with a guy in front of others—but by the end of the night, through dinner and afterwards, he was sitting closer, his fingers skimming the back of my neck or his hand on my thigh.

He and Cass got on particularly well. Both Hartbridge locals forever, both local business owners, and both similar in a lot of ways. Above all that, it was good for Clay to see that hanging out with queer people was fun and completely normal. And the very best part for me was getting to see him be his true self.

But then he said he should go. "I gotta be up and at it before six tomorrow. Last Monday before Christmas."

I pouted.

"Walk me out?" he asked. He thanked Cass and Jayden for everything, and I walked him to the mudroom. He cupped my face in his huge hands and kissed me, so soft and sweet. "I had the best day," he whispered.

"You can stay?" What I meant was that he could stay, yes. In my bed, inside me.

He understood because he groaned. "God, I want to."

"But?"

"Well, you're too sore," he replied. "I don't wanna do anything that'd hurt you even more."

As much as I wanted him, he wasn't wrong about that.

"And I'm a guest in someone else's house," he added. "And that feels weird to me. I want our first time to be special and private. I know that's probably weird to you, but I'm not used to that."

He looked genuinely torn about it. "Clay, it's fine," I

reassured him, my palm to his cheek. "To be honest, it's refreshing and sweet that you want to wait and do it right. It's not like it's a *long* wait, by any means. Everything going well, I should be in my new house on Tuesday night and won't be so sore. You could spend my first night there with me." I ran my finger along his bottom lip. "I'll need my boyfriend there to keep me warm."

That made him smile. "Tuesday," he murmured before he kissed me.

I sighed happily. Happier than I had been in a long, long time. "Let me know when you get home."

About fifteen minutes later, my phone beeped with a message.

Two more sleeps.

CHAPTER SIXTEEN

CLAY

I STOPPED by Gunter's house on Monday afternoon. He'd told me to use the back door and I could see why when I got there. He had a dropcloth over the floor in the mudroom, and after weeks of being a construction zone, it was now a shoes-off zone.

The new floors looked amazing.

So did the new double-roller shades he'd just finished installing. A gray to match the floor, inside the window frame, one roller thermal blackout, the other sheer.

Just amazing.

"Oh, I'm so glad you're here," he said. "Can you hold this for me?"

So I stood there, holding the higher-up, hard-for-him-to-reach shade while he drilled and installed the last one over the kitchen sink.

I really liked that he was so hands-on, so willing to just get in and get it done.

The countertops were still covered, but once he got down off the ladder, I pulled him around and pressed him up against the island, kissing him.

He broke away, laughing. "What was that for?"

"You looked like you needed kissing." I kissed him again. "And I'm just testing out these new countertops."

"One more sleep," he said, waggling his eyebrows.

"How's your backside from all that falling over yesterday?"

"It's fine. I rubbed in some heat cream after my shower this morning."

I lifted his chin and kissed him again, sweeping his mouth with my tongue. When I broke the kiss, he looked a little drunk. "One more sleep."

"Kiss me like that again and it'll be right now, bent over this island counter."

Dang.

"I've been watching a lot of—" *How should I say this?* "—helpful tutorials online. On how to make it good for you."

Gunter snorted. "Helpful tutorials. You mean porn?"

I grinned. "Educational videos."

He waggled his eyebrows again. "Hmm. Any particular favorites?"

"Well, so far, all of them."

He chuckled. "We'll be fine."

"I hope so. I ain't nervous at all. You know, having exactly no experience."

He laughed again but leaned up on his toes to kiss me. "Clay, we'll be fine," he said again, his eyes locked on mine. "There's no pressure. If it happens, it happens. If it doesn't, that's okay."

I leaned down and whispered in his ear. "I want it to happen."

He moaned and his hand fisted my coat, but a car pulling up at the house made us stop and take a step apart.

Hamish came in through the mudroom, grinning. "Please tell me I'm interrupting something," he whispered.

Gunter laughed. "Yes, you are. And he's here alone so you don't need to whisper."

He handed a package of screws to Gunter. "Ren said to use these instead."

"Oh perfect, thank you."

"Perks of having a hardware husband. And you got the kitchen shades installed. My god, Gunter, I was only gone for thirty minutes."

"I had some help," he replied, smiling up at me.

Hamish hummed and looked me up and down. "I can see that. You weren't kidding when you said he was all man."

Oh my god.

Gunter went three shades of red. "Hamish! I did not say that!"

Hamish raised an eyebrow. "You absolutely did."

"Okay, so I did," he admitted, holding my arm. "Clay, my darling boyfriend, it's not a lie. You are, and I bragged to them. I'm sorry."

I laughed. "It's okay. I'm flattered. I think." He just called me his darling boyfriend, so it wasn't like I could be mad.

"Wait," Hamish said, his smile fading. "Hold on a minute. Boyfriend?" He stared at Gunter, both eyebrows now near his hairline. "Something you forgot to tell me, perhaps?"

I laughed. "Okay, on that note, I'll leave you both to it. What time are the movers getting here tomorrow?"

"Should be around ten," he answered.

"Then I'll be here at ten."

"Are you sure? I don't want you to miss work. I know you're busy this close to Christmas."

"'Course I'm sure." I went into the mudroom and pulled my boots on. "I'll call you later."

His smile was cute and kinda dreamy. "'Kay."

With a wave to Hamish, I saw myself out, and I wasn't even down the back steps before I heard Hamish's voice. "You are so smitten! Look at your face!"

I didn't stick around to hear any more. I was fairly certain Gunter was about to get interrogated about the boyfriend thing, but hearing him accuse Gunter of being smitten made me ridiculously happy.

I was more than smitten with him. I'd gone and fallen in love with him, and having someone else see that Gunter might be falling for me too?

Well, that had me smiling like a fool.

So much so that Dad took one look at my face when I got back to work and shook his head. "If you're that happy, you can cook dinner."

I didn't even care. "Okay."

He eyed me. "Will someone be joining us?"

"Nope. I'm seeing him tomorrow. Helping him move his stuff in, and I'll probably stay the night."

Dad gave a nod. "Don't forget the garlic bread."

I HAD MOST of my day's work done before ten o'clock, but I left everything in Dad and Rusty's very capable hands. "Do you need help lifting stuff?" Rusty asked. "I can swing by for a few minutes."

His offer meant a lot to me. It really showed me that

he'd accepted me and Gunter. "Nah. We should be fine. But thanks, man."

"Well, if you get stuck, give us a yell."

"Will do."

I grabbed my overnight bag, threw it in my truck, and went on my way. The movers beat me by ten minutes, and they'd just started bringing in boxes and stuff.

Gunter was so excited.

"I can't believe this is finally happening," he said. "My new house."

"And it's amazing, Gunter. You've done a great job and you should be proud."

"I am proud of myself," he said. "Starting over and fixing up an old house. People must have thought I was crazy . . . Oh, my dining table." He did a cute little jig as two guys carried it in. Then someone else came in with a box. "Oh, in the kitchen, please. Not on the countertop. Just on the floor is fine!"

There were couches, rolled up rugs, two beds and mattresses, wrapped frames—which I quickly found out were wall art when Gunter begged them to pleeeeease be careful with them—a washer and dryer, and a lot of boxes.

Everything looked real expensive, though I expected nothing else from Gunter. He was a stylish guy. Not that he ever flaunted it. Hell, he was so down to earth, he joked about finding the box with the toilet paper in it first.

But the movers were gone soon enough, leaving us alone with a lot of unpacking to do.

The movers had put stuff in the right rooms, but we still had to move some stuff around. Like the couches, so he could put the rug down and then the coffee tables. We hooked up his washer and dryer, got the low cabinet situated, and plugged in his flat screen TV.

"I don't know if I want to keep this here," he said, head tilted, looking at a hall stand type of cabinet. It was in the living room along the wall, and it kinda made sense to have it there so you could put keys and stuff down on it once you'd walked in. But it wasn't my decision. He looked up at me. "What do you think?"

I put my arm around his shoulder and we faced the hall stand. "I think this is your place and you can put it wherever you want. If you wanna keep it here, perfect. If you wanna move it tomorrow, I'll move it for you tomorrow. If you wanna move it next month, I'll move it for you then." I kissed the side of his head. "If you wanna change it a hundred times, you just say the word."

His eyes softened. "Thank you."

I pulled him into a hug, my arms around his shoulders. "This is your house. You can do whatever you want."

He pressed his forehead to my chin. "You are the best boyfriend ever."

I kissed the top of his head. "Did Hamish give you a hard time yesterday about the boyfriend thing?"

He pulled back and sighed. "I don't know how it happened, but I've been adopted by two young Australian guys who, one, torment the shit out of me. And two, are the best two friends I could ask for."

"They seem fun."

"They are. They've taken it upon themselves to see that I'm happy here, whether I want to be or not."

"Are you? Happy here?"

"Yes. More than I ever remember being. But Hamish and Jayden have taken me under their little Aussie wings, and now, without even realizing it, I know what a 'fair dinkum' is and Hamish said he had to 'do a servo run for milk' and so help me, I understood him."

And as if speaking of them manifested them into being, Hamish's car pulled into the driveway. Hamish was chattering away as they walked in and Jayden came in carrying a bag of something that smelled really good.

"Oh my god, look at everything," Hamish cried. "Gunter, it's all perfect."

"It's all still in boxes," Gunter replied, confused. "How can you tell?"

Hamish grinned at me. "I'm talking about your boyfriend. Good afternoon, handsome."

I nodded, surprised I wasn't embarrassed. "Afternoon."

"And I come bearing gifts," Jayden said. "Brisket subs. And leftover lasagna from the diner for your dinner because I knew you wouldn't have any food here."

"You didn't have to do that," Gunter said. "Though I'm glad you did and I won't say no."

"Like you didn't have to pay such a big tip when you moved out of the bed and breakfast today," Jayden replied to him, pouting his lips.

"I paid what I thought it was worth," Gunter said.

"Well, you didn't have to do that," he said, handing out the sandwiches. "Though I'm glad you did and I won't say no."

They laughed and chatted as we ate our subs, talking about Gunter's sofas, and his dining table, and the kitchen counters they hadn't actually seen yet because they were still wrapped, and yes, the hall stand Gunter had worried about before it was in the best position exactly where it was.

But after we ate, they got stuck unpacking boxes. And I mean they were like a military-style mission to get shit done. Beds were made, the kitchen cupboards were filled, and the dishwasher was rewashing silverware, plates, and glassware because Jayden insisted. Books were stacked, lamps were plugged in, closets filled, cushions patted and plumped.

Not even two hours later, every single thing was unpacked, cleaned, and in its rightful place. The packing boxes were flattened, and new towels were in the dryer.

"We have to get going," Jayden said. "We have new clients coming tonight. I need to get home." Then he frowned. "I'm gonna miss not having you there," he said, giving Gunter a hug. "But congrats on your new home. It's beautiful. Be proud and enjoy your first night."

"I will," Gunter replied.

"Will you be at the lights festival tomorrow night?" Hamish asked.

"Yes, for sure!" Gunter answered. Then he looked up at me, questioning, hopeful. "Yes?"

"Absolutely. Anything you want," I replied.

"Speaking of getting what you want," Jayden said. "Is your ass still sore?"

"Jayden!" Hamish said. "Jeez."

Gunter laughed. "I will see you both tomorrow evening at the festival. Thank you for all your help today. And over the last three weeks. It really means a lot. I couldn't have done this without either of you."

"But you're looking forward to starting your first night in your new home," Jayden said suggestively. Then he looked right at me. "That Hartbridge Christmas Cupid really got him good."

I laughed. "What?"

"The Christmas Cupid," Jayden said. "Anyone that moves here at Christmastime gets hit." He mimicked pulling back a bow and releasing the arrow, then gestured to himself, to Hamish and Gunter. "We're all victims."

Hamish held up his ring finger where his wedding ring glinted, and he nodded. "True story."

Gunter laughed but shooed them out, thanking them again and again, closing the door behind them. He took my hand and led me to the couch where he pulled me onto it with him, him fitting perfectly under my arm. "Oh my god, I'm so tired. I'm absolutely beat. They just don't stop. Do you remember having that amount of energy in your twenties?"

"I'm not sure I ever had that amount of energy."

His laugh became a sigh. "Can you believe they got all that done? I was going to spend most of my day tomorrow unpacking everything. Now I don't know what I'll do."

"Sleep in?"

He laughed. "Maybe. I will have to make a trip to get groceries. I'm gonna miss not having a chef at my beck and call."

I laughed and kissed the side of his head. "I should put some more wood on the fire," I noted. "Don't want you to be cold on your first night here."

"With you in my bed, pretty sure it won't be."

Hmm. I'd almost forgotten about that.

Almost.

"So," I said, kissing the side of his head again. "Just how tired are you?"

He sat up. "Not too tired. But if you want to fix the fire while I have a quick shower, I won't complain."

"Oooh, first shower in your new house." I hummed.

His eyes met mine. "Think there'll be a lot of firsts in this house, don't you think? Starting now?"

Oh, hell yes.

He stood up and walked down the hall. "I won't be long in here."

Take a breath, Clay.

I added some wood to the fire, locked the doors, and turned the lights off, then went to Gunter's room. I hadn't really seen it since they'd unpacked everything. The bed was one of those super soft-looking expensive ones. The bed covers were white and looked luxurious and pillowy, the cushions on the bed were gray, with a dark gray headboard, and the whole thing looked like something out of a magazine.

Way more fancier than my bed.

God, we were really gonna do this.

I sat on the edge of the bed, trying to remember everything I'd learned in these last few weeks. How to make it good for him, and how to be considerate to a male lover.

"You look worried," Gunter said from the door. He had a towel around his waist and nothing else. His hair was damp, his skin looked flush like the water was a touch too hot. His lean body was the perfect mix of soft lines and muscle.

Dang, he was sexy.

"Just trying not to overthink," I said. I stood up. "You're gonna get cold standing there."

He flipped the light off, leaving enough light from the hall, and he walked toward me. "Then you better keep me warm. I'm not sure about overthinking, but you're very over-dressed." He unbuttoned my shirt and pulled at the buttons on my jeans. I lifted his chin and captured his mouth with mine as he finished undressing me, and when I was completely naked, I pulled his towel away.

Feeling his naked body against mine, the heat, the hardness, fueled a fire in me.

I kissed down his jaw. "Will you show me what to do?"

He melted into me. "Yes."

I sucked his earlobe into my mouth. "Will you show me how you like it?"

He whined out a breath. "God, Clay. Yes."

He pulled back the covers and laid down the towel. Then from the bedside table, he produced lube and a foil packet and he threw them beside the towel.

Oh boy, this was getting real.

He lay down on his front, legs spread. He urged me to kneel between his thighs, rub him down, massage his shoulders, his back, his ass, and feel how his body responded to my touch. He told me to use the lube and press a finger in, soft and slow. Add more lube, add a second finger.

He rocked his hips. "Yeah, like that," he moaned. "Open me up like that."

Jesus.

I kissed his shoulder and the back of his neck, breathed behind his ear. I was rocking with him, using my fingers on him until my cock would be ignored no longer.

I pulled out and rolled the condom on my aching hard cock, giving myself a hard squeeze before I applied lube to myself and more for him.

But then he rolled over and hooked his legs over mine. His cheeks were flushed, his lips parted. *Dang, those lips.* I leaned forward to kiss him, to plunge my tongue into his mouth, and he pushed his hips up, offering me his ass.

My cock slid against his hole and he whined, rocking us both.

"Clay, give it to me. Nice and slow. I want you inside me."

I'd had sex with women, and yeah, while I wanted to ram home and sink all the way in, I couldn't. I had a pretty big dick. I had to go slow at first, but I'd never done anal before. And this was Gunter. The man I loved. If I hurt him . . .

I kissed him softly. "Tell me if I need to stop," I whispered.

He nodded, and pressing against his hole, I slowly pushed in. His eyes went wide and he gasped as the head slipped in, and he whined as I pushed in slow.

He was tight and hot, his body welcoming mine, every inch slow and torturous.

And so divine.

I wanted to push harder. I wanted to thrust and release that coil that was wound so tight. I groaned with the need to make him truly mine.

Then his hands on my face drew me back into focus, and he pulled down me for a kiss. He rolled his hips a little, encouraging me to move. I began to pull out only to slide back in, deeper, giving him my tongue at the same time.

He groaned and he gasped, whined and cried out with every pass. The more I gave, the louder he was. He dug his fingers into my back, and his legs drew higher.

Sinking me deeper inside him.

His eyes flew open. "Fuck," he gasped against my mouth. "Clay. Yes, there."

I did it again and again, and he clawed his nails into my back as I gave him what he wanted. What I wanted. Climbing and climbing that impossible height of pleasure. So close.

It was so fucking close.

He felt too good. This was all too much, and with every thrust, I went harder, deeper, as deep as his body would take me.

Then Gunter grunted and he convulsed, his mouth

open, his eyes rolled closed, and his back arched under me as his load spilled between us.

Seeing the pleasure on his face, buried in him to the hilt, I couldn't hold it back anymore. The way his body engulfed me, how he took me, my cock surged and pulsed, and I couldn't go any higher.

The fall into ecstasy was sublime.

My orgasm obliterated my senses. The room spun, and the only thing I knew was Gunter.

His arms around me, his kisses along my shoulder and my neck. I was still inside him, and I never wanted to leave.

I began to rock us, a slow rhythm, and I kissed him much the same. For the longest time, I prolonged this moment. This feeling, being joined with him.

I searched his eyes, and a depth of wonder looked back at me. He looked utterly serene. Was it too soon to tell him I loved him? Surely he could see it in my eyes, feel it; this connection, this emotion.

I wanted to tell him so bad.

But I didn't want to ruin the moment, so I kissed him instead.

CHAPTER SEVENTEEN

GUNTER

THE HARTBRIDGE CHRISTMAS light festival looked like something out of a dream. It wasn't just a Hallmark movie. It was Disney and Hallmark and Hollywood all rolled into one. Main Street was blocked off, filled with people and kids. There were train rides, a whole Santa photo set up like a wonderland, Christmas music, and so many Christmas lights.

Walking through crowds of townsfolk with Cliff Henderson was akin to walking with a celebrity. Every single person said hello, shook his hand, wished him a very merry Christmas, and chatted for a moment before we went onto the next person.

Of course they said hello to Clay too, and I was introduced as well. Mostly as "this is Gunter Zuniga. He bought the old Nolan house" and there was instant recognition with variations of "oooh yes, how lovely" and "so glad to see it being restored." By the time we made our way to Carl's Diner, I think I'd met the entire district population.

I knew Clay wasn't up for displays of affection just yet.

Especially in front of the entire town, and he did seem a little nervous.

"Are you okay?" I asked.

He gave me a sad smile. "Yeah. It's just . . . I wish it was easier. Being in public, ya know?"

"You have to know, Clay," I said. "I understand, and I don't expect you to do anything you're not comfortable with."

He groaned in frustration. "That's just the thing. I should be able to put my arm around you . . . I want to."

I smiled up at him. "It will get easier."

He let out a deep breath, and his shoulders relaxed. "Thank you."

"Ho ho ho," Hamish said, coming over with Ren. "Speaking of hos, look at how cute Jayden is."

Jayden was behind the food stall, wearing a full elf outfit. Cass was nearby with his kids and an older couple who I could safely assume were his parents.

"I can't believe how amazing this is," I said.

"I know, right?" Hamish said. "And speaking of amazing," he added suggestively, looking between me and Clay. "How was your first night in your new house?"

My cheeks flushed warm despite the cold, and I didn't even get a word out.

Hamish gasped and grabbed my arm. "Oh my god, no words necessary. Your face says it all."

I laughed and glanced up at Clay. He smirked, embarrassed, and shook his head. But then he rubbed my back and gave my shoulder a squeeze.

An intimate touch. A public display of affection.

Brief, but he did it.

Then he and Ren got chatting, and Hamish and I ordered some food from Jayden. His permanent grin was perfect in that elf outfit, and he promised he'd see us when the stall closed.

We'd just finished our food when a lady rushed over and took Cliff's arm. She was maybe sixty years old, pretty and petite, wearing a purple coat with a fake fur-trimmed hood, cinched in at the waist, with slim black pants and purple boots.

"Oh, Cliff," she said. "I'm glad you're here. There's been an incident with Santa."

We all looked over toward the Santa Wonderland area, to the empty Santa seat and a long line of disappointed kids.

"What happened?" Cliff asked. "Old Harold on the sauce again?"

She patted his arm. "No time for rumors. We need a Santa, pronto! And you're . . . well." She gestured to his somewhat round tummy and his white beard. She sidled in closer to him, almost purring. "You're perfect."

Oh, okay. Wow.

"Santa?" he cried.

Clay laughed really loudly. "Oh, this is good."

Cliff shot him a glare.

"Think of the children, Dad." Clay grinned. "Evening, Cordelia. I think it's a great idea."

She winked. Actually winked.

I tried not to laugh, and Cliff looked utterly bamboozled as Cordelia led him back to the Wonderland.

Clay laughed. "I'm one hundred percent gonna get a photo sitting on his knee."

We walked over and stood at the side, watching kids all cheer when they announced Santa had arrived and would be just a minute. And sure enough, a few moments later, Cliff came out wearing the red Santa suit. No fake tummy, no fake beard; he was the real deal. Even his rosy cheeks were real.

Clay thought it was the funniest thing he'd ever seen.

But his laughter became a fond smile as he watched kid after kid have their photo taken and pop a letter in a big red mailbox.

Cordelia came back to us. "Oh Clay, your dad is just the sweetest thing. Look at him," she drawled. Then she looked at me. "I don't believe we've met."

"Cordelia, this is Gunter," Clay said. "Gunter, Cordelia Gray."

"Ooh," she said, her eyes lighting up. "Clay, Cliff told me you have a new man." She held out her hand for me to shake. "How nice to meet you!"

Wow. Cliff said what? Just how friendly are they?

But all that aside, I wondered for a stricken moment how this would end and how she would react. How this would affect Clay.

How Clay was feeling.

Trying to hide my surprise, I shook her hand. "Likewise," I said.

I wanted to reach for Clay's hand. I wanted to ask him if he was okay. If it was all a bit too much, if he wanted to leave.

I was surprised when Clay put his hand on my shoulder instead.

Another touch. Another show of affection.

It sent a wave of warmth through me.

She watched Cliff for another moment, then winked at me. "These Henderson men *are* quite the catch."

I met Clay's eyes and tried not to laugh. "They certainly are."

"So, Clay," she continued. "Your dad tells me he makes a mean bowl of chili."

And yes, this interaction was unexpected and a little weird, but just like that, there was absolutely no judgment, no questions, no anything.

And then another familiar face appeared. "Here he is, the big fella," Rusty said, shaking Clay's hand.

Clay smiled at the woman. "Trina, Merry Christmas."

"Same to you," she said.

"Rus, you remember Gunter," Clay said.

"Yeah, of course," he said with a smile and a nod. "Nice to see you again." Then Rusty gestured from his wife to me. "Trina, this is Gunter. I was telling you about him."

She smiled warmly. "Nice to meet you! How are you settling into Hartbridge?"

"I love it here," I said. "Not one thing I would change."

Then Clay did it again. He put his hand on my shoulder. It made me so happy I could have cried.

"Hey, where's your old man?" Rusty asked, searching the crowd.

Clay nodded toward Santa, and Rusty looked. Then he looked again. Then he busted up laughing.

Clay chuckled. "We should get a photo with him and put it up in the office."

And that's exactly what they did.

It was Clay standing on one side, Rusty on the other, both laughing, and Cliff scowling at the camera.

Perfection.

The whole night was perfection.

My life in Hartbridge was perfection.

Cordelia stayed to help Cliff finish up. "I think Dad's got himself a girlfriend," Clay murmured. "I think, and this is pure speculation, that he's been delivering her wood after hours, if you know what I mean."

I laughed. "Good for them. Speaking of wood deliveries, I think I'm due for another delivery when we get home."

He smiled and leaned in as if to kiss me, but he stopped himself. "Yeah, maybe we should call it a night."

I nodded. "You know, I'm pretty sure the whole town saw us together tonight. How's the rumor mill in Hartbridge?"

Clay laughed. "If it was plugged into the grid, it could power the whole state of Montana." He sighed. "You know what? I don't care what they think. I don't care what they say. Being here with you tonight was special for me. I never had anyone to bring here before, and if my Dad can put his arm around Cordelia and no one bats an eye, why can't I do that with you?"

I wanted to kiss him so bad. "I'm proud of you, Clay."

His gaze went from my eyes to my lips and back again. "Yeah, I think we should go." He looked around for Cliff, who was now out of the Santa outfit, talking to Cordelia. "Dad? You about ready to go?"

Cliff looked at us, then at Cordelia, and he smiled. "I have a ride home tonight," he said. "You boys be good."

Clay looked a little proud. "Okay, Dad. See you at work at 6:00 a.m."

Cliff made a face. "Yeah, it might be seven."

Clay laughed, and as we walked back to the truck, he slipped his arm around my shoulder. The lights were so pretty, Christmas music still played, and a light sprinkle of snow began to fall.

And like that wasn't perfect enough, when we got back to my place, we made love. Slow and tender. There was emotion in every touch, every kiss. The way he held me, the way his arms wrapped around me, the way his eyes said all the words I wanted to say.

The way he whispered my name as he climaxed deep inside me. The way he watched me in awe as I came.

The way he held me as he slept.

I woke up on Christmas Eve happy, contented, and very much in love.

I WENT to Home Mart and bought an entire pantry and fridge full of food and things like aluminum foil and freezer bags. I puttered around the house, not that there was much to do. Just some laundry and putting things where I wanted them. I was hanging a frame when I heard Clay's truck pull into the driveway.

It was just after lunchtime, and I worried that something was wrong . . .

Until I saw him smiling as he came up the front steps. I opened the door. "Hey you."

"Hey," he said. "Got something for you. Might want to put down a dropcloth." He gestured to the floor.

"Why?"

"Just do it."

I saw past him and Rusty was getting something out of the truck. It was half a wooden barrel . . . ?

I laid the dropcloth near the door. Then Clay and Rusty carried the wooden barrel thing up the stairs and put it in the corner of my living room. I could see what it was now.

A Christmas tree stand that just looked like the base of a wooden wine barrel.

Then they came back in with a Christmas tree. It was

all bound up, but it was tall and looked plump. "I noticed you didn't have one," Clay said.

I was speechless. "It's beautiful. I wasn't expecting this," I said, blinking back tears. "I wasn't going to get a tree because it was so close to Christmas and I was so busy with everything else. Oh my god, I can smell it already. It smells like Christmas."

Clay pulled me into a one-arm hug, holding my face to his chest and he laughed. "You weren't supposed to cry."

"He spent an hour lookin' for the right one," Rusty said. "Had to be perfect."

I slid my arms around Clay. "It *is* perfect. Thank you so much."

"Might wanna put some water in the base," Rusty added. He smiled at me before he disappeared out the front door.

Clay lifted my chin and kissed me. "Merry Christmas. I gotta go back to work. The boys are all finishing early but I gotta stick around, so I'll see you tonight?"

I nodded. "I'll be at your place at six."

He kissed me again. "Dad's cooking, so I'll just apologize now."

I laughed. "I'll bring the wine."

I WALKED BACK into the Home Mart for two things: wine and Christmas tree decorations. I didn't have high hopes for the quality of either.

"Back again," Rosie said.

"Yes, can't stay away," I joked.

"Thought you bought one of everything earlier."

"Almost."

I almost had. But I was stocking a kitchen from scratch.

I found what was left of the Christmas decorations and chose some wine that wasn't too bad, and I knew Rosie was going to say something. I could just feel it.

"So," she began. "Did you enjoy the festival last night?"

Yep, she saw us.

"I had a great time," I replied. "What about you?"

"Oh yes, it's my favorite night of the holidays."

She paused, smiling, holding the wine hostage. "Spending the holidays with anyone special?" she asked.

I resisted sighing. She knew. She must have seen me and Clay last night, or maybe she just heard because the whole town was talking about us.

"Yes, I will be," I replied. "What about you?"

"Yes, yes." She was still holding the wine, and it was just tearing her up that I wasn't giving any details. "So, I heard a little rumor about yourself and a certain Clay Henderson."

Aaaaand there it is.

"He's just the sweetest man," she said. "We're all just happy he's finally found someone."

Oh dear.

She said *we're*. "We're all? Who is we?"

"The whole town, of course."

I nodded slowly. "Of course."

"Let me tell you something about this town," she said, finally putting the wine into a bag. "We love our own in this town. It takes all kinds and we just adore them all."

Not what I was expecting. "Well, that's nice."

"And I heard that Cliff and Cordelia might have been seen together too. Santa's been busy bringing love to town this year. Isn't it wonderful?"

"It sure is." I took my purchases. "Have a lovely Christmas," I said.

"Yes, you too. Give my best to Clay and his dad."

"I will."

Oh boy. I got into my car, reminding myself that this is what small-town life was like. I'd gone from being isolated and feeling very alone in my old life, to now having an entire town knowing all my business.

It would take some getting used to, I had no doubt.

But it was also kind of nice.

I walked into my house and was hit by the smell of pine, and I was reminded that all the small-town weirdness was heavily outweighed by the wonderfulness that was now my life.

Smiling, I decorated the tree with the terrible mismatched decorations and lights, and it was soon time to go to Clay's.

Christmas Eve dinner was a tradition for him and his dad, and I was honored to be invited. But it wasn't just me. Cordelia would be arriving any minute too. Cliff was dressed up, his hair brushed, and his place looked a little cleaner. And he was clearly nervous.

Clay was trying not to smile. "Dad, relax. You'll be fine."

"I know," he said gruffly. "It's just . . . been a long time since your mother . . ."

Clay sighed and clapped his dad on the shoulder. "You deserve some happiness, Dad. And Mom would be happy for you."

"You just be on your best behavior," he grumped. "Don't embarrass me in front of her."

"Like you didn't try to embarrass me when I first started seeing Gunter."

It was too late to argue because her car pulled out front.

And dinner was lovely. And it was cute to watch Cliff and Cordelia blush and gush around each other.

I guessed me and Clay were much the same. He kept his hand on my knee under the table, or around my shoulder, or he'd softly thumb the back of my neck.

Cordelia was actually really sweet and she clearly adored Cliff. After Clay and I had cleared away the plates and had a moment of privacy, he pointed his chin toward his dad. "I think we should leave them."

I nodded. "Good idea."

Clay went and stood behind his dad, his hand on his shoulder. "Thank you for dinner, but we have to go. You two kids behave yourselves." We got to the door and Clay stopped. "Oh Dad, did you need some garlic bread? I have some extra at my place."

Then Clay pulled me out the door, laughing, before Cliff could throw something at him.

He grinned all the way back to my place, and when we got inside, he saw the tree and pulled me in for a hug. "I think today might be one of the best days of my life," he murmured.

I pulled back so I could see his face. "Honestly?"

He nodded. "Waking up with you this morning. Seeing your face when I gave you this tree. Seeing my dad happy. Does it get any better than this?"

I linked my arms around his neck. "I don't think it does." Then I remembered something . . . "Oh. Rosie at the store said she heard about us, so I think it's safe to assume the whole town knows. She said she was happy for you and that Hartbridge locals love their own, no matter what, but I just thought you should know."

He bumped his nose to mine. "I don't care. Let them say whatever they want. I will happily tell them all that I'm in love with you. Maybe it's too soon, and I don't mean to scare you off."

My heart galloped at the word.

"You love me?"

"I think I fell in love with you that day out in front of the diner. When you were wearing your red coat and shoes, when I'd been an idiot and tried to fight what I was feeling, and you smiled at me." He cupped my face. "Right then and there, I fell in love with you."

My eyes stung with tears and my heart felt far too big for my chest. "Clay."

"It's okay if you don't feel the same," he said, still smiling. "That's not why I told you. I told you because it's true for me. You deserve to be loved and to be treated right."

A tear escaped my eye. "But I do feel the same. I thought it might be too soon as well, or it might be too rushed, or that maybe I needed to be on my own for a while. But then I met you. And everything that was wrong with my life became right. You were everything I didn't know I needed. I didn't expect to fall in love. I didn't expect to be loved like this. I didn't know that love could be like this."

He pressed his lips to mine. "I didn't expect love in my life at all. But then I met you."

"Take me to bed, Clay," I whispered.

CHAPTER EIGHTEEN

CLAY

WAKING up in bed with Gunter was heaven. Waking up in bed with Gunter on Christmas morning was a special kinda magic. His bed was soft, the sheets and blankets were expensive and fluffy, and he fit against me like a missing puzzle piece.

What he'd said last night rang true for me too. I never knew love could be like this. I never had a clue it could feel so right. And it wasn't just the sex—as absolutely mind-blowing as it was—it was about the intimacy, the gift he gave me every time he took me inside him, the trust and the love.

I never wanted this feeling to end.

"Merry Christmas," he said, his voice croaking. He was watching me through sleepy eyes. "Sleep okay?"

"Perfect. You?"

His smile disappeared into his pillow as he covered his face and laughed. "You can work me over like you did last night. I slept so good."

I rolled him over and into my arms, his face on my chest, so I could kiss the side of his head. "Merry Christmas."

He ran his fingers through the hairs on my chest, and he hummed his contentment.

Until my stomach growled.

"Come on, let's get you fed," he said. "You do the fire, I'll do breakfast."

Twenty minutes later, we had a warm fire, fresh coffee, and eggs, bacon, and toast. There was fresh snow outside, Gunter put Christmas music on the TV, and it was just all kinds of perfect.

"Do you want your present now?" Gunter asked.

"Well, I have yours but Dad's going to bring it after lunch. Can we wait till we can exchange? Is that okay?"

"Perfect. What did you get me?"

I laughed. "I'm not saying. You gotta wait."

"Can I have a clue?"

"Oh my god, you're one of those kinda people who needs to know," I said with a laugh.

"Not even a clue?"

"Will you give me a clue about mine?"

"I will give you the whole gift right now if you want."

I laughed again and tilted his head so I could kiss his neck. "I wanna wait."

He sighed. "Only if you keep kissing my neck like that, mister."

I kept kissing and we ended up in the shower together.

Hamish and Ren dropped by with a plate of Christmas cookies, and Cass and Jayden dropped by on their way to Christmas lunch at Cass's parents' house after all the guests had gone, and then Dad arrived mid-afternoon.

Gunter wanted to try out his new oven by cooking Christmas dinner, so he slow-roasted beef and double-baked potatoes with brown gravy and beans, and it kept him pretty busy in the kitchen.

I brought my gift for him out of Dad's truck and put it under the tree. His gift for me was in a huge box and there were even a few smaller ones for my dad.

He bought gifts for my dad.

Could he be any more perfect?

Christmas dinner was delicious, and we had fresh coffee and Christmas cookies for dessert. Dad loved the house and Gunter asked him a hundred construction questions for fixing up the outside.

I loved that he didn't invite my dad just to be polite. He invited him because he really liked him. He wanted us to spend Christmas together, and he wanted to include my dad in his life.

In our lives.

"Before we open our presents," Gunter said, "I just want to thank you both for being here. I was fully prepared to spend Christmas by myself this year. After my dad passed away and I had my entire life upended and bought an old house in the mountains, I couldn't have imagined how this day would've ended up. I had the foresight to order a whole truckload of firewood so I didn't freeze to death while I tried to renovate my hundred year old house." He smiled at me. "And who should deliver my firewood but a ruggedly gorgeous man who offered to check my chimney."

"Smooth, Clay," Cliff mumbled.

"Shut up," he grumbled back.

"Thank you both," Gunter said. "Mostly Clay. No offense, Cliff."

I laughed. "And thank you for making me realize who I am." I kissed him. "I love you."

"I love you too," he whispered.

"You guys wanna do presents or wanna be left alone?" Cliff said.

"Presents," Gunter said. He handed Dad his first, and Dad honestly wasn't expecting anything. His shock was clear on his face.

"Oh, I didn't . . . ," he tried to say.

"Merry Christmas, Cliff."

He opened it to reveal a white photo frame with the Santa photos from the Christmas festival the other day when Dad played Santa. I was sitting on his knee, grinning, and even though Dad had grumbled at the time, he was smiling in this photo.

"It's just a photo I took on my phone. It was too perfect."

It was kinda funny, kinda sweet, and absolutely one hundred percent us. Dad was so happy. "Thank you, Gunter. I'm just sorry I didn't know we were exchangin' gifts."

Gunter shook his head. "No need. The memory of the garlic-bread swap will live in my heart forever."

Dad belly laughed, and Gunter looked so pleased.

Ah, jeez. They were really peas in a pod.

"Okay, yours is next," I said, handing Gunter his.

It was a fair size, but he was shocked when he felt it. "Oh, it's heavy."

"I didn't know what to get you," I said. "So I made it."

His eyes met mine. "You made this?"

I nodded and he ripped into the paper, and when he saw what it was, he looked up at me. "Clay . . ."

It was two wooden cutting boards. "I used the cut outs of your countertops so they'd match perfectly. I had to treat 'em and seal 'em—"

He kissed me, teary-eyed again. "So perfect. I love them. So much." He put them down so he could hand me my gift. "I hope you like it."

I opened the box, and when I saw what it was, I laughed. I pulled out the things on top first. They were vinyl albums. "Two David Bowie albums and Annie Lennox."

"And a record player," he added, taking the bottom box out. "They're back in style now, so I could order it pretty easily. Do you like it?"

I looked over the Ziggy Stardust cover, knowing he gave this to me because it was how I learned that being bi was okay. He was telling me now that he knew the real me and that these albums, what they signified, were something I'd longed for half my life, and now they were my reality. My heart did that thing where it grew big enough for two, and it made me a little emotional. "Gunter, I love it. And I love you."

He put his arms around me. "Merry Christmas, Clay."

I kissed the side of his head. "Merry Christmas."

"No more wasted days."

"Not a one."

EPILOGUE
GUNTER

I WAS face down on the bed with my feet on the floor and Clay was standing behind me. Well, correction. My feet *had been* on the floor. It was somewhat difficult to keep my feet on the floor when he was railing me.

He was used to waking up around five thirty for work, so when he'd stay over, I'd usually wake up to kisses on my shoulder, warm hands on my body, and gentle murmurs in my ear. He'd lube me up and get me ready so he could slide his monster cock into me.

It was my favorite way to start the day.

And on the weekends, when he didn't have to rush off to work, he could take his sweet time.

And boy, did he ever.

Like this day.

Just after 6:00 a.m., I was bent over the bed, gripping the blankets while Clay stood, gripping my hips while he sank his cock into my ass. Over and over, balls deep. Every massive inch of him.

"Fuck," I bit out as he drove into me. "God, yes."

Clay leaned forward, one hand on the bed near my head, his other hand still holding my hip.

The change of angle was divine.

"You feel too good," he groaned. He kissed the back of my neck as he pushed all the way in. "Wanna stay inside you forever."

"Yes," I panted. "Like this."

His fingers dug into my hip and he grunted as he thrust into me, over and over. But then he slowed to a stop, laying his weight on top of me. He was so far inside me, just slowly rolling his hips. "Don't wanna come yet," he murmured, his breaths rough. Then he kissed behind my ear, his beard soft and scratchy. "Fuck, Gunter, you feel so good."

I clenched my ass around him and flexed my hips, wanting, needing him to move.

He took the hint.

"Ugh," he grunted as he pulled out and drove back in, again and again, taking me to that place only he could take me.

"Oh yeah, right there," I gasped as he struck the fireworks inside me.

He gripped my hips harder. He fucked me deeper, over and over, sparking pleasure along every nerve in my body until heat exploded low in my belly, and I came.

He held my hips, keeping me impaled on him while my orgasm rocketed through me. And then, with a few final thrusts, his cock impossibly hard and swollen, inside me to the hilt, he came with a roar.

I could feel the pulse of his come filling me, the way he twitched with the aftershocks. He collapsed on my back, rough breathing in my ear, and slowly pulled out of me. He kneeled on the bed beside me, dragged me up the bed so he could wrap his arms around me and hold me properly, my back to his front.

His barely softened cock pressed against my ass, and I wiggled, trying to get it where I wanted it. "More," I murmured.

He chuckled. "Haven't you had enough?"

Since we'd foregone condoms? "Never."

He rolled on top of me, pressing me face down on the mattress. He spread my legs, pressed his cock against my still-slick hole and sunk into me again.

I moaned like the whore I was, apparently.

I'd never wanted sex this much. I'd never felt so sexy. I'd never felt so wanted, so loved. I never knew sex and love could be like this.

"Just stay in me," I murmured.

His dick twitched, and he groaned out a chuckle. "I was gonna make you coffee and breakfast, but damn, Gunter, I could almost go again."

I spread my legs and raised my hips, giving him better access. "Breakfast later. Give me more of you first," I mumbled.

LATE APRIL in Hartbridge was the prettiest time of the year. Then again, I said that about December, January, February, and March.

Instead of Christmas trees, Main Street was now filled with flowerpots of all kinds of colors, all the trees had green leaves and blossoms. There was still snow on the mountaintops, but everything else was coming to life. There were kids on bikes, people walking dogs, and so many birds.

And on Saturdays, the entire length of Main Street was

filled with townsfolk, shopping, chatting and drinking coffee, and the tourists who'd made the drive for a cutesy and quaint day out in the mountains.

I loved it here.

I'd been widely and warmly accepted into Hartbridge, and Clay's coming out as bi experience was largely positive. There was one guy at the sawmill who didn't particularly like it and had something to say, but Cliff put a stop to that real fast.

And so, our lives had been utterly blissful for the last four months.

I'd been working on my house, getting the outside fixed, sanded, primed, and painted. I decided I wanted to build a huge covered deck area off the back of the house. I needed to fix the shed, and build a garage before next winter, which would be joined by a covered walkway to the back deck, and then I could do the driveway but first I had to clear away some trees . . . just as well I knew a certain lumberjack who could do that for me.

Clay had been busy with work, and I had to wonder if there was a not-busy time at the lumberyard. He didn't spend every night at my house, and sometimes I didn't see him for a day or two, but that really worked for us. He got to have some father/son dinners with Cliff, and I got some much needed—and appreciated—time to myself.

I was, after all, not ready to dive straight back into a full-on, live-in relationship. What Clay and I had was perfect just the way it was. We each appreciated our independence and didn't need to get married to prove anything.

Even if Hamish was still gloating about how fabulous it was, and Jayden was starting to drop hints to Ren . . .

It just wasn't something I needed to jump back into.

"You okay?" Clay asked as we pulled up to Bridge

Street by the river. The park area was already filled with stall owners setting up. "You got a bit quiet."

"Just thinking," I said.

"About?"

"About how pretty this whole freaking town is and how moving here was the best decision I ever made."

This was not a lie.

"Thanks again for doing this today," Clay said. "I really do appreciate it."

"Are you kidding? It's a great cause. It's an absolutely gorgeous day, and there's a coffee stall and pastries right here."

He laughed and we got out, taking no time at all to set up the table with the trays and trays of saplings. Clay's regeneration program which he did every year was a great idea, not just for the environment and the sustainability of his industry, but also for the community.

The elementary school did a fundraising drive for new school equipment. The local boy and girl scouts had "green day" in conjunction with the national park and planted a few hundred trees to earn a new badge. And today was the big Hartbridge Arbor Day celebration. The local council ran a community day where local residents cleaned up trash and planted trees along the river, and they grilled hotdogs, and there were stalls for food, cake, crafts, face painting, and pets.

All of these amazing initiatives, and Clay was involved in all of them.

It was easy to see why he and his dad were so loved in Hartbridge.

"Oh my god," Jayden said, carrying over two cups of coffee. "Look at you two in your matching shirts."

I looked down at mine and then at Clay's shirt. They

were forest green with Hartbridge Arbor Day on the front. I turned around so he could see the back. It had the Henderson's name and logo in big yellow print, though Clay's shirt was twice the size of mine and it was still tight around his chest and arms.

I may or may not have done that deliberately.

"Hmm," Jayden said, totally checking him out. "I can see Gunter sized your shirt perfectly, Clay."

I preened and Clay grumbled, and Jayden laughed. "Enjoy your coffee," he said with a wink. "I better get back. The crowd is starting to come in."

They really were. People from all over the district, apparently. Cars started to file into town and there were people already walking down toward the stalls, and within the hour, everyone was busy.

Cliff and Cordelia soon joined us, and while Cordelia and I stayed behind the stall, handing out saplings and generally being the most awesome salespeople ever, Clay and Cliff charmed the crowd with how the lumberyard replanted scores of trees every year, how they repurposed lumber, how they believed in sustainability. They petted dogs, made children laugh, and charmed women and men alike.

Cordelia clucked her tongue at them. "Have you ever met two more magnetic men?"

Magnetic. I liked that term.

I chuckled. "My dad would have said they could charm the leg off a chair."

"So true." She smiled, looking at Cliff fondly. "Ooh, he's such a sweet-talker."

"Yeah, I don't think the apple fell too far from the tree."

She laughed, her hand on my arm. "I hope for your sake it didn't fall far at all."

I really liked Cordelia. She was in her sixties, if I had to guess. Always dressed impeccably well, always with her hair and make-up done, always with a smile on her face. She was an insatiable flirt and didn't give one damn what people in this town said about her . . . In fact, I think she liked it when they gossiped about her, even if it was all lies.

Flirt, yes. A bit sultry and a bit fun. But she only had eyes for Cliff Henderson.

"You two wouldn't be ogling the father and son duo, no?" Hamish asked, coming up behind us. He had Chutney on a leash, and they were wearing matching shirts.

"We absolutely are," I admitted. "Discussing apples falling from trees."

He laughed and looked around at the crowd. "This is an incredible turn out."

"Where is that gorgeous husband of yours?" Cordelia asked.

"He's working." Hamish pouted. "He's actually pretty busy. I said I'd grab him something to eat."

"Well, Jayden's been swamped over there," I said. "But there's a taco truck and a steamed dumpling truck further down. I heard someone mention poutine—"

"Gunter, don't turn around," Hamish said, fake smiling. "But there's a man over there staring at you. And I mean *staring* . . . aaaaand he's coming over."

"Gunter?"

I turned around, even though I didn't have to. I knew that voice. It was my ex-husband. "Scott," I said, surprised to see him, but oh my god, what did he do to his hair? Was black box dye on special? Oh please don't tell me he paid for that? "Wow."

"Yeah, what a surprise," he said.

I was talking about your hair. And possibly the whole North Face outfit. And the spray tan.

"You look great," he said, clearly surprised.

No, I look happy.

"What are you doing here?"

"Oh, you know . . ."

"No, I don't. That's why I asked."

He smiled at Cordelia, then gave Hamish a once over, settling on Chutney. "Oh, cute dog," he said. "I'm Scott Bassinger."

Oh my god. Did he think Hamish and I were together?

"Bassinger? Like Kim," Hamish said. Then his eyes went wide. "Scott. Oh, that Scott. Oh my god." Hamish, bewildered, turned to me. "*That* Scott."

I tried to convey with my eyes to him that yes, it was *that* Scott.

I collected myself and gestured to Cordelia. "And this is Cordelia."

She gave him a none-too-impressed smile. "Hello." There was no *pleased to meet you coming* from her for him, clearly able to detect smarmy when she saw it.

Then Scott noticed my shirt. He looked appalled. "Oh, are you *working* here?"

"Here? As in Hartbridge? Yes, I live here now."

His eyebrows shot up to his disastrous hairline. Really, what was he thinking? "Oh, I didn't know that."

"No, how would you? Because you left *so* suddenly."

I noticed Hamish trying to launch his eyeballs over at someone . . . No, not someone. At Clay.

Great.

"Ah yeah, about that," Scott said, just as a kid came up and put his arm around him. Okay, so *kid* might have been unfair. He was twenty, maybe nineteen. Rather fit looking.

Also wearing North Face from head to foot. Wow, did they win a store voucher or something?

Christ, did he still have acne?

"Scotty," the kid whined. "I'm starving but the only food here is terrible. It's all carbs and saturated fats. Can we go?"

Wow.

Scotty?

Jesus have mercy.

And the food here was not terrible, petulant child.

Scott smiled. "Oh, this is Tad. He wanted to do the hike through the national park." He didn't even have the decency to be ashamed. "We drove up from Mossley and were just passing through and saw the markets. So . . . quaint."

Tad.

Of course his name was Tad.

The much younger guy certainly explained Scott's hair dye and his desperation in trying to look twenty years younger.

"Hi, Tad," I said cheerfully. "That's an unusual name. Is it short for a tad young?"

Tad, bless his cotton socks, said, "No, my last name is Bertram."

Hamish snorted while Cordelia coughed and pretended to be interested in the saplings. Scott shot me a warning look.

Then Clay was beside me but looking between me and Scott. "Everything okay here?"

I looked up at him and slid my arm around his waist. "Oh sure, everything's fine. Let me introduce you. Clay, this is Scott, my ex-husband. Scott, this is Clay Henderson, the very wonderful love of my life."

Scott blinked at me, then had to physically look up at Clay just as Clay tucked me in under his arm.

I smiled at the look on Scott's face, extra glad I insisted Clay wear the tight shirt.

Tad turned to Scott. "Ex-husband? You never told me you were married."

Oh, that poor boy. That was going to be a fun car trip home.

I sighed. "I really should thank you, Scott. I mean that sincerely. If it weren't for you leaving, I wouldn't have the life I have now. I wouldn't be this happy. So thank you. And Tad," I added, for this poor little gayby. "You deserve to be treated better, settle only for the truth. Or make him buy you a new car or something."

Scott glared at me, but Tad's whole face lit up, excited, as he batted his eyelids at Scott. "Really? A new car?"

Scott's gaze burned in my direction with unspoken rage.

Cordelia handed Tad a tubed sapling. "Have a tree, dear."

Hamish coughed to cover his laugh.

Cliff came over, grin wide and voice booming. He clapped Clay on the back. "Just volunteered us for a wood chopping competition. Go get your ax, son." Then he noticed we had company, in particular, Scott. "We gotta keep these youngins in check. Am I right?"

I would have found it hilarious that Cliff assumed Scott fell into his age category if Tad didn't take one look at Cliff and swoon. "Oh. Hi there," he breathed.

Okay, woooow.

"Oh my god," Clay said.

Cordelia took the tree off Tad. "Wrong tree, honey."

Hamish hid behind me and I could hear him wheeze-laughing.

"We'll be going," Scott said flatly.

I smiled at him. "Okay. I do hope you find what you're looking for." And that was the truth, because under that fake tan and terrible hair dye looked a miserable man. "Say hello to your mom and dad for me."

We all stood there and watched them walk away. It sounded like Tad was already talking about a Jeep Wrangler, and I buried my face into Clay's chest and laughed. "Oh my god."

"A new car? Really?" Clay asked.

I looked up at him and shrugged. "He can afford it. And he lied to that poor boy."

"That poor boy just purred at my old man," Clay said, unimpressed. "I never heard a man purr before."

Hamish had to wipe his tears from laughing so much.

Cliff preened, chest out. "Yep. I still got it."

Clay sighed. "I'm going to get my ax from the truck."

"Is there really going to be a wood chopping contest?" I asked, probably way more excited than was normal.

Yes, there was.

Quite the crowd gathered around to watch Clay and Cliff compete against each other. They had to split and chop wood, and Clay won—because of course he did—but wow, Cliff gave him a run for his money.

At the end of the day, when all the crowds were gone and all the stalls were packed up, we gathered around the booth at the pizzeria. Clay and I, Hamish and Ren, Jayden and Cass, several half-eaten pizzas and a few beers later, and of course talk turned to Scott.

I shook my head, still disbelieving he'd turned up. "In my defense," I said. "The hair and the spray tan . . . he never used to look like that."

Jayden frowned. "I wish I'd seen him."

Hamish laughed. "Just picture a cross between Danny Zuko and an Oompa Loompa."

We all laughed again.

"I really tried to feel sorry for him," I said. "And I thought I'd forgiven him, but I guess I still have some residual resentment."

Clay snorted, his arm around my shoulder. "He left you the day after your father's funeral. He deserves every ounce of resentment. He also deserves his new fake boyfriend."

"Oh my god," Hamish said. "The tad young comment. Gunter, I was dying. And Scott's face when he met Clay. He took one look at you, mighty mountain lumberjack man in that tight shirt, and he almost swallowed his tongue."

I laughed and Clay kissed the side of my head. "And you told him I was the love of your life, so . . ."

I met his gaze. "Just telling the truth."

He kissed my forehead and hid his face behind my head, embarrassed.

Jayden sipped his glass of pop. "God, we're like a real-life version of *Friends*."

I sighed. "I would have said *St. Elmo's Fire*, but sure."

"Okay, old man," Jayden said with a laugh.

"Heyyyy," Clay and Cass cried. Cass was obviously offended because his age was closest to mine, and Clay was defending me, but all I could do was laugh.

Ren nodded over toward the counter. "Deputy Price," he said.

We all turned to look. He was out of uniform, and I probably wouldn't have recognized him. He was tall, maybe thirty, clearly worked out. "Gentlemen," he said with a nod. There was a sadness in his eyes, almost.

No, not sadness. It was longing.

"Could you please settle an argument for us?" I asked.

He walked over. "I can try," he said, smiling more genuinely now.

"Which is better? The TV show *Friends* or the movie *St. Elmo's Fire*?"

He made a face. "Gotta go with *St. Elmo's Fire*."

"See?" I crowed.

"I mean, you gotta pick the old classics, right?"

"Old?" I faked being struck in the heart. "Old?"

Everyone laughed, and Clay's arm around me tightened just a little. "Pull up a seat," Clay said to him.

"Oh no, I can't," Price said. "I have to get going . . ."

"Pizza," the girl said, walking out to give him his pizza box.

"Thanks, Ellie," he said, giving her a bright smile. He gave us a wave. "Enjoy your night."

We all watched him leave, and when he was gone, Cass made a thoughtful face, Hamish raised one eyebrow, and Jayden gave me a nod.

"I thought so too," I whispered.

Clay groaned. "I don't see it. I don't have that built-in detection thing that you guys seem to have."

Ren leaned in and whispered, "You mean a gaydar?"

"Is there such a thing as bi-dar?" Clay asked. "'Cause I don't have that either."

I laughed and slid out of the booth. "On that note, Mr. Bi-dar, it's time for you to get this old man home."

Clay groaned as he got out of the booth, stretching his back. "Who's the old man? God, I'm sore."

I rubbed his shoulder. "Because you tried to show your dad up in the wood chopping contest."

"He nearly beat me too." He smiled at them all. "Thanks for all your help today, guys. It means a lot."

"Anytime," Ren said.

Hamish swatted his arm. "You didn't do anything."

Jayden laughed. "Yeah, we gotta get going too."

We threw some twenties on the table and said goodbye in the street before Clay and I climbed into his truck.

"I'm ready for a hot shower and bed," he said as we drove down Main Street.

"Same," I agreed. "I had such a great day. I'm glad the seedling drive went so well, but I'm really sorry you had to meet Scott. Especially under those circumstances. I certainly wasn't expecting to see him."

"Oh, it was no problem for me. I was more worried about you seeing him. It had to be rough."

I sighed and smiled at him in the darkened cab. "I was shocked to see him, but honestly, it really reinforced that he did the right thing. For me, I mean. Not really for him. He looked miserable under all that façade of trying to be twenty-five. It was kinda sad. And I do wish him happiness, I do. I was probably a bit harsh with him, but—"

"No you weren't."

I snorted. "I hope he's happy with Tad Young."

Clay smiled. "I hope the kid gets a new car."

I chuckled. "Same." I reached over and ran my fingers along the back of his neck. "I meant what I said to him. You are the love of my life; I do believe that. You are every single thing he's not."

He patted his hair. "I got some printer toner at the office if you want me to color my hair like him."

I burst out laughing. "Please don't ever."

He gestured to his face. "And some wood stain, if you like that orange look."

"Oh my god, it was bad, wasn't it?"

Clay smiled warmly at me. "You're the love of my life too, Gunter. There won't ever be anyone else like you."

His words spread warmth through me, settling in my chest. I was so freaking happy with him, with this new me, my new life.

He pulled his truck up by my house and followed me inside, and as soon as I put my wallet on the counter, he pulled me into his arms. "I love you. And I know we haven't been together for that long, and you have a whole history with that douchebag I met today and—"

"History, yes. But my future is with you."

"I was just gonna say that." He smiled. "Gunter, when I'm with you, my world feels right."

"Oh, Clay."

He kissed me softly, his eyes so full of love. He murmured, "When I look at you, I see forever."

His gaze, his words, unleashed butterflies in my belly. "I met my forever the day I met you, Clay. You delivered a load of firewood and got out of that truck and you smiled at me and bam! That Hartbridge Christmas Cupid got me good."

Clay chuckled. "He got me too."

I shrugged. "But then Santa gave me my very own lumberjack for Christmas, so it was fine."

He cupped my face and pressed his forehead to mine. "And you were the best Christmas gift I ever coulda asked for."

I kissed his nose. "Well, I am the gift that keeps on giving."

He chuckled. "Yes you are."

"But I'm not returnable, just so you know."

He grinned and kissed me. "The forever kind of gift."

I snuggled my head against his chest; his strong arms wrapped me up. "Forever."

ABOUT THE AUTHOR

N.R. Walker is an Australian author, who loves her genre of gay romance. She loves writing and spends far too much time doing it, but wouldn't have it any other way.

She is many things: a mother, a wife, a sister, a writer. She has pretty, pretty boys who live in her head, who don't let her sleep at night unless she gives them life with words.

She likes it when they do dirty, dirty things... but likes it even more when they fall in love.

She used to think having people in her head talking to her was weird, until one day she happened across other writers who told her it was normal.

She's been writing ever since...

ALSO BY N.R. WALKER

Blind Faith

Through These Eyes (Blind Faith #2)

Blindside: Mark's Story (Blind Faith #3)

Ten in the Bin

Gay Sex Club Stories 1

Gay Sex Club Stories 2

Point of No Return – Turning Point #1

Breaking Point – Turning Point #2

Starting Point – Turning Point #3

Element of Retrofit – Thomas Elkin Series #1

Clarity of Lines – Thomas Elkin Series #2

Sense of Place – Thomas Elkin Series #3

Taxes and TARDIS

Three's Company

Red Dirt Heart

Red Dirt Heart 2

Red Dirt Heart 3

Red Dirt Heart 4

Red Dirt Christmas

Cronin's Key

Cronin's Key II

Cronin's Key III

Cronin's Key IV - Kennard's Story

Exchange of Hearts

The Spencer Cohen Series, Book One

The Spencer Cohen Series, Book Two

The Spencer Cohen Series, Book Three

The Spencer Cohen Series, Yanni's Story

Blood & Milk

The Weight Of It All

A Very Henry Christmas (The Weight of It All 1.5)

Perfect Catch

Switched

Imago

Imagines

Imagoes

Red Dirt Heart Imago

On Davis Row

Finders Keepers

Evolved

Galaxies and Oceans

Private Charter

Nova Praetorian

A Soldier's Wish

Upside Down

The Hate You Drink

Sir

Tallowwood

Reindeer Games

The Dichotomy of Angels

Throwing Hearts

Pieces of You - Missing Pieces #1

Pieces of Me - Missing Pieces #2

Pieces of Us - Missing Pieces #3

Lacuna

Tic-Tac-Mistletoe

Bossy

Code Red

Dearest Milton James

Dearest Malachi Keogh

Christmas Wish List

Code Blue

Davo

The Kite

Learning Curve

Titles in Audio:

Cronin's Key

Cronin's Key II

Cronin's Key III

Red Dirt Heart

Red Dirt Heart 2

Red Dirt Heart 3

Red Dirt Heart 4

The Weight Of It All

Switched

Point of No Return

Breaking Point

Starting Point

Spencer Cohen Book One

Spencer Cohen Book Two

Spencer Cohen Book Three

Yanni's Story

On Davis Row

Evolved

Elements of Retrofit

Clarity of Lines

Sense of Place

Blind Faith

Through These Eyes

Blindside

Finders Keepers

Galaxies and Oceans

Nova Praetorian

Upside Down

Sir

Tallowwood

Imago

Throwing Hearts

Sixty Five Hours

Taxes and TARDIS

The Dichotomy of Angels

The Hate You Drink

Pieces of You

Pieces of Me

Pieces of Us

Tic-Tac-Mistletoe

Lacuna

Bossy

Code Red

Learning to Feel

Dearest Milton James

Dearest Malachi Keogh

Three's Company

Christmas Wish List

Code Blue

Davo

The Kite

Learning Curve

Series Collections:

Red Dirt Heart Series

Turning Point Series

Thomas Elkin Series

Spencer Cohen Series

Imago Series

Blind Faith Series

Free Reads:

Sixty Five Hours

Learning to Feel

His Grandfather's Watch (And The Story of Billy and Hale)

The Twelfth of Never (Blind Faith 3.5)

Twelve Days of Christmas (Sixty Five Hours Christmas)

Best of Both Worlds

Translated Titles:

Italian

Fiducia Cieca (Blind Faith)

Attraverso Questi Occhi (Through These Eyes)

Preso alla Sprovvista (Blindside)

Il giorno del Mai (Blind Faith 3.5)

Cuore di Terra Rossa Serie (Red Dirt Heart Series)

Natale di terra rossa (Red dirt Christmas)

Intervento di Retrofit (Elements of Retrofit)

A Chiare Linee (Clarity of Lines)

Senso D'appartenenza (Sense of Place)

Spencer Cohen Serie (including Yanni's Story)

Punto di non Ritorno (Point of No Return)

Punto di Rottura (Breaking Point)

Punto di Partenza (Starting Point)

Imago (Imago)

Il desiderio di un soldato (A Soldier's Wish)

Scambiato (Switched)

Galassie e Oceani (Galaxies and Oceans)

French

Confiance Aveugle (Blind Faith)

A travers ces yeux: Confiance Aveugle 2 (Through These Eyes)

Aveugle: Confiance Aveugle 3 (Blindside)

À Jamais (Blind Faith 3.5)

Cronin's Key Series

Au Coeur de Sutton Station (Red Dirt Heart)

Partir ou rester (Red Dirt Heart 2)

Faire Face (Red Dirt Heart 3)

Trouver sa Place (Red Dirt Heart 4)

Le Poids de Sentiments (The Weight of It All)

Un Noël à la sauce Henry (A Very Henry Christmas)

Une vie à Refaire (Switched)

Evolution (Evolved)

Galaxies & Océans

Qui Trouve, Garde (Finders Keepers)

Sens Dessus Dessous (Upside Down)

Spencer Cohen Series

German

Flammende Erde (Red Dirt Heart)

Lodernde Erde (Red Dirt Heart 2)

Sengende Erde (Red Dirt Heart 3)

Ungezähmte Erde (Red Dirt Heart 4)

Vier Pfoten und ein bisschen Zufall (Finders Keepers)

Ein Kleines bisschen Versuchung (The Weight of It All)

Ein Kleines Bisschen Fur Immer (A Very Henry Christmas)

Weil Leibe uns immer Bliebt (Switched)

Drei Herzen eine Leibe (Three's Company)

Über uns die Sterne, zwischen uns die Liebe (Galaxies and Oceans)

Unnahbares Herz (Blind Faith 1)

Sehendes Herz (Blind Faith 2)

Hoffnungsvolles Herz (Blind Faith 3)

Verträumtes Herz (Blind Faith 3.5)

Thomas Elkin: Verlangen in neuem Design

Thai

Sixty Five Hours (Thai translation)

Finders Keepers (Thai translation)

Spanish

Sesenta y Cinco Horas (Sixty Five Hours)

Código Rojo (Code Red)

Código Azul (Code Blue)

Queridísimo Milton James

Queridísimo Malachi Keogh

El Peso de Todo (The Weight of it All)

Tres Muérdagos en Raya: Serie Navidad en Hartbridge

Lista De Deseos Navideños: Serie Navidad en Hartbridge

Spencer Cohen Libro Uno

Spencer Cohen Libro Dos

Spencer Cohen Libro Tres

Davo

Chinese

Blind Faith

Printed in Great Britain
by Amazon